PERFECTION

Eternally Three

Kris Cook

MENAGE AMOUR

Siren Publishing, Inc.
www.SirenPublishing.com

A SIREN PUBLISHING BOOK
IMPRINT: Ménage Amour

PERFECTION
Copyright © 2010 by Kris Cook

ISBN-10: 1-60601-553-2
ISBN-13: 978-1-60601-553-7

First Printing: February 2010

Cover design by Jinger Heaston
All cover art and logo copyright © 2010 by Siren Publishing, Inc.

Printed in the U.S.A.

PUBLISHER
Siren Publishing, Inc.
www.SirenPublishing.com

DEDICATION

To all my friends and family who allow me to prattle on and on about writing,

To my advance readers, Steve, Juanita and Angelina,

To my author buddies, Melissa Schroeder and Nikki Duncan,

To my editor, Devin Govaere,

To my alliance warrior, Stephen,

And to my mentor and longtime friend, author Shayla Black.

PERFECTION

Eternally Three

KRIS COOK
Copyright © 2010

Chapter 1

I met Lillian only a week ago. Now, she is dead. I know for certain that she wasn't crazy. If I don't figure out how to stop what is happening, I will be dead in three months, Micki in nineteen. How do I tell her?

Eric's Flash Drive: day 7—entry 1

* * * *

Breathe, Micki Langley instructed herself.

On any other day, Zone Three's reputation of catering to a clientele with specific sexual tastes would have intrigued her. But her reason for being at the club now had nothing to do with this particular curiosity. Not by a long shot.

Her brother, Eric, had fallen off the face of the earth. The only clue to his disappearance led here.

As her eyes adjusted to the bar's dim lighting, she glanced around. The place presented a strange mix of sixties-style and high-tech decor. Red velvet sofas surrounded the perimeter, and large hi-def flat screens hung every few feet on the walls. The decibel levels of the DJ's tunes impeded conversation. At each corner of the dance floor, mirrored platforms served as mini-stages for hot dancers, male and female, wearing as close to nothing as legally possible.

The building vibrated from the crowd of people not just dancing, but kissing, touching. If it weren't for their clothes, she would've sworn they were actually having sex. The action on the sofas burned even hotter. Lovers writhed on them with no hesitation.

Ohmigod! Is that guy's head actually under that woman's skirt?

Being here completely intimidated Micki, threatening her ability to intake oxygen. The meditation exercise she'd learned in yoga helped her gain the slightest composure. Still, a flurry of butterflies continued to swarm inside her. Worry cramped her gut. What if she didn't find Eric?

No, she must. She wouldn't think otherwise.

Shocked that she'd actually made it past the long line, red rope, and massive, muscled bouncer outside, she drew in a shaky breath. Maybe her new outfit had done the trick? Doubtful, though. A mini wasn't her normal choice, but she'd wanted to blend in. Looking at the other women, Micki knew she still stood out, if only because her skirt, for Zone Three, fell on the conservative side.

The fact she'd made it inside couldn't have been because of her looks. The other women roaming the club, all tens, flattened out any hope of a bell curve. On good days, she could pass as an eight.

Maybe Zone Three's gatekeeper let her in because she had no escort. Most likely. Fresh meat. Whatever. She'd made it inside. Now she could begin her search.

Micki hadn't spoken to Eric in a week, five days longer than ever before. In a funny sort of way, he acted as her anchor. Her rock. Rescuing him from his craziness kept her in control. But now that he was nowhere to be found, she couldn't get her bearings, adrift in uncharted waters.

She walked right, away from the dance floor, alert for any sign of him. No luck. Instead she saw off-the-charts sexy men in every direction. If she'd been trolling the club for a date, she would've been like an ice cube in the desert—melting in the hot environment.

Moving near the back wall, she spotted stairs, another rope and a bouncer more menacing than the last. Nothing said keep out more clearly.

Where did the stairs lead? VIP rooms? The sign hanging from the rope stated: *by invitation only.* Given the racy conduct of the club goers in the public areas, Micki could only imagine what went on up there.

Did Eric really know these people? He'd had some wild friends over the years, but… Could he actually be up there? How would she get past the guard to find out? The bouncer didn't look as accommodating as his buddy outside. Best to check downstairs first before sneaking into the more exclusive areas of Zone Three. She'd think of something later, if necessary, to finagle an invitation past that rope.

People jostled and shoved their way around her as she trekked around the club, but none took notice of her. And none of them her brother, her only living relative. She tried not to succumb to the panic ricocheting through her system.

Micki had been just four and a half, Eric six, when their mother had died at twenty-nine. They'd endured a rough childhood, but they'd done it together. This last week without him had nearly crushed her.

No matter how many times she reminded herself that Eric's voicemail had instructed her to come here with his flash drive and give it to some guy named David, her anxiety mushroomed. Why here? And if David hung out at Zone Three, what kind of man did that make Eric's friend? Could her brother be in real trouble this time?

She opened her purse and found her cell, mints, and Eric's flash drive. She took out her phone, knowing she would have no missed calls or text messages, but she should check just in case.

The cell's screen mocked her with the words: *mailbox empty.*

She'd tried to reach Eric all day before finally giving in to the crazy message he'd left.

God, how she wished she'd been at least able to reach his girlfriend, Brooke. But every attempt to contact her went straight to voicemail. Even text messages went unanswered.

Brooke normally knew how to find Eric, even when he jaunted off on one of his crazy excursions. And if Brooke hadn't known where he might be this time, she would have insisted on accompanying Micki to Zone Three to try to find him. Micki would have loved having the other woman here to bolster her courage. Unless... Eric and Brooke had left together on a spontaneous vacation, but it wasn't like him not to take Micki's calls. His message had said nothing about a cozy few days with his girlfriend.

This was one of those times Micki wished she had a man in her life to lean on, but she'd given up on that possibility after she and her last boyfriend called it quits three years ago. Relationships just didn't work out for her. And sex? Well, the fantasy always seemed to far exceed her reality.

So Micki had come to Zone Three alone, filled with uncertainty. What if Eric had stumbled into something dangerous?

Micki hoped that he would call her or appear so that she could exit the club and get a cab home. No matter how interesting the place, no matter her recent torrid dreams of two incredible men making love to her, this sort of thing wasn't for her.

If she found Eric and this turned out to be a joke, then she'd punch her shit-of-a-brother as hard as she could. The apprehension gnawing at Micki told her that wasn't going to happen.

In his odd message, he'd asked her not to call the police. She'd ignored his instructions, but they'd only informed her that not enough time had elapsed to file a missing persons report. The on-duty sergeant had instructed her to come back in two days.

Something kept scratching at her mind that her brother didn't have two days.

If she didn't find her brother or this David character Eric

mentioned in his voicemail, she would call the police again in the morning and demand they do something.

On Eric's message, his voice had sounded strange, like he somehow wasn't himself. Eric didn't take drugs. At least he'd never before. Looking around Zone Three, she wondered how much she *really* knew about his life.

She'd circled the perimeter of the club, but still saw no sign of Eric. Finally, she turned to two women who stood nearby.

"Excuse me. Do you know a guy named Eric or David?"

The women didn't acknowledge her. Didn't act as if they'd heard her. Maybe the music's volume kept them from hearing?

Micki spoke up, "Excuse me."

During several more attempts, she tried to ask other nearby women, but like the first two, they ignored her. What kind of customers did this place cater to? Did Zone Three's brand of whiskey make everyone rude?

As more and more people crowded into the club, she continued scanning again for her brother. Still, no sign of him anywhere. *Damn. Where the hell can he be?*

Suddenly, a bolt of electricity shot through her. Starting in her chest, the sensation expanded through her to her hands and feet, along her skin. Every part of her body heated up. The fire inside made her tremble. *Strange.* Probably just nerves.

As she moved through the throng, she noticed several men turn toward her and hungrily stare as if she'd suddenly become USDA prime choice steak. Until now, no one had bothered to notice her. What changed? It didn't matter. Though discomfited by the undue attention, she would use it to her advantage and see if, unlike the women, the men would answer her.

Searching the smoky room for the least intimidating male face, a pair of piercing dark eyes snagged her attention from across the room and didn't let go. Wolfish eyes, definitely intimidating. And the rest of his face—square jaw, sexy mouth, and oddly familiar.

Her eyes must be playing tricks on her.

Midnight hair hung to his shoulders and surrounded his rugged features. Six foot two. A black leather jacket—not the kind purchased at a designer store, but one roughened by a life on the road—covered his powerful shoulders and arms. Clearly, a motorcycle waited outside for him.

He reminded Micki of one of the men created in her sleep: a biker, a loner, and a man who would take her with few words and leave her weak and satisfied. The star of her most vivid, wicked dreams.

Fate? She'd never believed in it. Coincidence? That seemed unlikely, as well. He leaned against the bar with lust-filled eyes, just like in her dreams.

His presence, his magnetism, hit her like a sledgehammer. Heat flushed her from head to toe, and electricity rushed her. A missile of sensuality sizzled up her spine. She stumbled at his impact.

Micki grabbed the back of the closest sofa to steady herself as the man's gaze caused her fluttering butterflies to intensify their attacks on her insides like kamikaze pilots.

Could he be the David that Eric had instructed her to find and give the flash drive to? The likelihood of that seemed razor thin. Best to check with others before moving closer.

As she tried to pry her gaze away, his masculinity blasted her. The only thing between her and the floor—her grip on the sofa.

What's happening to me?

Suddenly, the club's music exploded around her, touching every exposed part of her skin and vibrating through the silky fabric of her top. Tangled in his dark stare, she felt helpless.

Deep, low notes pulled her toward the bar, closer to the leather-clad bad boy. Where she'd been warm before, now a blistering fever spread throughout her body.

But she wasn't here to make her dreams a reality. Eric needed her. So Micki tore her eyes from the provocative male and scanned Zone Three's crowd again for her brother.

* * * *

I've read until my eyes burn. It seems that immortals need humans for life essence. But it takes a triad, similar to the laws of electricity and the flow between positive, negative, and conduit. In this case, an angel, a jinn, and a human. If I try to tell anyone this, will they believe me?

Eric's Flash Drive: day 9—entry 3

* * * *

When the human dropped her gaze from his, the self-control Jared had relied on for the last two hundred years crumbled. He'd better suck it up, or someone would suffer. Maybe even him. He hadn't felt that deeply—hell, felt anything—in so long that it hurt. He tried to raise his shields again, but something about her made that impossible.

Fuck!

Dark hair cascaded down her shoulders. A white silk top embraced her full breasts. Smooth legs extended from her skirt, longer than the micro-minis the other women wore. He liked her choice of attire, its mystery and promise. Next to her, he would tower over the woman by more nearly a foot. Every inch of her kept him enthralled. Though he tried to resist her allure, he couldn't devour her enough with his stare.

He'd given up humans two centuries ago, but Jared couldn't help wondering what it would be like to fuck her.

Transfixed, he followed her every move.

His gut tightened when he spotted energy flaring from the woman like dancing red flames. He frowned. That wasn't possible. Humans only produced slight energy, and never enough to create color. Even when aroused, the largest display he'd ever seen from most mortals amounted to no more than a wispy smoky gray. But he couldn't deny her red—a color in the immortal plane he'd never seen before, except once.

And that one treacherous time, he'd never forget.

When his eyes had locked with the sexy female, his body had heated. Now, his cock enlarged. In his very long existence, he'd never gotten that hard that fast. Ever. Jared couldn't seem to clear his head. He'd seen a photo of Ms. Micki Langley a few days ago. Her picture had proven her beauty. Up close and in person? She flattened his restraint like a steamroller.

Where the hell is David so I can call this little payback done?

Synthesized tunes, synchronized perfectly to the multicolored flashing lights and fog machines, continued to clang against his eardrums. He watched her move unconsciously to the beat of the music. Though he detested the iPod, preferring his vinyls, he wished he had one now so he could drown out the sickening *thump*—and his own lust for the woman—with Korn or Zeppelin.

He seemed to be alone in his opinion, as the dance floor overflowed with immortals, both jinn and angel, and their soon-to-be human lovers. A trio in the center twisted together, the men sucking on the woman's bare breasts. His jinn-starvation, pulsing for satiation, clawed at his insides. He knew it well, but would never answer its call again, especially not with Micki Langley, no matter how much his dick disagreed.

She looked into her purse for the third time. He could tell by watching her that her insides danced with agitation. David's message didn't say how he'd lured her to Zone Three, but clearly something besides the sex most humans expected had brought her here tonight.

Jared considered cloaking himself in invisibility and sidling up next to her, but decided against it. He'd been tasked with keeping her here until David showed. Until then, she could walk around the club freely. He didn't trust himself to get close to her. Even from this distance, he doubted his willpower to resist. A single touch might unleash the darkness inside him.

She tapped one of the waitresses on the shoulder and spoke. Jared had watched her trying to engage some of the other women and witnessed their total disregard. Same old Alliance. Distrustful of all outsiders. At their slight, Micki's face showed worry. For what? Or whom?

Though Jared hated to admit it, a part of him howled in frustrated denial that Micki no longer looked at him. Damn it, why did he want her so much, naked and writhing in screaming delight beneath him? He hated himself for it.

"What are you doing here, jinn? You dare show your face?" boomed a bass voice from behind the bar.

Jared looked up and saw someone familiar. Greg, an angel warrior, posed as a human bartender.

He couldn't disagree with Greg. He'd no business being here.

Where the fuck was David? What game did he play, asking Jared to come to a stronghold of the Alliance when most who knew him saw him as an enemy? Why hadn't David chosen someone like Greg to make sure Micki stayed put?

"You'll have to ask your boss that, junior," Jared stated in an accent perfectly modern and local to the region.

Like all immortals, mimicry came easily for him, a much needed skill to conceal oneself from the short-lived and ever-changing mortal world.

The angel wore a gray t-shirt with Zone Three's logo, but underneath the fabric lived the muscled chest of a warrior.

"You're dreaming bullshit if you think I trust anything you say."

Jared mocked, "For in that sleep of death what dreams may come?"

Or nightmares?

He doubted the angel would recognize the line from *Hamlet*. The irony of the phrase wasn't wasted on Jared. Even when immortal death would finally take him to the Ether, he wouldn't be free from his guilt. The horror of the terrible night that'd been his downfall and had earned him the Alliance's disgrace would haunt him forever.

He felt the sensation of sparks coming from Greg preparing to attack. With a power bolt? A magic weapon?

Bring it on. Battle would bring Jared back to his senses and prevent him from doing the unthinkable with Micki Langley. He hoped.

"Giving me a lesson on the Ether by quoting Shakespeare? I'll kick your dark-loving ass into the Eternal Prison myself!"

Jared tried to gather his own power to counter whatever the angel brought. Even then, he couldn't rip his thoughts completely away from Micki.

Greg! The mental message from Nash hit Jared's brain like a bolt.

The angry angel growled back and still focused his power. Several patrons stepped away from the bar. Immortals. Most, too young to know Jared or his dark past, seemed confused, but he had no doubt they would back up their buddy should the angel need them.

But Nash… he *knew* Jared.

Greg, stop! That is an order!

Greg's icy stare remained full of righteous rage. *He shouldn't be here.*

It is not for you to decide. Stand down, soldier!

Greg's power eased up, but his gaze remained filled with distrust. *Nash, you, more than anyone, should want this scumbag destroyed.*

Jared agreed with Greg. Nash had the most compelling reason to want him dead.

That is my concern. Not yours.

But—

David has his motives, and you don't have to know them. Leave the jinn alone. Do you understand?

Yessir! Greg sent back to his commander, even as he glowered at Jared.

Did Nash stand in some dark corner, watching them?

Greg walked to the sink behind the bar and turned to glare over his shoulder. *Don't expect me to serve you a drink, asshole!*

"I'm not thirsty."

Greg's Alliance friends must've also gotten their orders from Nash as they walked away, leaving three barstools on either side of Jared empty. Even so, they still stared daggers at him. The rest of the crowd seemed unaware of the drama. Nash, instead of broadcasting wide, must've been selective in sending his messages. A well-trained commander.

Jared looked around for Nash. He'd not seen his former student since that terrible night when he'd fallen from the Alliance's grace and shared a nasty handshake with the dark side he'd never known he had. Now, Nash commanded Alliance troops. The old Jared would've been proud. Today, he didn't give a shit, not after everything that'd happened.

No sign of Nash anywhere. Damn.

With nowhere else to focus, Jared lasered his gaze back to Micki. Once he honed in on her, another wave of lust washed over him. In the next instant, the red flames around her pulsed brighter. What the hell did that mean?

Her hips swayed ever so slightly as she continued walking around the club. Several male immortals nearby took notice of her, their stares decidedly carnal. Fury exploded inside of him, a possessive fire that made no sense. She provided him the opportunity to do some much-owed penitence, nothing more. Best to get off this impending train wreck and find someone trustworthy to finish the job.

Jared sent out, *Nash, where the fuck are you?*

I am close.

Has David lost his mind asking me to protect her? Jared clenched his jaw.

Nash did not respond.

Jared knew well the evil that sought Ms. Langley.

Did you hear me, Nash? You know this isn't the right job for me.

Silence. Damn! Jared's anger melded into urges more powerful than any mortal could survive. He'd resisted them for two centuries, but he didn't know how he could withstand the onslaught of lust inside him tonight. How incredible would it be to flick his tongue against her clit as he readied her for his cock? The hunger she roused devoured his will. A dangerous need pushed him, and he wasn't sure how much longer he could control it.

David and Nash may have gone mad since he'd last seen them, but Jared had to keep it together, regroup his control. If he didn't, Ms. Langley could end up dead.

Chapter 2

I've learned from the book that the Alliance and the Dark are sworn enemies. Where does the Bloodline fall into this scenario?
Eric's Flash Drive: day 13—entry 1

* * * *

Hidden in a dark corner, warrior angel Bradley intently watched the woman David had assigned him to protect.

Legs, long and tanned. Round, full breasts. Pouty red lips. Micki Langley. Everything about her called to him to take her sexy body and press it against his own, but he had a mission to complete.

He scanned the room for darklings, but found none. It'd been over a century since demons had broken into an Alliance stronghold, and Zone Three's first line defenses tonight included Trey at the door and invisible sentries flying above the club. He doubted the Dark would mount a frontal attack, but he remained on guard.

He also watched Jared, the traitor. How had *he* made it past Trey?

Practically salivating, the jinn eagerly studied Micki. Bradley wasn't surprised, given his own reaction to her. Understandable or not, Jared wasn't to be trusted, especially with Micki Langley.

Bradley had seen the confrontation between Greg and Jared. Why hadn't his fellow warrior taken the disgraced jinn down? Greg knew Jared's past. Something, someone, had suddenly made Greg stand down.

It'd been many years since Bradley had seen Jared, and he planned on making tonight the last time. Though not a direct objective of his assignment, killing the jinn seemed justified. Jared had betrayed everything the Alliance stood for and had made no apologies or restitution. Jared coming out of his two hundred year seclusion on the very night Micki Langley came to Zone Three wasn't an incredible coincidence. Ms. Langley definitely didn't need to be in the crosshairs of the dangerous jinn.

"He's here at David's request." Out of green jinn smoke, Nash materialized next to him. Just over six feet tall with bulging muscles, he was a warrior everyone took seriously. In his former mortal life, Nash must've come from Persia or Babylon. Olive skin, dark hair and brown eyes. Human women flocked to him, though Nash mostly kept to himself.

While Bradley trusted Nash, he could hardly fathom David's reason for inviting a snake into their lair. "Why?"

"To protect her."

Jared, protect *her*? How could David be so blind, so reckless? The archangel's colossal arrogance would get Micki killed. Though Bradley respected his commander, he also knew David dispensed orders in a high and mighty manner. Redundancy in missions assured a greater chance of success, yes, but giving Jared a mission after he'd broken the Alliance vow? Much too risky. If Bradley didn't know that David was an archangel, he would have sworn at times the guy was the Devil himself.

"Nash, my orders are to keep her out of the Dark's reach. Now, I also have to protect her from him?" Once he said it, he wished he hadn't. He knew the pain the jinn at his side carried. All warriors who'd been in that cavern that terrible night knew what Nash suffered.

After a long sigh, "I guess you do, soldier."

Bradley smiled at the thought. Time to kick some traitor jinn ass. "I guess I do."

"Given that, you'd better tuck in those wings of yours and do it quick."

"What do you mean?"

Nash shook his head. "Don't be a fool, Bradley. Whatever David has in mind is in the best interest of the Alliance. Don't forget that."

"I won't." Though he wasn't so sure about David's judgment.

"Then why are you standing here open-mouthed, ogling the human you're to protect and glaring at the other immortal assigned to this mission? Can you not see the energy she's emitting?"

Bradley scanned Micki again. His eyes widened. She broadcasted to the entire immortal world like a flashing sign, Las Vegas style. Red flames, unseen by human eyes, encircled her entire body.

Nash added, "If her energy keeps growing and you don't reduce some of her output, every immortal, both Dark and Light, will be fighting for a chance at her."

True. Her power impacted him in ways he'd never felt. It magnetized him. He wanted to taste her depths, to spread her legs wide for his tongue, to provide her with a night of incomparable orgasms. Keeping his distance proved to be a difficult task, as if she put him under some spell that threatened his restraint. He'd never been so unsettled.

I've never seen anything like that from a human. Have you, Nash?

Once, a long time ago.

How's it possible?

That's a good question for David.

"What should I do to get her power under control?"

Nash's stare scolded him. "That is a question I would expect from a newly risen angel, not you."

"You want me to arrange a tripling with her?" Everything below the waist stood up and saluted that suggestion.

"That *is* the obvious answer."

True, but who else would join them to—

"Triple with Micki—and him?" Bradley pointed at Jared in horror.

"Do you have a better plan?"

"There are other jinn here. Surely—"

"But no other jinn David assigned to her."

His jaw clenched tight at the thought of tripling with the traitor. Nash seemed unfazed by the idea. Nothing made any sense at all.

There must be a better tactic. "She doesn't appear to be here for sex, and sharing a human with him, forget it."

"Abandoning your mission?"

Bradley winced. Put like that, no.

"You're a jinn. Why don't you stay and take his place?"

"You have your orders, and I have mine." Then the jinn commander dematerialized in a haze of smoke.

Bradley cursed. At least this might give him the opportunity to deal a little Alliance retribution to the traitor. As he pushed away from the wall to move closer to Micki and the jinn, the thought made him smile.

* * * *

Micki swallowed, shoving aside her curiosity and overactive imagination magnified by the dim lights of the club. The heat and electricity that'd almost knocked her off her feet earlier still swirled around her. Added to that, the memories of her recent dreams provided the ingredients for her weak knees and aching pussy. That must be it.

Either that or the hot biker staring at her like he craved her more than his next breath.

Micki shook off the shiver of trepidation and excitement. She hadn't come here for the hunk. Now, she should focus on her task. Find Eric or David. *Unless against all odds, the hunk is David?* Her nerves threatened to sever her control in half, as if she'd attacked them with a cleaver.

She drew in a calming breath, then another. Surely, she wasn't the man's focus. Most likely, he'd been looking past her at the door for someone else to arrive.

Though annoyed and a little frightened, unable to resist, she looked for the biker who'd haunted her dreams, but couldn't see him through the machine-generated fog. She imagined his eyes still on her, staring from behind the warm vapor. Her temperature rose rapidly at the thought of him. A predator. Concealed, ravenous. The sort of man she'd always avoided, knowing they'd only stamp pain over her untried heart.

Most likely, the yummy biker had moved on to more willing prey. Still, warmth continued to go up inside her as she recalled her recent dreams, the ones in which he touched her in every sinful way she'd ever imagined. Tongues diving into her greedy mouth, hands squeezing her hard nipples, cocks invading her hot core. He and the other hunk fulfilling her desires together.

Not waiting for the invisibility the smoke provided to fade, Micki found her way to the opposite side of the bar, away from the dark-eyed beast. Maybe one of the bartenders would be of help in her search and would know if the hottie was David. She couldn't imagine coming within his reach until she knew for certain.

She sat on one of the few empty barstools and noticed the fog clearing. She couldn't refuse herself one more peek at Mr. Intense. She looked back where she'd first seen him. His unblinking dark eyes pierced her. Hungry. Unwavering. She sucked in a roomful of air. Oh, dear God.

Again, electricity zapped her when she spotted him. It crackled and popped inside her, pulsing, like flames that licked at her chest, belly and clit.

She tried to clear her head, but instead trembled from head to toe. She wrapped her arms around her middle, trying to stop it with absolutely no success. No time to figure out why; she needed help, now.

Micki averted her gaze from the sexy biker. *Please, mister, look at someone else. I must stay on task.*

She'd already scrapped the idea of asking the hunk first. She needed answers, yes, but before approaching him, she'd ask someone less threatening.

"Excuse me, sir?" she shouted over the noise, trying to get the bartender's attention.

The bartender closest to her rinsed martini glasses, but never looked up. If the biker with the lusty eyes could ignore her like the guy slinging drinks, she would breathe much easier.

"Sir!"

He still didn't acknowledge her. Rather, he set down the glasses and took the order of a nearby man with two women stuck to him like parasitic remora fish clinging to a shark.

In fact, Zone Three's inky waters teamed with carnivorous creatures. And a great white with forcible eyes was still zeroing in on her. She couldn't muster the courage to meet his stare.

When the bartender finished, Micki called to him again, but he seemed deaf and blind to her. She shook her head in frustration. Zone Three got under her skin and not in the good way. The few singles around her mingled, trying to make connections. Since Micki sat alone, no wonder she felt *way* out of place.

She took in a long, slow breath. When she gathered her courage, she glanced at the other side of the bar and found the hot biker's seat empty. Relief and disappointment mingled inside her—until she felt more than saw him edge up to her left. He didn't sit in the empty barstool next to her. Instead, he hovered close, closer. Her pulse picked up speed. It took all of her effort not to glance at him over her shoulder, but it was impossible not to *feel* him.

Micki waved again to the bartender, who continued to ignore her, unlike this man. Warm currents of his exhalations stirred her hair and skated over her exposed neck. A flash of excitement spread over her skin. The electric charge swirled around her and down to her mound. If she'd been standing, she would've fallen to the floor.

Garnering a little daring, she peeked over her shoulder at him. *Oh,*

God. Not a mirage brought on by distance, artificial smoke and colored lights. Up close, he looked exactly like one of the hunks in her recent erotic dreams—a three-dimensional embodiment of her sleep-born fantasy.

When Micki met his gaze, full-blown lust shot back at her. He had eyes of night she could lose herself in forever.

He didn't speak.

She dropped her gaze and found that his expanding denim could barely contain his desire for her.

"Do you approve?" The stud baited her.

She jerked her head up and met his dark stare. He'd caught her looking at his—

Damn.

The blood rushed to her cheeks.

Time to fade into the background. Unlike spotlight-hogging Eric, she liked her invisibility. Besides, she had a purpose for being here and eye-fucking the biker wasn't it.

The swirling heat sizzled her, charging every cell in her body. Her heart pounded faster in her chest, mirroring the rhythm of the music.

Boom. Boom. Boom.

"Ummm. Are you David?" The words came out more like a squeak. Micki felt warmth fill her cheeks.

His eyes hinted at danger. He didn't answer. The silent treatment at Zone Three pissed her off. Still, she must keep trying for Eric's sake.

"I'll take that as a *no.* Do you know Eric Langley? Or a guy named David? I don't know his last name, but I've been told he comes here most weekends."

The stud nodded, then lifted his leather-clad arm, calling the bartender to him. She wanted to tell him not to waste his time, but she couldn't find her voice when the hunk's dark stare centered on her, drawing out shivering heat from her wherever it landed.

Why did she react so strongly to him? She'd never been very

sexual, but being near this beast ignited some chemical reaction inside her unlike anything she'd ever experienced. The ache sharpened in her pussy.

He pulled off his jacket, revealing monster biceps shooting out of a tight, black t-shirt. His bronzed skin bespoke a love of sun on his body, and she wanted to touch his black hair with her fingers, kiss his square-jawed face, feel his hands on her. A unique tattoo of three interlocked triangles decorated his upper arm. A fantasy in the flesh.

Without a word, he placed the jacket in her lap. It smelled of him—sin and heat and male. Was Mr. Dark, Mysterious, and Dangerous indicating to everyone—and to her—that she was his for the night?

He moved his hand to her bare leg, resting it possessively just below her skirt and above her knee. Her gut tightened. Guess that settled the question.

Why wasn't she objecting? She should take his hand and remove it. Instead, she gripped his coat. Under her fingers, the leather felt worn and rough. So did his hand on her thigh, which added to her growing arousal.

"Jared," he finally offered.

He isn't David.

His bass voice rocketed to her core. A blistering-hot current shot up her spine. She'd never had this reaction to any man's voice. A word from him and—*Bang!* A breath away from orgasm.

"Jared. That's a good name." She squirmed, squeezing her thighs together, feeling the delicious discomfort deepen. "I'm Micki."

"Pleasure."

Get a grip, Micki. Stay focused.

She'd come to find Eric. Nothing else.

* * * *

"You know Eric Langley?" Micki's tone changed from sultry to serious, but it still stirred Jared's cock. Her sexy-hot body stirred him even more. Her scent, jasmine coupled with a hint of vanilla, filled his nostrils. Breathing her essence drove him wild.

Fuck!

Eric Langley. Same last name as Micki. Her husband? Foolish, but fresh resentment demolished Jared's reason. He burned hot at the idea of her belonging to someone else.

Somehow David had used Eric to get her here. Same angelic prick he'd always been.

Though Jared had originally decided to stay away from her, as more and more immortals had begun noticing her and her growing red aura, he'd moved closer. Jared wasn't sure why, but he had the most insane urge to protect her.

As he inched his way to her, the unusual red flames around her flared.

Though he knew the risk—both to her and his sanity—he caressed Micki's legs in the hopes her energy would cool. He felt her shiver, but he didn't stop. He wasn't sure, but if he could just siphon off some of her power, then the other immortals' attention would divert back to the human regulars at Zone Three.

The more her power ran across his fingers, the more he wanted to taste it, take it in, but only tripling could provide what he craved. Not that any warrior here would agree to join him in a triad and a needed renewal of immortal power.

He clenched his jaw tight.

Once David showed up, he would pass Micki off to the archangel's care. After a few choice words, he'd hop on his Harley and head back to Montana, away from all this Alliance crap and humankind. Away from Micki Langley and his perilous desire for her.

"Did you hear my question?"

He repressed a smile. Even her impatience thrilled him. So very sexy.

"I've heard of Eric Langley," Jared lied. "Don't know him

personally."

"Do you know where he is? Is he safe? Do you know how to reach him?" Micki's panicky words shot out like bullets from a machine gun.

"No."

Her eyes pleaded with him though she didn't shed a tear. This one had moxie, which made her all the more intriguing. Like he needed gasoline on the fire.

"Can you tell me how to find David?" she demanded more than asked.

Greg moved toward them and barked, "What do you want with David, woman?"

"Do you know David? Is he here?" Micki shot back at the angel.

"I know him. And no, he's not here," Greg answered.

Micki's eyes filled with anxiety. "Do you expect him soon?"

"David keeps his own calendar."

She wrung her hands. "How can I contact him?"

"You can't. How do *you* know David?"

"I don't. My brother does. Eric Langley. Do you know him? Have you seen him recently?" Micki asked the angel. The slight quiver in her voice would have been lost on human ears but not Jared's.

She didn't know David, and Eric wasn't her husband. Jared felt relief creep through his body, and he hated himself for it. She could never be anything to him.

"No. Never heard of him."

Is that true? Jared shot to Greg.

Jinn, you may be on a mission for David, but I don't have to share information with you.

"Damn." Micki bit her lip. "Do you know anyone else I can ask about my brother?"

Greg moved to the sink and turned on the faucet, looking back dubiously at them. Jared felt sure that the angel knew Eric. Why was the jackass being so cagey?

Greg pointed at him and asked Micki, "You with this worthless piece of shit?"

Micki tensed at the angel's words. Did she expect him to react, to jump up and punch Greg? The old Jared would've already had the guy on the ground, beating the pulp out of him for the insolence. Now, well, Jared's shame had been boiled into his bones. He deserved the angel's indignation, and more.

Still, Jared would make sure Micki didn't leave until David showed up. He owed Micki and the Alliance that, at the very least.

"It's a public place," she shot back at Greg. "We are allowed to be here just like anyone else."

Silently, Jared sent to the angel, *Don't forget what Nash told you.*

Greg didn't respond. Instead, he tossed an empty glass into the sink, splashing soapsuds everywhere. "If you run with the likes of him, you'll get much more than you bargained for. I have half-a-mind to slap some sense into you."

"Shut your mouth. Now," Jared warned, then added, *If you lay a finger on her, angel-boy, she will be the last human you ever touch.*

Green smoke beat at Jared's insides, dying for release. He held it at bay. He curled his left hand on Micki's leg into a fist, ready for whatever Greg dished out.

The angel could say anything he wanted to him, and Jared wouldn't blame him, but the asshole would not scare Micki. It had nothing to do with following David's orders. Something primal beat inside him, and he would pulverize Greg if the angel dared to test him.

Damn. I feel like I'm on a playground with schoolboys. This isn't helping me find my brother.

Jared whipped his shocked stare to Micki. How had he heard her thoughts? A human?

Chapter 3

Brooke just walked in and found me reading. She didn't ask me about the book, thank God. It's late, and she suggested I come to bed.

I want to tell her and Micki everything—I really do. But how? They would think I've flipped out. They wouldn't be far from wrong. I have my own doubts about this. What if Lillian was mistaken? But my visit to the doctor's office didn't prove her incorrect. While I'm physically in great shape, I feel like I'm dying on the inside. He suggested a psychiatrist. The clock is ticking. I don't have much time left—nor does Micki.

Eric's Flash Drive: day 13—entry 12

* * * *

Jared shook his head. Micki Langley didn't fit the mold of any human he'd known before. Sure, immortals sent thoughts freely to one another. But humans? That only happened during a full sexual connection. But he *had* heard her thoughts. They weren't the random bits of mind junk he'd gleaned from humans before. Her thoughts came to him clear and complete.

"Thanks for the advice," she said tartly to the angel. "If you don't know anything, then—"

"Get her a Corona with lime," Jared ordered Greg, hoping it would keep her side a bit longer.

Micki turned to him with a frown. "That's my favorite drink. How did you know?"

Jared could think of no explanation other than their weird

connection. He shrugged.

"In a glass or a bottle?" Greg groused.

She looked back at the angel. "Bottle."

Everything about her exhilarated Jared. He wanted her like hell, and the very ground shook because of it. David better get his ass here quickly.

"And he wants two shots of tequila," she commanded. *Just like my dream biker would want.*

Greg snorted a response before turning to get their drinks.

Had the angel also heard her thoughts? Jared wasn't sure. He considered asking the warrior, but decided against it. Besides, Greg wouldn't tell him anything except to go to hell—where he belonged.

Another reflection from Micki blared to him. *Why am I ordering drinks? I should be asking questions.*

Jared closed off his thoughts, just in case she could read them. Usually not possible with a human, but better safe than sorry.

Who else could hear her mind-speak? Jared glanced around the room. From several directions, immortals glared back at him, but none acted as if they'd heard her musings.

He turned his gaze back to Micki. His effort to reduce her outpouring of energy through touch wasn't working. What more could he do—besides finding an angel to help him fuck her breathless? He better figure it out fast or those searching for her would soon pick up her signal. Following orders now included getting her output controlled. His gut wrenched at the thought. *Damn!*

David's message, along with a photo of Micki, had ensured Jared complied. The Dark wanted her, just like another woman he'd known—and lost. Had the archangel brought Jared into this debacle as some kind of joke? Whenever the guy finally did show up, Jared would rip his wings right off.

Micki shifted under his hands and need clutched his soul. He resumed rubbing her thighs, hoping to strip off more of her power and to keep her focused on him. He'd seen her impatience with Greg. If he didn't keep her engaged, she'd likely move on to someone else. That would be dangerous.

His dormant skills resurfaced with every moment. He would keep her here, vibrating under his touch, raising the stakes with more seductive caresses, controlling more of her heat. He would keep trying to reduce her power to something manageable until David showed his face. It had to work.

Greg delivered a bottle, a lime sticking out of its neck, and the two shots. Jared couldn't wait to see Micki's lips on the long glass bottle and imagined her lips on his cock. The battle inside him raged between his anemic willpower and his heavy-duty desire. He detested his weakness.

Forgoing lime and salt, Jared slammed one of the tequilas.

"Fourteen fifty," Greg announced.

So like the strongholds he'd known centuries earlier, the Alliance also kept up pretenses here.

Micki pulled out a credit card from her purse. *Back to the task of getting the answers I need.* "What can you tell me about David? Is he one of your regulars?"

He admired her mettle. Could the tricks at his disposal keep her next to him?

Even as unanswered questions assailed him, Jared grabbed her wrist, silently informing her she wasn't paying. Ensuring Micki couldn't see, he conjured a twenty in his other hand, then he slapped it onto the bar. Micki's submissive expression thrilled him. She placed her card back into her purse. Heat stampeded to his cock.

"He is," Greg answered.

"And? Please," she pleaded. "My brother is missing. I'm worried about him."

Greg sighed and took Jared's bill. "David left hours ago. Some emergency. But I expect him back after midnight."

"Are you sure?" Jared's irritation swelled.

His plan to ditch the place and the woman depended on David

being there. Being available. Same old David.

"Quite sure."

Fuck! Now what? Did David expect him to stay half the night with Micki? No way. His willpower wouldn't last. If he couldn't stop the pulsing red energy from radiating from her, he couldn't keep her safe.

Micki's hazel-gold eyes glistened with tears. Her faithfulness and courage for her brother astounded him and added to her off-the-charts appeal.

He pressed his legs into her thighs to comfort and distract her.

His touches mitigated a small part of her energy, but not enough. The danger wasn't just around them. Their skin-to-skin contact incited his lust into a supernova fervor. Jared's cock engorged with every pulse of her heartbeat. The dangerous combination—the urge to protect, tangling with the need to possess—spun in his head.

She needed a tripling. A willing angel would be easy to find, as long as it was with a different willing jinn. *Fuck!* The image of another jinn touching Micki razed his reason.

He downed the other tequila.

Her heat pulled at Jared, and the immortal hunger he'd been able to keep at bay for so long juiced up to life inside of him. He shifted his hands under her tight skirt. She froze, paused.

Her breathing sped up. Her skin flushed.

Then her thoughts danced into his head.

It feels so good. My whole body is on fire. He's so strong, so very sexy. I need him inside me. No. I need to focus on the fact Jared or the bartender might be my last hope of finding Eric. Or David. God, his touch is so good!

He agreed that touching her felt good. He needed to keep doing it to bring her power down, distract her. Unfortunately for him, each of Micki's passionate thoughts only added to his own.

Jared pushed his fingers farther up her skirt, stroking her upper thighs. Her firm flesh and soft skin felt amazing. He wanted to rip her skirt right off to bare her hot cunt for him to consume.

Suddenly, Micki gasped. More heat boiled out of her.

Before he could discern why, a male voice interrupted Jared's thoughts. *So, are you ready to triple?*

Jared looked past Micki to a dark corner of the club. Glaring back at him stood Bradley, one of David's most prized angelic soldiers. A warrior to the core, brimming with Alliance fervor.

Grimacing, Jared looked away. He wanted to triple. God knew he did, but... *No.*

Had David, due to the late hour, sent Bradley to relieve him of his duty to Micki?

Bradley sent, *Look at the energy she's producing. She's become a beacon for every immortal in the area on both sides of the war. We have to get her off the power grid now!*

Jared turned back to Micki. In the last few seconds, her aura had grown to frightening levels, shining bright. What could be causing that?

My job is to keep her here until David shows. That's all.

Bradley crossed his arms over his chest. *My job is to protect her, asshole!*

Then do it, but I won't triple with anyone.

Bradley scowled. *Your hands are all over her and you want to refuse?*

I am only touching her to shave off some of her power.

Jared knew that wasn't his only reason.

He should have returned an instant 'no' to David and his mission, rejected this task. When he'd opened the package with the photo of Micki and the written message from David, his soul had fractured.

Bradley growled, *Your feeble attempts aren't working. Time to move horizontal.*

Find someone else, angel. Do whatever you need to do to keep Micki Langley safe. My only job is to keep her here. Mission accomplished.

That's idiotic, jinn. She's in danger and putting the stronghold in danger. Let's get her out of here.

And disobey David's orders? Jared hoped Bradley would detect his sarcasm.

Jared wasn't letting Micki out of his sight or out of the club.

Good point. Let's get her upstairs.

Jared knew that would be where a stronghold like this would have the rooms to—

Triple. That's right, jinn. But I don't trust you. The angel started walking toward Micki and Jared.

Good. Then find another jinn for your plan. I won't complete the triangle.

He said the words with conviction, though everything inside Jared screamed that he was a liar.

* * * *

Micki tried to regain some of her composure, but she might as well have tried to swim up a river's category five rapids. She couldn't remember ever being so stimulated and jumpy.

Seconds ago, another bolt of electricity had shot through her body. Different than the one earlier when she'd had to grab the sofa to steady herself, more like a crisp current that made her skin tingle and her tongue taste chocolate.

Jared's stare drifted back over her. Mindlessly, she looked in her purse for something—anything. She needed to ground herself, find some kind of footing, but every brush of his hands over her skin took her higher. How could she be this aroused when he'd done nothing more than caress her legs?

The flash drive jabbed her palm, bringing her back to her task. Eric's task. And reality. Fantasy or not, she had to find an escape from Jared's powers over her.

"How do you know David?" she asked. "What's his last name?

How can I reach him?"

"How many questions are you going to ask before you let me answer?" Jared chided.

"Depends. Do you know any of the answers?"

"One. Nobody here has a last name."

That didn't surprise Micki, given the wild crowd.

As he leaned into her, Jared's long black hair touched her shoulders. Her heart picked up pace. Was he going to kiss her? No. Instead, his eyes drifted behind her. What was he looking at? Or whom?

Some other woman must've demanded his attention, giving Micki an opportunity to exit. Even if some part of her wanted to stay, she really should take the cue.

Still she hesitated. Jared's shifting glance over her shoulder said to her that the sexual interaction between them had ended, but his left hand stroking her leg shouted that they'd just begun.

She turned to see who Jared looked at and nearly fainted. *It's not possible!*

What felt like a hundred thousand volts bore into her as she stared at someone eerily like the other man from her dreams: her sun-soaked, hard-bodied soldier.

Dizziness seized her and she thought she might slip from the barstool to the floor. Micki tightly closed her eyes. Would her other fantasy man disappear when she opened them again? She wished she could blame her delusions on the beer, but she hadn't even taken the first sip.

When she opened her eyes, he was still there in all his sexiness. A brown camouflage tank pulled tight around his ripped torso and cargo shorts covered massive, muscled thighs. Six foot four. Blond hair cut razor-short. Her gaze caught his, and she saw baby blues looking back with a ferocious hunger.

I need to pinch myself.

Had she completely lost every sensibility? If Jared could help find

Eric, great. If not, she must look for David by herself. Her fantasies would have to wait, even though something about these two made her body scream out for the fulfillment in the worst way.

Micki turned back to Jared. He stared at her breasts. Normally, she'd be insulted if a virtual stranger checked her out so obviously. With Jared, her desire simply deepened. She licked her lips, imagining the soldier and biker touching every part of her in tandem, one vigorous and arousing, the other masterful and demanding. She barely stifled a moan as moisture seeped from her pussy.

She pushed the lime into her bottle of beer. Some of its contents erupted over the lip and down the sides. She dove to lick the liquid off before it spilled on the bar top. She wiped the neck of the bottle with a bar napkin and took a long drink. Then she caught Jared watching her with a fixed stare. Her hands shook as she placed the bottle back on the bar.

Heat moved through her. Sinful sex. Men wanting to seduce her for her body and give her pleasure like she'd only imagined.

She needed perspective and fast.

Difficult when Jared continued his arousing caresses. Her legs felt weak. She wasn't sure she could stand on her own after his expert handling. Her natural cautions gave way to deeper passions, burning as Jared hypnotized her with his fingers, moving up her thighs—*closer, closer, closer...*

Pounding with excitement, Micki turned back to the blue-eyed soldier. Utter Adonis—able to charm or kill as need be. Even at their current distance, his stare revealed unabashed desire. And a mouth-watering body.

Focus! "Jared, do you know anyone who might help me find Eric or David?"

He pointed at the soldier. Fire erupted deep inside her when she saw the man march toward them.

Micki turned back to Jared, whose palm caressed her legs—and very nearly between them. "You know him?"

He nodded.

The music changed tempo, speeding to overdrive, just like her heartbeat. Two more steps and the blond god would be next to them. Things sped faster and faster.

BOOM! BOOM! BOOM!

"I really need to find David now!" she said nearly shouting. "I can't wait for him to return."

BOOM! BOOM! BOOM!

Jared slipped a finger between her thighs, almost touching her *there*. Micki held her breath and tensed, waiting for what she shouldn't want.

"He's gone for the night," the sexy blond stud stated as he stepped right beside her where he could see clearly each and every one of Jared's touches. "He'll be back tomorrow,"

His eyes blazed and his face filled with lust. Excitement wrapped itself around her, squeezing more liquid from her channel.

"Oh." She stared up at the new arrival "Do you know the number to his cell? Or his address?"

"I don't think David owns a cell, and he stays lots of places. I'm Bradley," the soldier added, watching Jared's every move with hot eyes.

She should be shocked at Bradley's rapt attention to her and Jared. Instead, heat spread through her body like warm chocolate.

If Jared had a Harley waiting for him, Bradley had a Hummer or a tank, and a bed with silk sheets. Alluring in a different way than Jared, Bradley seemed deliberate, rather than moody. Battle ready, rather than road-hardened.

She spotted the tattoo on Bradley's upper arm. Three interlocked triangles—an exact twin of Jared's. She reached out to touch the tat on the soldier's upper arm, but then pulled back. Heat burned up and down her spine.

"Don't stop, sweetheart. Feel free to touch me any way you want."

She didn't. The thought of touching him scared and intrigued her.

Maybe these two worked together—like a seduction tag team—persuading women, night after night, to share their bed.

Bradley glared at Jared. From the contentious look between them, Micki realized they weren't a seduction duo. Not even friends. Enemies? She couldn't tell, but the vibe between them ran hostile. Did they pursue her separately or together?

Either way, Jared's palm inched up her thigh again, sending shivers of delight through her body. She loved his touch. Bradley still watched with a rapt gaze. Would they fight? They looked capable of anything.

Her gut broiled like an oven on high. Her recent dreams of them aroused her, but as thrilling as exploring fantasies would be, that wasn't why she'd come.

"How do you two know each other?" she asked.

Neither answered.

Standing beside her, Bradley's body heat loomed on her shoulder. Jared's hot eyes sent her silent commands that incited cravings. Her body began to demand satisfaction. Heat rose from her skin, centered between her legs, melting her.

Then Bradley cupped her cheek, fingertips caressing her neck, while Jared nearly touched her intimately. Tingles erupted. Warm wetness soaked her panties.

"What's your name, sweetheart?" Bradley asked.

"Micki."

Jared's free hand slipped under her shirt and brushed across her bare back. Sensations ripped through her entire body. Combustion. She shivered.

Bradley looked at her, his stare burning with suggestion. She wanted him to drink all of her up with his hot mouth, but she needed to focus.

"Do you know Eric Langley?" Micki asked Bradley.

He cut a quick glance to Jared before looking her way again.

"Yes. But I'm not sure if he's here, either."

Bradley knew Eric! "Thank God! Where is he? Is he safe?"

Another pause. "I don't know."

Jared and Bradley's hesitation troubled her. She suspected they knew more than they'd told her. Plus, strange as it was, as her worry for Eric grew, so did her desire for these two men. Did the nice folks in white coats need to whisk her away?

Unease skittered through her. "If you don't know, I can't just sit here. I need to be looking for him."

She should get up, resume her search, but Bradley's piercing blue eyes zeroing in on her mouth paralyzed her.

She swallowed hard. *Bring on the straight jacket.*

"You look like you need to be kissed," he murmured.

Heat flared inside her, but she tensed. When she glanced back at her biker, he showed no sign of rage—not even slight annoyance. Instead, he seemed revved up by Bradley's suggestion.

Micki sucked in a shocked breath.

She could name a thousand reasons not to take Bradley's dangled bait, but the moment crashed over her reserve. She could exit the ride later, before the big drop. Now, she burned to taste Bradley's lips, revel in Jared's touch. Feel their need and let them feel hers.

It's only a kiss, right?

If Eric watched from the shadows, though she doubted he did, kissing Bradley might bring him out of hiding, either in full big-brother mode or thrilled that his prank had worked. If not, her best hope would be to soften against Bradley and Jared a little to learn what they *really* knew about her brother.

Slowly, she leaned forward, offering Bradley her mouth. His full lips met hers, just touching. Moist and firm. He tasted of mint. Then he pulled away and smiled at her showing perfect white teeth.

A shiver ran through her as he leaned in again and pressed his mouth against hers for a second time, harder now. Her toes curled as he cupped a hand around her nape and coaxed her tongue into dancing with his. Skilled. Devastating. Bradley impacted her senses like a velvet jackhammer. A shiver ran from their lips all the way down to her clit. She squeezed her thighs together trying desperately to curb the ache.

Jared cupped her left breast. She sucked in a breath. Hot. Delicious. The rush of pleasure amazed her—as did her brazen behavior. But something inside her would not be quieted. Desire? Instinct? Regardless, whatever awoke obliterated logic.

Previously, her few erotic dreams ran to the more vanilla flavors, but for the past several nights she'd been dreaming of two men ravaging her. Since the very first multi-flavored dream, her hunger had been growing. Seething. Voracious. Unappeased—until now.

Her body felt like the tide coming in and out, rippling from where Jared's hand latched and Bradley's mouth pressed, all the way through her. She groaned softly.

One of Jared's hands wandered across her shoulders, down her back, and stopped at the clasp of her bra. With one pinch, it came undone. Seconds later, his hand locked back onto her breast, but this time, skin touched skin. A thunderbolt shock shot through her, warming every cell. His thumb drifted across the bare nipple. Her ache multiplied. Micki swallowed hard. Her appetite for them demanded more with each pass of his thumb over her nipples now hot and tight. *Can anyone see us?*

She scanned the room. Everyone's activities passed every boundary she'd ever known. While unusual for her, not unusual for here. Her skin warmed even more.

Jared's other hand, still between her thighs, eased past the remaining inch to her soaking panties. His finger dipped under the elastic and teased around her swollen pussy. Micki gasped. Her gut tightened, and she flushed hot. *Oh God!* No way of hiding her want now. With that touch, he knew. His fingers pressed against her clit, pulling another moan from deep in her throat. She felt really alive for the first time.

She tore her mouth from Bradley's. What the hell had she been thinking? Doing?

She knew exactly why she'd come to Zone Three, and it hadn't been for sex.

Renewed fear cramped her belly. "I've got to stop this. I need to find my brother."

Chapter 4

Why do bloodliners die so young? It doesn't make sense. I cannot figure it out. I need to find someone to help me understand this, but whom?

Eric's Flash Drive: day 15—entry 3

* * * *

"We'll help you, Micki." Bradley kissed her ear hoping it might diffuse some of her power.

With the jinn refusing to go upstairs, he caressed Micki. But nothing they did worked. He buzzed with energy from their hot kiss. Even more strange, he could hear Micki's thoughts.

Could the jinn be duping him somehow?

Micki sighed. Her concern for Eric weighted her spirit down, but still, her energy continued to intensify. He must do something, and fast.

"Won't we help her, Jared?"

The jinn didn't reply, just stared with a hot gaze that revealed his starvation and Micki looked like the ten-course meal he craved.

Bradley glared at the jinn. *What the hell are you doing?*

Trying to get her power output controlled.

It hasn't worked. The only chance we have is to get her upstairs and triple.

Listen to me, Mr. Alliance. I'm not going upstairs. She's staying here until David shows up. Then you can do whatever you want with her.

Damn, he wanted to introduce Jared's jaw to his fists.

"Will you help me?" Micki asked the jinn.

No response.

Answer her or I swear I'll send your ass to the Ether myself. Bradley's patience dissolved.

Try it, warrior!

Bradley's jaw clenched tight, but he kept nodding and smiling at Micki. *You're a fool, jinn. You obviously aren't smart enough to realize that everything we've tried on Micki has failed. Her energy is like a solar flare.*

Jared glanced back at him. *Perhaps we have to do more.*

The jinn's hand moved underneath Micki's skirt.

She glared at Jared. "Stop!"

Not only is your attempt to use foreplay not working now, she's ready to bolt. Is that what you want, Jared?

The jinn's eyes went dark. Then the nefarious immortal turned to Micki and asked, "Which part of you is saying stop, you or your soaked little panties?"

She blushed.

Bradley's cock hardened with the need to have her spread out and open to all he ached to give her, to pleasure her beyond her wildest dreams. Images of her enraptured by his touch engulfed all thought.

He could sense Jared's lust growing,. Green, smoky flames circled the jinn.

Bradley looked down at his own body. The familiar blue light surrounded him, but this time, it swirled faster than he'd ever seen. *So bizarre.*

He needed to clear his mind, get back to the task and the mission.

"I don't care about my panties right now, just my brother."

Bradley sent to the jinn, *We have to move upstairs, now!*

She's not leaving my sight until David shows up. Or do you think you can change my mind about that, angel? With a pointed brow raised, Jared removed Micki's bra in an instant, pulling it out from under her blouse. Micki's jaw dropped.

Jared held the garment aloft in his fist in defiance. *Take a look at her energy output, angel.*

Bradley scanned her. The jinn's action had reduced the red flames back about half of what they'd been. Bradley let out a long, slow breath.

Seconds later, the red flared up reaching the ceiling and four feet around them, nearly double the previous max for the night. Fingers began pointing and voices began whispering throughout the club.

Damn!

Bradley needed to take action. Instead he fixated on Micki's nipples jutting from behind the silk of her blouse. How he longed to taste her ripe berries.

His mind would not quiet. But it wasn't just her state of undress that pulled at him. Her thoughts flooded into him. How she cherished her brother. Her ability to conquer her fear with courage astounded him. How alone she felt without him, a feeling he understood. He'd stamped his own emotions down on the day he'd risen into immortality, the memory of his human life and family erased completely. The same day he'd sworn his allegiance to the Alliance— his new purpose for the past two hundred and twenty-nine years.

Each moment with Micki, his connection to her deepened. He could feel it in the tightening of his skin, the heavy thump of his heart. Was it her red flames that drew him in deeper? Or was it something else about her?

Uncontrollable need for her consumed Bradley, more need than he could conceive. He craved pleasing her until he could barely think.

He forced the feeling away.

"Give my bra back," Micki breathed to Jared.

Instead, the jinn stuffed it into his back pocket, letting the split straps hang out.

Jared, her power is expanding beyond the dangerous.

The jinn frowned, showing he knew it.

"Fine. Keep it," she stated, her hands trembling. "But if you won't help me find my brother, then I need to go."

He sent to Jared, *Enough of this. I'll find another jinn.*

Jared glared back at him and then leaned into Micki. "You're not leaving until I get my other prize."

"Other prize?" she panted.

"Your panties."

What the hell are you doing? he sent to Jared.

Micki's cheeks flushed a gorgeous, rosy red. "Please. I really need help."

Jared's message reached him, *No other jinn is gonna touch her tonight.*

Again, Bradley wondered at the jinn's motives. He couldn't blame Jared for taking the bra, a perfect token to remember her essence. Tokens of victory would have to come later, after they'd earned such a victory. His mission: ensure her safety.

First mission objective: get Micki upstairs to a place he could secure. The club floor remained too wide open, too crowded. Colored lights, flashing strobes, bodies rubbing together—all could hide danger. With his power askew, the feasibility of guarding her here fell far from optimal.

"Eric might be upstairs," he lied.

Micki whipped her gaze in his direction. "Upstairs?"

"Yeah," Jared answered waving to the crowd, "where most of these pricks go to—"

"Unwind," Bradley finished. *Get on board, Jared! Stop trying to scare her off.*

Micki's thought pierced him, *Unwind. Code for sex.* She swallowed. *If I go upstairs, with them, I should call someone. Let them know where I am, just in case I have to...unwind to find out anything else about Eric.*

"For privacy, you can go to the hall outside the ladies room," Bradley offered. "It's quiet enough to make a call on your cell."

He watched Micki's cheeks flush and her body shiver. More red flames poured out of her.

"How? Did you read my mind, Bradley?" she asked.

He winced at his stupid mistake, but his thoughts whirled with images of Micki under him, no clothes, just soft skin, his cock sliding in and out of her pussy, her screaming in satisfaction.

He shook off the thought. *Focus on your mission!* "Just thought you might want to check to see if you could reach your brother."

"O-okay," Micki said skeptically.

Bradley, you can hear her thoughts, too?

Yes. How is that possible?

Jared shrugged.

Micki looked back and forth between Jared and him. "Bradley, you really think Eric might be somewhere upstairs?"

"Yes, sweetheart." The lie almost stuck in his throat. Deceiving her felt like a stab to his chest, but unfortunately a necessary one. Second objective: reduce Micki's energy outflow, and fast. That meant tripling.

It had to be done or every immortal, dark or light, would be drawn to her. Might as well paint a target on her chest. Zone Three wasn't completely secure from the Dark. If they saw her and wanted her badly enough, they would attack. Siphoning energy from her would be no hardship. He could just imagine latching on to a swollen nipple with her writhing underneath him.

"Go make your call," Jared ordered her.

He sent back, *I'll follow her to make sure she's safe. You stay here in case David returns.*

Like giving orders, angel?

Bradley didn't take the bait.

Clearly, the jinn also knew they had to keep an eye on her at all times. Bradley had taken an oath to the Alliance, and he took it very seriously. The tattoo on Jared's arm indicated that the jinn had also taken the same oath.

I swear my eternal allegiance to the Alliance and to its leaders in the Council of Seven. I swear to protect mortal and immortal from the Dark.

Bradley knew that Jared had broken it.

Micki brushed up against him. Her feminine powers ensnared every one of his senses. *Intentional?* he wondered, but her touch made him crave the orgasms he would draw out of her with his hands, his tongue, his cock.

"Thank you, guys. I will call someone. I'll be back." She bounced away, her hot ass tempting him with each step.

When Micki got out of earshot, but not eyesight, Bradley told the jinn, "Don't think I am letting my guard down with you."

"You'd better not."

A threat? The remark left Bradley uneasy and thoroughly pissed off.

Bradley asked, "You staying or going AWOL on us?"

"Staying. Until David shows his fucking ass."

"Good. Make yourself useful and size up the room, especially by the stairs."

"I am not going upstairs with her."

Bradley needed to get Jared's attention and fast.

He got within an inch of the jinn's nose. "Soon, her power will call to every immortal within a hundred miles if we don't triple with her. You want her in that kind of danger?"

"Back off, or you will find out exactly what I am capable of."

Bradley visualized his sword. If he needed to conjure the weapon, it would be in his hands instantly. "Darklings are probably already picking up her signature."

"Don't you think I know that?"

"Then we have to get her upstairs."

Jared glared. "You better follow her, soldier."

He looked up and saw Micki duck into the hallway out of his line of sight. He cloaked himself in invisibility and teleported next to her, leaving Jared to brood. He couldn't tell if the jinn would finally surrender and go upstairs or not. If Jared didn't agree once Micki returned, he would find another jinn, and gladly.

As he moved closer to Micki, he could actually *feel* her desire. It seized him, adding to the pressing need stiffening his cock. Her fragrance intoxicated him. Though he was duty bound to protect her, he wouldn't decline the chance to sate the lust that threatened to consume him. No other woman would suffice. Not tonight.

* * * *

Energy vibrated throughout Micki. Walking away from Jared and Bradley turned out to be quite difficult. She had to concentrate on putting one foot in front of the other to keep from running back to them. The urges these men called forth screamed for more, demanding submission to both their desires—and hers. She shoved them aside.

When Micki finally reached the hallway, she darted into the ladies room, away from the roar of the music.

Three women stood at the mirrors reapplying makeup, straightening outfits, and chatting. Doubting they'd give her an answer, she asked, "Can you tell me what to expect *upstairs*?"

Surprisingly, they answered her, and she wondered what had changed. Maybe just asking about the second floor had done it. Did she look different?

Shit, no bra! Could that be it?

They all said it was very safe and connected to the club. They even made recommendations on which room to choose. *Choose a room?*

"My fave is the Cave room. But it isn't for the skittish," the one in the vinyl orange mini told her.

"Mava, you're gonna scare the girl. Can't you tell this is her first time?" the woman with the brightest red lipstick asked.

The one with the hazel-gold eyes like Micki's own added, "A virgin? How exciting. You should try the Pirate room."

Micki blinked. The girl could've been mistaken for her younger sister—clearly experienced in Zone Three's activities.

"Eve, you always suggest that one. How about the one that looks like a castle? What's it called, Daphne?" Mava asked.

"The Royal room," red lipstick informed.

Apparently, the floors above contained several chambers with themes. *An erotic playhouse.* Uneasiness took hold of her. Could she really go up those stairs? With Jared and Bradley?

On the other hand, if that's what it was, Eric would be there, maybe even with Brooke. Another reason that Micki had to check it out.

Thanks for the suggestions," she answered them.

So, she needed to pick a room and at least pretend to agree to unwind with Jared and Bradley. The scared part of her wanted to run out the door and hail a cab home. Tonight had become far-fetched, wild. A steamy place for threesomes and her two fantasy men appearing in the flesh. Micki took a deep breath. Crazy, but she couldn't leave without knowing what'd happened to Eric. Now she had to make sure Jared and Bradley helped with something besides helping her out of her panties.

"Have a great time," Eve told her.

"May I ask you another question?"

"Shoot."

"When I first came into the club not a single woman would give me so much as a friendly wave. But you are talking with me and giving me advice. Why?"

Eve laughed. "You are truly a virgin."

Micki felt the heat in her cheeks.

Daphne scolded, "Stop teasing the girl."

"Sorry," Eve said.

Daphne continued, "You're with Bradley. The other guy we don't know. But if Bradley thinks you're okay, then so do we."

Micki's anxiety pushed her on. "Do any of you know a guy named Eric Langley?"

"No," they answered in unison.

"How about a guy called David?"

"Everyone knows David," Mava informed her.

"Is he here tonight?"

"I haven't seen him," Daphne answered.

"Me either," Eve echoed.

Mava chimed in. "Ditto here."

Micki thought about asking these women to help her. Before she could, the women all fell into a whispered conversation as they exited, leaving Micki alone in the restroom.

Apprehension threaded itself throughout her body, but she stilled it with thoughts of Jared and Bradley. They both looked so capable— of orgasms, yes, but also of helping her find her brother.

Maybe she would go upstairs with Jared and Bradley. She could just imagine what *upstairs* might be like.

Did she dare trust them? That would be crazy and definitely not logical. Not like her at all. Still, given the bouncer and the *by invitation only sign,* she couldn't go up there by herself.

While going upstairs with Jared and Bradley terrified her and also ignited her, she needed them with her as she searched for Eric in the uncharted waters upstairs.

As long as her flirtations kept them interested, she could extract more facts. Find out what they *really* knew.

Should she? Being a tease with these men would be like walking a tightrope that crossed a raging fire with no net. She'd risk their fires to find her brother.

She recalled Eric's voicemail:

Micki, I have a favor to ask of you. I have been working on a very secret project. Go to my place and get anything that might have research on it. Also, if you know where I have put an antique book, get it.

Take everything to Zone Three Friday night at nine. Find David. Everyone knows him. Give everything to him.

That is all. Be Safe.

And Micki, don't call the police.

She'd found the flash drive where he kept all his most personal items in their mother's shoebox at the back of his closet. It looked so innocuous.

No book, though.

At her apartment, she'd hooked the flash drive up to her laptop. All the documents were password protected. The one that caught her eye: *Research.* She'd tried a few words Eric might've used as passwords, but none of them worked. She wondered what he'd gotten himself into and what could be so precious on the flash drive. She wouldn't get any answers without following the instructions in his voicemail. She'd investigate more, but she had to be smart. Logical.

Who should she call for back up?

She pulled out her cell from her purse.

Immediately, she tried Eric. No answer. Her heart sunk deeper.

Next, she dialed Brooke.

"Hello?" Brooke's voice answered.

Micki felt hope rush in like a strong wind.

"Brooke, it's Micki."

"Hi, Micki. Everything okay?" Brooke's voice sounded concerned.

"Where have you been?" she asked, unable to hide her anxiety.

"At my mom's home in Denver until today. Landed a couple of hours ago. Are you okay?"

"Did you get my messages?" Micki failed to keep her agitation out of her voice. She wished she could have, but her worry for Eric didn't allow it.

"No. My battery died at my mom's and I forgot to pack my charger. I took it off the charger and just turned it back on."

"Have you heard from Eric?"

"Not since I left."

Hope plummeted. "Oh, God."

Micki leaned against one of the sinks, her legs shaking. Eric might be in real trouble. "You haven't heard from him either."

"No. Not in over a week."

"Micki, you know how Eric is."

"Yes. But this is different. He's nowhere to be found."

"It is just Eric's way. I know this is longer than he's ever dropped off the map, but—"

"I got a voicemail this morning. He sent me on one of his cryptic goose chases."

"Then he's okay. Just another one of his pranks."

"Maybe. But he sounded—"

"What?" Brooke asked.

His voicemail had thrown Micki. "Strange."

No teasing. No tone of jocularity. Even his phrasing seemed wrong, odd. If she hadn't recognized his voice, she would've never believed it to be her brother's.

Brooke choked. "He did?"

Micki hated that she had to share her worry with Brooke. She'd always hoped the woman would be her sister-in-law one day. But what if she told Brooke that she might find Eric at an erotic playhouse?

"Brooke, I'll tell you more later. Can I give you the address where I am?"

"Okay."

Micki rattled it off.

"Got it. Micki, what's going on?"

Just a quick look-around on the upper floor. Then she'd tell Brooke everything. Unless…

"Do you know a friend of Eric's named David?" Micki held her breath.

"David? No."

"Well, I'm going to check to see if he or Eric are upstairs."

Brooke asked, "Upstairs? Where are you?"

"A club called Zone Three. Have you been here with Eric before?"

"No. Never heard of it."

That didn't fill Micki with a warm fuzzy feeling. "Wait for me to call. I'll be leaving shortly. Too much to tell now but I will later."

Jared and Bradley would help her and go upstairs with her. A dangerous choice but she couldn't go up without them.

"Micki, don't be stupid. I can be there—"

"If you don't hear from me in thirty minutes, call my cell." She asked Brooke to be her lifeline. *God, what am I doing?*

"Micki, what's really going on?"

"I'll tell you. Soon."

"And if you don't answer in thirty minutes?"

"Call again."

"No, I'll call the police."

"They won't do anything about Eric for another day. I tried."

Brooke paused, then her voice began to shake. "You really think Eric's in trouble?"

"I'm not sure. Maybe."

"If you find him."

"I'll call you," Micki promised. "Talk to you in a little bit."

Micki hoped everything would be all right, but her nerves said otherwise.

She left the restroom and headed back to where she'd left Jared and Bradley. As she approached them, both men stood. Sexy, gallant beasts. She couldn't keep herself from reaching out and touching Jared's hair. He didn't move her hand or his head, letting her stroke it at will. She expected this wolf to purr. He didn't. Instead, he mustered a rumbling growl.

Bradley cupped her chin. "Let's go upstairs."

Her mind kept wandering to images of her fantasy men giving her more than just information. The hot electricity grew and the ache in her sex expanded.

"I'll go upstairs with you, but only to search for my brother."

"Okay." Bradley extended his arm for her to take. She took it and looked at Jared—and the pink bra straps of her bra dangling from his pocket.

Chapter 5

"Wait," Jared stated, his mind whirling.

He felt his self-restraint stretched to the limits from the smell of Micki's sweetness, from the sight of her curves, the sound of her sexy voice. He needed to haul ass away from her. But he couldn't. He shouldn't do this, but all paths led to upstairs to drain her energy.

Damn you, David. He doubted the archangel flew near enough to receive the message.

Micki kept her right arm in Bradley's, but offered her other arm to him. Instinctively, Jared reached for her waist, sliding his way down the curve of her hip. Her want, obvious by the vibrations and heat he felt from her body, promised more to come.

"Help me find my brother." She stared right into his eyes, imploring.

"If it takes all night, I'll be here for you," Bradley offered gently. Silently, the angel went on a rampage. *Are you crazy, jinn? We need to get her upstairs and transmute her power into our own.*

And what if we can't? Jared sent to the angel. *I've never seen power like this. Have you?*

No response, but the scowl on the soldier's face said he hadn't either. Jared wondered how Micki could contain such enormous energy. If they could expend some of it, would it last? Or would it just recharge? And if they took some of her massive power, what would it do to them?

Suddenly, a vivid image of her writhing naked between him and Bradley on a blanket under a full moon blasted his thoughts. The mind-movie continued with her fisting his hard dick with one hand

and Bradley's with the other. Heat sizzled down his spine when he realized the image wasn't his, but Micki's.

More of her thoughts marched into his head. Her fear and excitement about the upper floors. Her worry about her brother. Then back to images of the three of them interlacing their naked bodies together, this time with Bradley's cock driving deep into her wet cunt, and his dick slamming into her ass. Her mind turned faster and sharper than his motorcycle, the same speed that revved his heart.

Could my brother really be upstairs?

She moved closer into Jared. Only the thin material of her blouse and the cotton of his shirt separated their skin. Her chest rose with every breath, now bare beneath the silk. Blood pressed hard into his dick. He ached to be inside her, touching all her soft parts. His resistance shook under the onslaught of his desire for her, the thread of his vow of celibacy unraveling.

"Please go with us," she pleaded.

David's message had said to keep Micki at Zone Three until he arrived, safe from the threat that stalked her. But what if that threat was him?

He looked Micki up and down. Every part of her infused him with pure bliss and threatened to destroy his determination. Bradley should pick another. That would certainly solve his issue. Fuck David's orders. He couldn't bear thinking of another jinn touching her, his need growing to the levels of the power she displayed.

He could sense Micki's attempt to fool herself into thinking she *only* wanted to find her brother. Her arousal told a different story, buried underneath all the layers of insecurities and concern. Potent want.

He looked for an escape away from the stairs leading up to an imminent detonation. If he went upstairs with her, if he got close to her, he'd fuck her like a madman and not stop all night.

Out of the corner of his eye, he spotted someone he recognized from years ago. A male human. Not just any human. What was he named?

Connor.

He looked to be in his early-thirties, but Jared knew better. Filled with dark blood sustaining his body, his soul dead. One of the Dark's familiars. Here, at a fortress of the Alliance? Though his name seemed innocuous, Connor's expertise stretched all the way to murder and butchery.

Jared's blood went cold.

Connor, with some of his former humanity still present, made it past the alarms of the stronghold. He remembered the human at the cavern centuries ago. Connor's empty eyes, along with all the others, looking on as Jared had committed the ultimate sin.

Now, the cursed creature looked straight at Jared and smiled a sick toothy grin. Then he turned his gaze on Micki.

Anger thundered inside Jared, a lightning arc that caught fire.

"Let's go!" he ordered. "Upstairs. Now!"

"O-okay," Micki agreed.

What's wrong? Bradley sent.

Jared urged her to pick up the pace. *One of the Dark's pets just walked inside.*

Where?

He looked over his shoulder. Connor talked with two other humans. More Dark familiars?

Rather than point, he sent an image of Connor by the bar, *Over there.*

Bradley sent out, *Got it. Nash, are you still around?*

No answer.

He tried another. *Greg?*

The acknowledgement came, *I'm here.*

"Okay, guys, you can slow down." Micki's head turned back and forth from Bradley to him.

Bradley shook his head. "We might miss Eric if we don't hurry." Then sent to Greg, *See the guy with the goatee? He's a Dark familiar.*

What! Here?

Yes, Bradley confirmed. *There may be others. Take care of it and get word to David.*

Done.

Jared recognized the Alliance jinn standing by the stairs with his arms folded. He would pummel the guy to mush should he try to stop them.

Bradley smiled and unlatched the rope. "Nice to see you, Raf."

"He's going up there?" Raf questioned, pointing at Jared.

"He is." Bradley moved first. Jared followed, feeling the bouncer's suspicious gaze follow.

The staircase width allowed Micki to ascend between him and Bradley. Taking two steps at a stride, they lifted Micki by her elbows, her feet dangling.

"Cut it out!" she demanded.

When they topped the stairs, Jared looked back to locate the Dark familiar. Connor and his other partners were nowhere to be seen.

"Okay. You both like to leap stairs, great superhero imitations. Can we please slow down?" Micki asked.

Don't try anything stupid, jinn.

Jared glared. *Just do your duty. Connor is gone. It's possible he saw Micki's huge energy output and is sending for his masters.*

Bradley frowned. *I can't imagine the Dark staging a frontal attack at an Alliance stronghold.*

I can. Jared knew the Dark too well. When they wanted something badly enough they did whatever it took to get it.

Bradley sent, *We need to get Micki to a room.*

I agree.

"Are either of you listening to me?"

Jared, we need to triple with her. I don't like the idea of you being part of that any more than you do. But we can't wait. It's the only way to diffuse her energy. Even the walls of the stronghold won't be able to hide the power flowing inside her should we fail.

Jared looked at her. Her current energy signature would not be contained inside Zone Three for long. How could he triple again? How could he even consider it?

Because even though touching her might reawaken his nasty side, Jared knew she faced a certain, far uglier death if he didn't. *Fuck.*

"Hello?" Micki's irritation grew. "Am I invisible? Have you both lost your hearing?"

Bradley answered, "Sorry, sweetheart. It's loud. Let's find somewhere we can talk."

Her lips pursed. Lips Jared wanted to taste, to devour.

"Okay," Micki agreed. "But I'm here to find my brother. That's it."

"Eric Langley," Bradley answered. "We remember."

Jared shoved a thought at the angel, *I only need fifteen minutes.*

What? No fanfare?

He ignored the angel's sarcasm.

Fifteen minutes, an immortal quickie. When finished, he could fade into the background and protect her from a distance until David showed.

Bradley led them down one of the hallways, seeming to have a specific destination. The angel knew the place well. The strong blue light Jared viewed radiating from Bradley proved he'd tripled within the past few days. Unlike Jared, the angel had no need to form a triad.

"Where are you taking me?" she asked.

Bradley answered, "Somewhere safe."

The angel's curt responses threatened to end the evening with her making a run for the door, into Connor's arms. Jared watched Micki's hands tremble.

Safe? Micki's thoughts drifted into his head, *What am I getting myself into?*

Jared wanted to comfort her, keep her moving forward, away from the darkling pet. Comfort wasn't his strong suit.

Before he could try, Bradley got back in the game and stroked the back of Micki's neck. "I mean *quiet*. Everything will be okay. Trust me."

She relaxed a bit and her trembling subsided some.

Bradley stopped at the last door on the left.

The angel released a sliver of blue power through the door. Checking the room, no doubt. Very adept. Still, Jared checked for himself. It only took a tiny bit of the green energy left him.

Empty.

Subtly, Bradley waved his hand over the doorknob to disarm the magical booby-traps. *Very impressive.*

"You'll like this." Bradley stated to Micki.

"Who can we ask about my brother?"

All his muscles went taut, knowing that the Dark's bull's-eye painted Micki at its center. This was no time for bygone chivalry, not that he'd ever been accused of being civilized. He considered throwing her over his shoulder and dragging her into the chamber but thought better of it. His own anxiety over Connor and over what he must do to ensure Micki's safety eclipsed the smidgeon of politeness he possessed. "Just open the door!"

Let me do the talking! Bradley said aloud, "There's a phone in the room."

"A phone?"

"We'll call the on-duty manager. He'll know if your brother is up here."

Micki nodded shaky. "He will?"

The angel opened the door to a dimly lit suite. Soft pillows littered the place. Sensual music played quietly. A large, exotic bed filled the center of the room, draped in bright fuchsia, turquoise, and gold. Jared's gut tightened. The perfect setup for tripling, something Jared knew he shouldn't do. Still, he would for Micki's safety.

Bradley placed his hand on her back. "Once we get inside the room, Micki, we'll be able to get the answers you need."

Jared gladly let the angel take the lead. He didn't want to talk. He must concentrate on the next fifteen minutes.

Desire ripped through him. Pleasure called. Lust exploded through every part of him. He imagined diving down between Micki's thighs and lapping at her wet cunt. He felt more animal than immortal. Bradley needed to keep him in check.

Micki didn't move into the room. Instead, she stood trembling, her hazel-gold eyes unblinking.

Fifteen minutes, Jared reminded. *Don't give me anymore.*

I'll set the pace. We'll go as long as it takes to get her off the radar. You understand?

Fuck you! Don't give me orders. I said fifteen minutes. I will not stay any longer than necessary to get her power surge under control.

Bradley sent, *You will follow my lead or you can get the hell out of here, right now. Can't you see she could bolt at any minute? You know what's waiting for her if she does?*

Yes, Jared knew. He steeled his self-control and resigned himself to a very long fifteen minutes.

* * * *

Bradley's teeth pulled on Micki's earlobe sending tingles through her neck. He pressed a gentle hand on her back, urging her to enter the room. She planted her feet. The hallway seemed safer than the isolated room. Did it really have a phone? Shivers of uncertainty and desire ran down her spine.

Micki thought about the game she and Eric had often played as children. She wished this time he would appear if she yelled, "Olly olly oxen free!" Her head swirled with memories and emotions mixed like the contents in a blender.

"Micki, go in." Jared's stare burned and demanded.

Her knees went weak. Why couldn't she help but follow his command? Did she want to be dominated by him? Obediently, she took three steps and found herself in a beautiful place filled with trappings similar to her recent dreams, a domain fit for a wealthy sheik's palace.

Brightly colored pillows, in a variety of shapes and sizes, covered most of the floor. Sheer fabric fell from the tall ceiling, surrounding a large welcoming bed. Warm incense wafted in the air. Definitely a place designed for pleasure. Vacillating between excitement and nervousness, Micki felt her cheeks warm. Every nerve jumped like popping popcorn.

"Where's the phone?" she piped.

Bradley pointed to a table by the wall opposite the door. On it sat a white phone.

As she took a step toward it, he held up his hand. "Best to let me talk to the on-duty manager since I'm a member of the club."

Since her attempts to get information downstairs had been futile, she conceded to Bradley. She turned to Jared who'd taken one step into the room, but no farther. Strange.

She held out his jacket, hoping he'd come closer. He took it from her, slipped it on, and then stepped back again.

Very strange.

Bradley lit several candles. The flickering lights danced on his massive biceps each time he brought the wicks to life. A godlike creature. She could only imagine what he might bring to life in her.

Jared closed the door and turned the lock.

She sucked in a mouthful of air. *Ohmigod.*

Bradley glared at Jared and then turned to her with a softer expression. His blue eyes reassured her. "Don't worry. We just don't want to be interrupted."

Interrupted?

"What about my brother? That's the only reason I'm here."

But that wasn't totally true. Micki also wanted to be with these two fantasy men from her recent dreams, to have her body wrapped around them. Vibrations pulsed into her channel like electric currents. She'd never felt anything like it.

"We'll find out about your brother right now." Bradley went to the phone and picked up the receiver. He punched the zero.

Jared walked around the place by the walls, tapping each as he passed them. He seemed like a wild beast in a cage. Was he afraid of something? Micki couldn't imagine what. Jared was the type others feared.

"This is Bradley. I'm in the Persian Room. Can you tell me if Eric Langley is in the upper floors?"

"Or has been here in the past couple of days?" she requested.

"Or has been here any time this week?" Bradley added.

"Ask about David, too." Her heart beat wildly in her chest. Could she get the answers she so desperately needed from the person Bradley talked to?

He asked, "Or David?"

Jared did another lap around the suite. His tense prowl made her edgy.

"That will be fine," Bradley said and then put the receiver back on the cradle.

"What did they say?" she asked, aware of the shakiness in her voice.

"They're checking with the staff and then they'll get back to us."

"How long will that take?"

"No more than."

"Fifteen minutes," Jared finished.

In fifteen minutes, she would find Eric. She just had to.

"Micki, what do you do for a living?" Bradley flashed her a warm smile. Her mouth watered as if tasting warm chocolate.

"I work at a bank. I work on compliance issues with the Federal Reserve."

"Sounds interesting."

Micki suppressed a laugh. She knew he lied. Her job, on the best of days, barely edged passed dullsville. She'd never complained. It was a place she could disappear to, away from the world and its dangers.

Bradley sat on the bed. "Won't you sit by me?"

Boom! Boom! Boom!

Was that her heart or the music reverberating from downstairs? Bradley said he wanted to help her find her brother, but it seemed as if seduction held the top post of his mind.

She should leave. Now. Call Brooke and go. Instead, she sat down next to Bradley.

He grabbed her hand. Currents shot through her entire body.

Jared stood five feet away looking *hungry*. His gaze fixed on her, unwavering. His breathing sounded labored, but he wasn't moving. Instead, he seemed frozen in place. He wasn't trying to seduce her after coming on so strong downstairs. Jared mystified her.

"Compliance. Interesting," Bradley said.

She clasped her hands together nervously. "Not really."

"Sure it is. Don't you think so, Jared?"

She risked a glance at her biker. He didn't budge or acknowledge Bradley's question. Sweat dripped from Jared's forehead. Micki frowned. He acted like some internal struggle raged inside him. About what?

"So, you've met Eric before?" she asked Bradley.

"No. But I have seen him. With David."

"Who is this David? Tell me about him."

Bradley inched closer to her. More fire jetted through her and her clit swelled. She didn't know what to think, but the sexual part of her, the one she usually kept buried, recklessly disregarded caution. Despite that, she didn't want her time with Bradley and Jared to end. Or to stop with mere conversation.

"David is kind of the boss around here."

"He's an asshole!" Jared spat, jolting her.

She jumped to her feet.

"It's okay," Bradley murmured. "Sit back down, sweetheart."

She didn't. He gently pulled at her hand to coax her back beside him. Heat blasted her with that small touch. Her knees wobbled, forcing her to comply.

"Why don't you like David?" she asked Jared.

He merely tightened his jaw and looked away.

"David and Jared have some history they need to work out." Bradley paused, shooting her biker an angry stare. "Jared, why don't you come here and talk to us."

Something about her charmer's question and tone made her quiver violently. Her nerves threatened to suffocate her. What weren't they telling her?

After Bradley's request, Jared rolled his shoulders but looked more tense than ever. Still, he approached her.

Her dark-eyed biker paused for what seemed like an eternity before taking her other hand in his. An inferno jetted through her arm, down her chest, her stomach, into her mound, ending in her toes.

Jared took her other hand. Whatever had been keeping him back he'd put it aside. Only his hunger remained, alive in his intent gaze. The tension she'd sensed earlier between him and Bradley seemed to ease away. Clearly their touches and stares proved they'd set aside their animosity for each other and now wanted only to please her. Being the object of their absolute desire pleased her. Very odd that downstairs they'd been far from buddy-buddy, but up here, they wanted to work together. Maybe that's how it worked at Zone Three. Patrons set aside everything for a ménage.

Bradley touched her cheek, leaned in and planted a kiss on her mouth. He parted his lips, deepening to a hot oral embrace. His tongue pushed in deeper, dancing around the inside of her mouth. She loved it.

Ring. Ring.

She jumped up again. The phone. *Eric? Please let that be you.*

Bradley went to the phone. "Hello?"

Please. Oh, please.

"Yes."

She moved closer to him, away from the bed and Jared, hoping to hear the person on the other side. No luck.

Seconds crawled by like a slow moving centipede.

"Okay. Thanks." He put the phone back on the cradle.

"Tell me where Eric is!" she shouted.

Chapter 6

I just finished the passage about the Dark's deadliest attack on the Bloodline. According to the book, the Alliance wasn't of much help then. An entire family branch destroyed because of the Alliance leaders' ineptitude. Though the Seven were the most powerful of the Alliance, they were not invincible. Long ago when the Seven still met in the open, the Dark massacred four of them, hundreds of angels and jinn, and twenty-seven bloodliners under the Alliance's protection. That day, all immortals—Alliance and Dark—thought the Bloodline eradicated. But they were wrong.

Could it be that simple—bloodliners needing immortals as much as immortals need humans?

Eric's Flash Drive: day 30—entry 9

* * * *

Bradley held Micki's hand. Eyes anxious, she stared. His blood ran cold to utter the next words. "No one has seen or heard from him in three days. Also, no David tonight."

Micki's knees buckled. She would have hit the floor if he hadn't caught her.

"Where the hell is my brother!" Giant tears flowed out of her eyes. Her despair and growing energy filled the room and beyond.

Jared, we have to do this now!!!

The jinn looked at him. *The last thing she wants is sex.*

Bradley hated using a woman's pain to seduce her, but he must. *They* must. If not, she would be dead, or wishing she was, in short order.

He lifted her up into his arms and placed her on back the bed. More tears, ones she'd clearly been holding at bay. She put her head into the silk sheets, soaking them. Pent-up anxiety poured out of her. Her entire body rolled with each uncontrollable sob. His gut tightened. He hated seeing her suffer.

"Micki." Jared breathed gently.

"We'll help you," Bradley added. He rubbed her back, stroking her.

Slowly, her sobs subsided. With her between them, Bradley's instinct took over. Her feminine scent and the heat from her pussy lured him closer.

"How? I don't know what else you can do." She looked up from her make-shift tissue and turned to Jared. "Will you help me?"

The jinn nodded, his solemn gaze fixed on her. Bradley believed he meant it.

Even through her vulnerability, she persevered. She'd barely spent her tears and already her determination to find her brother had returned. Micki was both resilient and insistent. More arousal rushed into his cock. He wanted to kiss her, take her. Not just for duty and not just to get her off the grid or because his own lust demanded it. Something deeper demanded he devour all that she had to offer, then take more.

Without hesitation, he grasped both sides of her face and turned her to him. "We will help you find him. Searching for him alone is too much for one person, even a loving sister."

Micki's eyes filled up once again. For a moment, he thought she would say something. Instead, the tears fell. She closed her eyes and let go of his and Jared's hands. She pulled her arms around her chest, and rocked ever so slightly.

"Micki, we're here for you." Bradley leaned in and kissed her eyes, hoping to ease her worry.

The kiss broke for a moment. When it did, Micki cast a glance at

Jared. The jinn's face displayed a dichotomy of desire and second thoughts.

He couldn't let Jared falter. They had to get her energy consumed, so he resumed kissing her, moving to her mouth.

Don't fail her, Jared.

* * * *

Jared nodded to Bradley. He'd made his decision to break his vow and triple with the angel and Micki.

He watched their kissing intensify and his lust thundered for satiation. He feared what might be unleashed inside him, but he couldn't think of any other alternative to keep her alive.

Jared moved his hands under her skirt. He urged her to part her thighs for him. At first, she resisted, but as he massaged her legs, she slowly relaxed. His fingers eased under her panties and found her slick folds, brushed her moistness. He couldn't wait to taste her pussy. His blood pulsed hard and fast as he touched her warm invitation.

Amazingly, he could feel Micki's mind. *Oh, God! Where is Eric? I feel so alone. I've never been so afraid. I need Jared and Bradley. I need their strength to lean on. I must escape from myself just for tonight. Please.*

Lights flashed deep red. Jared wanted to quiet her mind and ease her fear. Where he touched her, he could feel her temperature rising. Sparks danced over all her skin.

I need them to drown everything out. I need them!

Her suffering sliced Jared in half. "Micki, do you like me touching you?"

"Yes."

His mind swirled with desire and his cock hardened again, making him grit his teeth. Could he really keep the dark lust that beat inside him at bay?

Bradley moved down from her mouth to her shoulders, licking the entire way.

Jared felt Micki's pulse quicken.

Don't stop, she thought.

"We won't stop." Bradley's blue power swirled around Micki's red.

"Not until you're dripping with desire." Jared sent his green energy to join with the blue and red surging around her. "Not until you're begging us to take and fill every part of you."

Ease off, Bradley warned.

Fuck you.

Micki turned to him. "I—I've never begged."

"By the time we're done, I promise you'll be very comfortable with it." Jared vowed, watching her shiver as the angel sucked on her lobe.

Her breasts demanded Jared's attention. He gladly complied, cupping them through her blouse. Taking both delectable taut nipples between his thumbs and forefingers he pressed. She gave a long moan and titled her head back, delighting him to his core. He pinched harder. She grabbed his forearms and gasped, blasting his centuries of self-denial to bits.

He released her nipples and caressed her gorgeous mounds. His reason scattered, overtaken by need. In the back of his head, he knew he must stay focused, but something about her made that impossible.

Bradley sent, *Slow down!*

Don't tell me how to triple, infant!

The angel reached around Micki's back and grabbed his shoulder and squeezed hard enough to break a human bone. But Jared wasn't human.

She wiggled between them, distracting them, flushed and unaware. Energy gathered and swirled at levels unlike anything Jared had ever seen or experienced. Her skin burned hot under his touch.

Mentally, he probed the power Micki radiated. An enormous jolt shot through him, stronger than anything he'd ever felt. They didn't have time to slow down. They must triple now.

"I'm nervous," Micki fidgeted.

"That's okay, sweetheart." The angel shot him a glare when Micki closed her eyes. "I understand, but you're safe."

Though Micki's red energy didn't shrink back, that would take a tripling, her worries faded from her expression.

The angel promised her, "This will be incredible for you."

And for us, Jared thought.

Micki opened her eyes. "I'm not sure how far I can go tonight. I didn't come here for…you know."

Her gaze burned him up to the core, and his insides threatened to explode. The need to move his mouth over hers, dip inside for another delectable taste, scorched him, leaving him weak-headed as all remaining blood rushed to his cock.

"We'll go only as far as you want," Bradley lied.

Jared looked up at Micki. "Believe me, you'll want everything we can give you."

He touched her soft lips with his forefinger before he replaced his finger with his mouth. She tasted wonderfully warm and sweet. He pressed harder into the kiss. Urgent need engulfed him.

Desire filled him for their coming orgasms and energy exchange. He puzzled over this new ache she'd brought forth, more compelling than any before. Her energy continued to grow, spanning the entire room. He wasn't sure he'd be able to consume it all. He must try for Micki, but unease gripped him. What if the tripling didn't work? What if he couldn't hold the seeds of darkness inside him from taking her last breath?

Still fully clothed, Bradley gently rolled Micki to her left side, then pulled her back toward his front. Was the angel testing him?

Her thoughts skated into his mind. *I can't believe my fantasy is really coming true. I've never been so turned on.*

Her silent confession summoned his need to dominate her. He unbuttoned her white silk shirt and found the mounds that had been tempting him all night long. Her firm, reddish nipples jutted out to him, begging to be touched, tasted. He took one at a time between his thumb and forefinger and pinched.

"Yes, yes, yes." she repeated and then screamed silently, *Please, take me!*

Jared hesitated. Could he control his hunger enough?

When Bradley rolled her nipples between his fingers, and Micki moaned his question dissipated. Jared leaned in, nipped the hard tips back and forth until his took in one quivering berry in his mouth and sucked hard. Micki's swirl of energy inundated him.

Jared sat Micki up and dropped to his knees in front of her. As he stared in hunger, Bradley sent a warning glare. He wondered if the angel had his sword ready to conjure.

Jared turned Micki's hips toward him and removed her skirt, leaving her soaked pink panties clinging to her swollen folds. Micki leaned back into Bradley.

As the angel tossed her shirt to the floor, Jared dipped down and licked Micki's inner thighs. She moaned. Jared delighted in the sounds roused by his and Bradley's fondling.

Micki's trembling revealed her passion and Jared couldn't wait another second to turn up the heat in her. He kissed her swollen mound under the fabric.

Rivers of light raced around them, a deluge of power. Desire. Passion. Ecstasy. All of it overwhelmed his better senses, trapping him in a vortex of Micki's sensual energy.

Jared struggled to remind himself to stay in control, to not loose all of his hunger, but when Micki's red color exploded inside his head, it obliterated all rationale.

He ripped Micki's panties from her body. His primal need twisted for release. He lapped her clit with his tongue.

Micki's moans brought a flood to his balls. He needed release, especially when Micki fisted her hands in his hair and pulled him in closer between her legs.

He tensed as the power coursed through him, totally explosive.

"Do you want more?" he said, spreading her legs wider apart.

"G-God, yes!"

He stood and pulled her off the bed to a standing position, away from Bradley. "We are going to split your pussy wide open. Then when you think you can't take anymore, we'll spread your legs so that we can take your virgin ass."

"O-Ohh!" Her moans grew louder with each of his verbal caresses.

"And finally, our cocks will drive so deep into you that you will scream for mercy." Jared spun Micki around. Her back to him, she now faced Bradley straight on. Then he growled in her ear, "We won't have any."

She squirmed. Her ass teased him, pressing against his hard cock screaming for release.

"Please," she panted.

He reached around her and pinched her taut nipples. "How bad do you want our dicks?"

"Very much." *So badly, it's burning me alive.*

"Show me."

Micki took his hand and guided it between her parted legs. She took hold of his index finger and pushed it deep inside her pussy where his tongue had just been. In and out. She clamped onto his finger, and he nearly lost his mind imagining how tight that passage would be on his dick.

"I'm not convinced," he teased.

Micki's head dropped back against his chest. Then she pulled his finger out of her slit, unfolded his middle finger to extend along side his index finger, then she shoved them deep into her sex.

"O-ohh…." she moaned.

As his fingers plunged deeper into her cunt, Micki's body undulated wildly.

He sent to Bradley, *You should get a taste of her pussy. She's delicious.*

Down the angel went to the floor on his knees.

Jared felt Micki's hand wrap around his wrist, pushing the fingers deeper into her sex. "You ready to beg like the vixen you are?"

Micki leaned back into his chest. "Really, you're going to make me?"

Jared put his lips next to her eye. "Yes, I am."

Micki's desires reverberated through Jared like the ripples from a pebble on a still pond. Everything inside him quickened. Every part of her, inside and out, tempted him. Sexy. Adventurous. Gutsy. Loyal. Delicious.

With both hands, he guided Micki's head and lips, demanding entrance. He tasted her mouth's warm moistness. Dizziness took hold of him. Jared liked the rush he felt as their kiss deepened.

He released Micki's lips, and she turned to look down at Bradley. He watched as she drove her hands into the angel's blond hair, and she shifted her hips forward toward the warrior to give him a deeper taste of her wet slit. Lust raged inside Jared.

Bradley apparently had skill. More moans exploded from Micki as the angel manipulated her clit with his tongue. The scent of the wet heat between her thighs added to Jared's own frenzy.

"Do you like him tasting your cunt?" he asked.

Stop, angel.

Bradley paused and looked up with a frown. Jared nodded at him, then whispered in Micki's ear, "You ready to beg yet?"

Micki panted, "Y-yess, please. More."

The exchange of power advanced. Tonight, nothing would keep him from taking all Micki had to offer him, not even his own guilt. He'd wanted to believe it was to protect her from the Dark, but he knew better. His need for her soared.

Her breathing turned shallow and fast. Jared kissed the back of her neck. He reached around and cupped both breasts. Her shudder of excitement vibrated his hands. He loved that he had the power to incite such heat in her. His breathing quickened as her need grew.

Micki, with her curves he was dying to explore, blocked out all reason. He traced the middle of her back with his lips, from the spot between her shoulders down to the curve above her sexy ass.

He felt her body tremble every place his mouth touched. At the end of the route, on his knees, he nipped her left round cheek and heard her moan. He loved the sound, craved hearing more from Micki as he felt more of her.

As Bradley tasted her wet folds, Jared touched her perfect round butt. The desire to be inside her was more than he could resist. He parted the two soft curves to get a view her back entrance.

The fingernail hold Jared had on self-control weakened, teetered.

Trying to reign in his thoughts, his animalistic lust, he swallowed, tightened his jaw.

Stay in control, Bradley barked.

Jared's hot green smoke seethed just under the surface. He dove into her—passed the tight ring—with his tongue, lubing up what he wanted. She burned like fire! Micki wanted him—them. He sensed it. felt it. She writhed as he and Bradley double-tongued her. The animal in Jared broke free, smashing its cage. He wanted Micki more than anyone he'd ever desired over the centuries.

Ohmigod! Micki's thoughts pushed into his mind. *Yes! Yes! Yeeesssss!*

The moans and gasps fell freely from her mouth. She would feel total release. They all would.

Micki swayed slightly.

Jared parted her cheeks wider. "I won't stop. Ever."

He licked her between them, and Micki pressed back against his face.

"Oh, Jared...Bradley, your mouths..." Micki's skin flushed, and she tensed against him—then screamed.

She let go to her first orgasm.

The last mental fingernail on the cliff of his control broke.

"More?" The angel had a feral smile as he pulled away, his ravenous gaze captivated by their shared woman.

Jared looked at Micki. Her red output flared up for a second, and then lessened. Neither he nor the angel had taken in her delicious energy—that would take the tripling—but they had peeled off enough of her power to reduce the beacon, at least until the real exchange.

Jared couldn't stop touching her. He risked so much, but the hunger in him would not be quieted.

His willpower disintegrated as he inhaled her essence. She intoxicated him, capturing every cell of his body. Waves of desire pushed him below the surface of his self-control to the place he'd feared to reach again. Deep inside him. A place of pure instinct unbridled by rules or conscious will. He didn't stop, couldn't stop. He went deeper and found new levels, a passion he'd never known before.

He shot to the angel, *Bradley?*

Yes?

Do whatever you have to do to me if I start to...

Trust me, I will.

Jared nodded, knowing if he lost his way in the process, Bradley would stop him should things go awry—for Micki's sake.

Chapter 7

The book has a list of the locations of the Alliance's strongholds and the Dark's lairs—present and past. Babylon, Atlantis, Pompeii, Camelot, Transylvania and others, each with their own secret immortal sites. Today, all the major cities have at least two—one from each side.

The outsiders, the Rogues, have no formal headquarters. They seem to congregate haphazardly.

Tomorrow, I'm going downtown to our city's Alliance stronghold.

Even though Lillian told me to avoid all immortals, going to Zone Three may be the only way to save my sister and me.

Eric's Flash Drive: day 32—entry 1

* * * *

"You want more of our tongues dipping into your pussy and backside?" Jared asked Micki.

Micki's eyes popped wide open. She'd played this game and Jared and Bradley thought her experienced, but she wasn't. What if she disappointed them once they moved to the horizontal? What if her lack of skill turned them off? Living her fantasy could become a complete disaster. It wasn't too late to exit, but she wanted them too badly to leave. What they'd awakened inside her would not free her until it got what it needed—complete satisfaction.

A red-hot sea of want boiled inside her.

She squirmed. "Do either of you have protection?"

"Don't be afraid. You have no need for a condom with us,"

Bradley said.

Micki raised a skeptical brow.

"We have no diseases," Bradley clarified.

"B-but I could get pregnant."

"Not possible with us." Jared massaged her ass. Her stomach flip-flopped. "Neither of us can impregnate you."

Micki frowned. Had they both gotten the *snip?* They seemed pretty young for that, but her instincts assured her that they would never harm her. They'd already tried to help her and had given her such pleasure. Their muscled fortress-like bodies surrounded her. She smiled. With them, she felt utterly protected.

"I want more of your pussy," Bradley whispered.

Desire amplified inside her at his admission. He deepened her need by flicking his tongue on her clit. Oh yeah, she wanted more. Wanted them.

Bradley tongued her, then he back away.

Please, she wailed, her body pulled tight with desire.

"That's the begging I hoped to hear," Jared growled.

Micki couldn't keep her thoughts straight. Bradley and Jared made her dizzy, overwrought. She needed them, despite everything.

"Tell me what you want." Bradley's hand moved up her thighs as he continued vibrating his tongue against her bud of nerve endings. Electricity pulsed through her. "Beg sweetly."

"I want you! God, please."

"Inside you? Slowly, very slowly, so you can feel every inch of my cock pressing in your pussy?"

"Y-yesss. Every inch inside me" she panted. "Pressing."

He pulled words out of her that she'd never uttered. The wild woman had escaped from Pandora's box. No logic. No internal deliberation. Just words flowing out as soon as they entered her mind, words of complete abandon and desire.

She is so fucking hot! Jared's voice echoed in her head.

But he hadn't spoken. Not aloud. So how had she heard it?

She shook her head. She was letting her imagination get the best of her. Why not go along with it? Take the big drop on this rollercoaster.

Why not? She could think of a million reasons why she shouldn't, but her want would not be denied. Not now. She had to have them, feel them, taste them and let them taste her. To give herself completely to them.

"Micki, come for me again," Bradley said between licks.

Jared rumbled low behind her. "I can't wait to bulldoze your tight little ass with my cock."

No holding back now. The train had left the thrill ride's boarding station. She would take this ride with no safety bars on the track to the very end. Take the big loops and incredible speeds with her hands held high above her head in pure delight.

Bradley reached for her sex. His fingers circled her clit while his other hand tweaked her right nipple. A massive pulse of longing in her body echoed his caresses on her skin. Her very soul burned, as did her body.

Mmm.

Bradley stood up in front of her, then kissed her deep and long. He took her shoulders and turned her to face Jared, still kneeling on the ground before her like a devotee of a mythic goddess. She leaned back into Bradley's hard chest. He felt good, strong and protective.

Instead of diving his mouth into her sex, Jared stood and took a single step back. He seemed to continue to grapple with whatever concerns troubled him.

"Jared, you like what you see?" Bradley asked him, smoothing his hand down her stomach to her wet curls. "I'll bet she wants to see what you have for her. Isn't that right, sweetheart?"

She nodded. She did want to see, to touch, to taste. "I really would like to see," Micki swallowed her nerves. "All of you."

"Prove it. Talk dirty, Micki." Jared growled at her. "Tell me what you want."

Leaning into Bradley, she had the perfect position to watch Jared undress. *Just for her.*

She choked out, "I want to see your penis."

Jared smiled. "You sound clinical, not passionate."

Micki bit her lip. *Did he her want her to say...* "Show me that long, hard dick."

"Why? What do you want me to do with it?"

"Fill me up. Fill my pussy up."

He rolled his shoulders, need pinging off his body. He didn't speak a word, just nodded roughly.

He didn't give her some choreographed strip performance. He ripped off his leather jacket like a wild mustang shaking off a poorly secured saddle. Tremors shook her as she saw him shed his shirt. A fine layer of sweat covered his six-pack. His hard, muscled biceps flexed. His powerful chest rose and fell, gathering air for what she imagined would be an assault of pure pleasure.

"You do the pants," he ordered her.

With trembling fingers, she rushed to comply.

She knelt in front of Jared and unbuttoned the first button on his jeans with shaking fingers. No zippers here, old school button flies all the way. Bradley moved to the side clearly to better enjoy the show she would be performing on Jared.

Lost to the buzz inside her, nothing else mattered but this moment inside this room, with these men. Jared and Bradley.

Her fingers freed another button. And another. And another. Then the last one, and his cock pulsed behind white cotton, right in front of her.

"Touch my dick," he ordered.

Jared's head dropped and his eyes closed as her hand touched his hard cock through his white briefs. Very old school.

"You could do this better with me on the bed," Jared told her, thinking *I want you on the bed with your hot cunt ready for my devouring.*

Again, her imagination led her to believe she heard his thoughts. Instead of troubling her, his silent wicked ponderings added to her excitement.

"I think s-so."

"She wants to be on the bed, too." Bradley put his hand on the small of her back. "Isn't that right, Micki?"

"Y-yes." She did. Wanted to be there with them. To lose herself and her fears, her pain and worry.

Jared urged her off the floor to stand before him. She loved his touch, his strength, his forcefulness.

He guided her to the bed, his fly wide apart, to sit before him.

"She's hot, isn't she, Jared?"

"Damn. Yeah." Jared removed his biker boots and jeans in a flash.

"You like this, sweetheart, don't you?" Bradley's lust-filled eyes fixed on her naked body. "Then let Jared know how much you want this. Pull out his cock."

Obediently, she slid her hand up Jared's ripped belly, playing with the single line of hair that shot up from his waistband of his briefs just below his navel.

In a microsecond, Jared took off his briefs and tossed them across the room.

Finally, the man she'd lusted for downstairs stood next to her, fully exposed for her enjoyment. Lightheadedness threatened her as she gazed at his massive arms and legs that could protect and shelter, his muscled torso that would turn any woman's head, and his rock-hard cock that revealed his complete desire to have her.

Wait for me to connect, Jared! You need to slow down, Bradley's thoughts raced through her head.

"Your tongue also tasted her tight, hot cunt. You have to know that there's no slowing down with her!" Jared growled at him and sat down beside her on the bed.

The outburst startled Micki. It sounded passionate, not angry.

Power coursed through her like rays of the sun—through her, to each of them, and back again. A red-hot sun.

Words. Thoughts. The voice of reason inside her head that normally yelled her into submission couldn't muster even a whisper. Besides, she loved them talking about her, *thinking about her.*

"And I'll taste more of her, too." Bradley stripped in jerky motions.

She looked her soldier up and down. Not an ounce of fat on his muscled body. He sported a marvelous physique and a large throbbing cock. Her knees went weak.

"I want you to have a taste of my dick, Micki. Take that pretty mouth of yours and find out what's in store for you, but take a taste of Jared's cock first."

She nodded and trembled with the anticipation. She bent over Jared and licked his shaft up to the tip, her tongue stopped at the tiny slit. Salty and warm. A living thing that wanted to pierce her to the core. Aching, she took the head in her mouth and sucked. Jared gripped her hair in his fists and moaned.

Bradley walked over to the bed and sat beside Jared. "Get on the floor, Micki. Now me. Suck my dick, sweetheart."

Micki slipped onto the floor and knelt before them. She grabbed Bradley's cock. It pulsed hot in her hand, and she began pumping. She felt it grow. *God, how big can he get?* A shiver of expectation shot through her gut.

"That's it. Get it real hard for that hot mouth of yours."

How could it get any harder? Micki would have sworn it grew another half inch.

"Suck me," Bradley ordered. "Sweet and smooth."

He and Jared had delighted her with their hands and mouths. Now she'd give them the same kind of devotion. Anticipation engulfed her as she leaned in.

Taking each of the cocks in her hands she moved her lips over one—then the other.

Mmm.

She pumped them and molten red-hot lava flowed inside her.

She licked Bradley's cock up the side, to the head, then down the other side.

"Oh, yes!" Bradley shouted. "Sweetheart, you're so unbelievably sexy."

Sexy. A word she'd never considered for herself. She did feel sexy, incredibly so.

"Enough!" Jared bellowed and stood.

He pulled her up and close, her slick folds slid against the top of his hard cock. It startled and thrilled her.

Ohmigod!

Jared's rock-solid body against her fueled more passion, desire, and heat than she thought possible. It grew, multiplied. Would she explode into a million pieces once it detonated?

Micki looked deep into those eyes she'd first seen downstairs. Dark, lusty. His intensity continued to grow.

Her mouth went dry. Could she satisfy such a man?

Then Jared flipped her face first on top of Bradley so that her pussy touched his hard cock. Blue eyes probed her. Another wave of warmth rolled through her. She wanted him and Jared inside her. Must have them.

Bradley guided his dick into her pussy. Pressure. His delicious pressure filled her, sliding against sensitive tissues that had her gasping and grabbing the sheets. If the trembles of need that started from her core and ended throughout her body could be measured, they would certainly hit the Richter scale.

"God, you're so wet and tight. Beautiful." Bradley's words warmed her body even more.

She rotated her hips, pushing hard against him as Jared massaged her butt. The warmth turned to a rolling thunder in her belly. In this moment, nothing mattered but satisfying her need.

Bradley began pumping into her. Guiding her up and down his cock, over and over. *Oh, God!* In her entire sexual experience, nothing came close to this. Impulsively, she pushed her pelvis into him hard, stroke for stroke. Drunk on desire, dizziness assailed her, threatening to take her to unconsciousness.

Bradley's thoughts pressed, *No, Jared. Not yet. Not until...*

She felt the tip of Jared's cock between the cheeks of her ass. Though at first a bit frightened, a spasm of craving ripped through her washing away all fear. Another spasm and another. She wanted them both, deep inside her. She wanted to share herself with them in a way she'd never shared with another lover.

The room began to spin, to vibrate. Almost audible, pleasure bombarded her with electric shocks. She felt like a powerful, sexual woman, feminine to her very soul.

Bradley leaned in and kissed her more tenderly than before. His cock pushing inside her drew out a whimper from her lips. Her entire body throbbed as she matched his speeding strokes. Her orgasm began as a long explosion. Goosebumps covered her skin, not from being cold but from being so very hot.

She felt Jared's cock slowly move up and down between her two cheeks, rubbing, but not entering. The teasing drove her wild. Could she let him take her that way? She'd never tried anal sex before.

"This okay?" Jared asked.

"It is." Though, she wasn't so sure.

"I'd never hurt you, Micki," he promised gruffly.

Bradley pulled out of her pussy. "Neither would I."

"I know."

Jared nibbled her earlobe, his breathing hard, rhythmic, hypnotic before the final plunge.

"Do it," Bradley shouted. "Before it's too late."

Too late? For what?

Jared's chest blanketed her back. His hair hung down touching her shoulders.

She whimpered and closed her eyes, lost in sensations that overwhelmed and drowned her. She melted into Bradley's rock hard body, grinding back and forth against his freed cock. She wanted him back inside her, thirsted, craved, would die if she didn't have both of them.

"Tell him what you want," Bradley ordered, his breathing labored.

"Jared, I want you inside me."

"Stop dancing around it. Tell him you want his hard cock in your virgin ass!"

"I do. I want that. I need that."

Still, he didn't enter her. Why was he holding back? She wanted him to plunge his dick deep inside her. Wanted him inside her more than anything she'd ever wanted before.

"Help him," Bradley said, his breathing labored. He pulled his dick out of her, but kept it pressing on the outside of her swollen mound. She ached for him to be back inside her channel.

Shakily, she reached around and grabbed Jared's erection. He answered her tugging with a groan.

As if on cue, Jared applied lubricant to his cock and her opening. Where had he found it? The room must've contained everything lovers needed hidden away in corners for the experienced like him. Heat rolled through her body.

"Relax, Micki." Bradley instructed her.

She couldn't resist his commands. Didn't want to.

Jared's fingers teased her entry with the slick lubricant. He didn't rush. Time seemed to roll on forever. Bit by bit, she felt desire rise up even more than her fear.

Then Jared pushed his finger past her ring. Tight and immense. She tensed and sucked in a breath. If his finger seemed big to her now, how could she continue?

"I don't think I can do this." Micki closed her eyes tight.

Bradley kissed her on the cheek and whispered, "You're seconds away from something amazing."

She trembled.

"Take a deep breath and then let it out," Bradley commanded.

She let out a long sigh and tried to unclench. Jared rubbed her back and shoulders with his free hand. She kept her eyes closed. Lights flashed at the back of her eyelids—blue, green, and red.

Jared moved his finger in and out of her. The previous pain eased back into arousal.

Another finger joined the first. Again, she felt a bit of pain but not as much as before. And a third finger. Then Jared slipped his fingers deeper into her. In and out. Miraculous sensations expanded inside her, as did her need for more.

"Do it, Jared!" Bradley shouted.

Could she actually take all of his enormous cock? Fear seized her, tensing her all her muscles.

Bradley gazed fixed on her. "Breathe, Micki."

She took in a deep breath, and let it out.

The fingers left her backside and Jared'd throbbing shaft became their massive replacement.

She swallowed hard against the shock. *Monstrous.* The pain thundered through her, exploding in her gut like bombs.

"It's okay, Micki." Bradley whispered in her ear. "The shock will pass in a moment."

Her biker paused, his cock throbbing inside her, while Bradley kissed her cheeks. She released the breath she'd been holding. She let it out like a slow leaking balloon. When her lungs emptied, the pain subsided, replaced by a growing lust.

"I'm in. Are you okay?" Jared asked, his deep voice filled with concern.

This mysterious man didn't move a muscle. His willpower amazed her. She could tell that every fiber of his being wanted to charge ahead like a high-performance racecar, but he waited.

"I'm okay." Something about this felt right. Like everything she'd ever done before led to this very moment. Again, her muscles tightened, but not from nervousness, from bliss. In readiness.

"That's it," Bradley murmured. "I can feel your release. Can you feel her, Jared?"

"Fuck yeah."

"Do you like cock inside you, sweetheart?" Bradley's muscles flexed, glistened.

Micki closed her eyes as sensations and desire washed over her. "Yes."

"I think you're ready for more."

"I am. Please."

The head of Bradley's cock touched her folds. *Oh, God! Can I really take them both at the same time?*

He pressed his dick up into her pussy, stretching her more than she knew possible, burning her with each and every inch he went. *So much! Oh God!* Both men inside her, filled completely by them. Her body pulsed violently.

Every nerve ending came alive. Unparalleled passion overtook her.

"What are you feeling? Tell me." Bradley accelerated his rhythm inside her. Deeper and deeper he went.

Micki felt as if scalding steam discharged through her, burning everything along its path.

"Now!" Bradley shouted.

Then Jared began hammering inside her, matching Bradley's rhythm.

Don't ever stop!

Only one thin layer of flesh separated their bulging dicks. They each hissed, cursed. Harder and faster. Faster. Harder. Deeper. *Harder! Deeper!*

"Yesssss! Ohmigod! Yesssss!" "

Minutes. Hours. Eternity. Time had no meaning as they plunged into her deepest recesses over and over again.

"That's it!" Jared yelled. "Squeeze my dick with your beautiful ass!"

Her heart pounded loud and hard. *Boom! Boom! Boom!*

Nothing existed outside this room. She was more alive than she'd ever been in her entire life. The moment was so right. Blissful.

She felt them tense and then jets of hot liquid spilled into her. Micki's ache flamed into a spasming climax as she hit a crescendo. Jared and Bradley stiffened and pushed hard into her, deeper still, filling her thoroughly.

Orgasmic waves rolled through her like warm shocks, sparking inside her. She couldn't possibly bear another. But another came, and another. When the last hit her, to her core, shaking her whole body and began to subside, Micki opened her eyes.

Jared's body became—hot green smoke?

Bradley changed, too. Not into smoke, but large white wings sprung from his back surrounded by blue light and folded around the three of them. Wings?

She looked down at her own body. First, she thought she saw red. Then it changed, turning into light show that mirrored the colors of the rainbow.

The rainbow, the smoke, the wings seemed so real. She smiled knowing the vision came out of her incredible orgasm. With eyes half closed, she smiled in sheer satisfaction.

Then a door appeared in the middle of the room. Not a door—an opening. To where? She strained to see through it. Wherever it led to seemed dark and terrifying—without substance. Her gut tightened.

She closed her eyes, praying the opening to the darkness would close. Then she felt Jared's hands rubbing her shoulders, Bradley's lips pressing against hers, igniting her body again.

When she popped her eyes open again, the door disappeared, along with the rainbow, wings and smoke.

Ohmigod! Multiple undulations exploded from deep inside her, moving throughout her entire being as another orgasm overtook her beginning at the spot behind her navel, down her clit, through her channel, echoing a vibrating response. Typhoon-like waves. Again and again until she couldn't breathe, couldn't think, couldn't be without them.

When the vibrations finally subsided, she fell back, dizzy from the most incredible sex she'd ever experienced. Totally spent. As Bradley and Jared withdrew, sweet unconsciousness called to her.

Before succumbing to a much-needed rest, she saw Jared's face fill with fear.

Micki tried, but couldn't keep her eyes open to ease his concern.

"What the fuck have I done?" His anguished question floated through her hazy mind.

Bradley tensed against her. "What did you do to her, you dark-loving son of a bitch?"

She wanted to tell them before sweet sleep swept her away, but she couldn't find her voice.

You've given me the best sex I could ever dream of.

Chapter 8

Tonight, I went to Zone Three. A very strange place. Met a guy named Greg. Asked him several questions but tried not to reveal too much about what I'd learned. He told me to come back in the morning to meet David. Seems David's the man in charge. Not sure who to trust, but I have no other choice.

Eric's Flash Drive: day 33—entry 6

* * * *

Jared leapt from the bed and threw on his clothes when Micki's eyes shut. Gingerly, he'd reached out to her mind. Nothing.

Was she injured or worse? His jaw clenched at the thought of her dying because of him. He had to get far away from her and fast.

Bradley remained underneath Micki. *What did you do to her, you dark-loving son of a bitch?*

Jared had no answer. Instead, he bolted from the room.

Was the nightmare happening again? He'd been unable to hold himself back, to control his darkest urges. In his lust, had he taken the last of her life force? Double the pleasure; double the guilt. His gut wrenched.

Fuck!

Like a criminal fleeing the scene, Jared turned invisible. He hated leaving Micki, longed to turn around and go back to her. If he did?

So, down the stairs he went stopping for no one, though only a few stragglers still hoping for a hook-up remained in Zone Three.

If Micki was dead, David would find him and mete out a justice well deserved. If he hadn't killed Micki, well, he couldn't be allowed near her again. Her very life depended on it.

As he approached the exit, he spotted Greg and Trey talking next to the door. They would sense him passing. He'd have to utilize some of his new power to transport out of the club.

He scanned the energy inside him. A basketball of green energy spun hotly inside him created from his tripling with Micki and Bradley. More energy than he'd ever received from any triad. This new sphere, created from sex with Micki and Bradley, would keep him satiated for centuries. *Fuck!* His new lifespan came at the too high price for Micki. His gut seized tight at the thought that she might be dead.

Power up. Battle. Form a triad. Power up. Repeat as needed. The cycle of immortality. For Jared, the cycle threatened any who joined with him—as Micki may have learned too late. He'd resisted the Dark's pull two centuries ago, but the taste endured still fresh in his mouth, an overwhelming seduction.

Resist all you want, Jared. Darkness will take you.

The voice of Terrok, a demon prince, had been rich and deep that fateful night. His words had haunted Jared ever since.

Remorse shredding him, Jared took a speck of the new energy and used it to transport next to his motorcycle. The early morning air slapped him in the face when he materialized in the parking lot.

He mounted his Harley and kicked it alive. It roared like a lion before quieting to a low, growling rumble. He turned the handle and sped down the deserted road. Riding his 1952 Panhead normally provided him with a hypnotic respite, but this time its spell failed to quiet his mind.

He'd only agreed to keep her at the club until David arrived and took her off his hands. Still, no sign of the damned archangel.

Jared would've never agreed to come to the stronghold if he'd known that he would break his personal vow and triple again.

He could still smell their lovemaking, her scent teasing him. His cock hardened, and he hated himself for it. He accelerated to the bike's top speed, not stopping for traffic lights. The more distance between him and the two he'd left at Zone Three the better.

He could try to rationalize that his tripling with Micki had been necessary to keep her safe, but he knew the real reason. From the moment he saw her, he'd been unable to contain his desire. Micki was the most passionate, amazing woman he'd ever encountered.

Damn!

Equally astonishing, what about the portal that had appeared during the final climax and energy exchange? He'd seen it first, then Micki, and finally Bradley. Instantly, he'd known it led to the Ether. No immortal had the power to open the Ether, or so he'd thought. How was that possible? Thankfully, the portal had closed before any evil escaped.

Jared's gut went tight all over again.

Could it have been the Dark's lust inside him that caused it to open? God, given that possibility, he would *never* triple with anyone ever again.

* * * *

In the dilapidated and abandoned four-story building across the street from Zone Three, dark figures stood behind one of the few unbroken windows on the third floor watching the jinn speed off on his motorcycle.

Discarded items of the building's bygone years floated freely in the dank spaces while rats scurried everywhere. The place suited them.

The menacing observers, two males and one female, sported black leather overcoats. The males carried Glocks with silencers on their right and swords in scabbards on their left. They wore military-style footwear. The female with eyes of violet had six daggers sheathed in a criss-cross harness around her full chest and a M16 hanging at her side. She wore the kind of hardware and thigh-high black boots that would give just about any red-blooded male a hard-on.

The threesome remained cautious staying a few feet from the window, not wanting to be seen by the Alliance's invisible sentries above.

Obeying their master's orders, they'd been watching for several days for a particular human—a woman. When the morsel had arrived, they'd sent Connor in. He'd returned with details about the angel and the jinn. They'd teleported Connor back to the lair to inform their master.

The three could no longer sense the mortal woman's energy but they still wanted to sample it. Hungered for it

"The human is still inside with the angel." The shortest male shuffled around the room. "She didn't blare that much energy when she first arrived. In fact, Pratt, she appeared as any other mortal."

"Irkon, I can't sense her life force any longer." Pratt turned to the female. "Can you, Azlian?"

The woman pulled out one of her knives and threw it to the wall. The blade stuck down to the hilt. "No doubt the jinn and angel tripled with her in that lackluster Alliance way and have taken the woman's energy into themselves."

Irkon's eyes darted from the female to the window. "If her power could reach such heights once, it could again."

Azlian nodded. "How sweet it would be to hear Micki Langley scream as we drained her energy."

"We should seize her now," Irkon said. "There are only two immortals left in the place."

"There are still seven sentries above. What about the Alliance energy barrier surrounding the stronghold?" Pratt asked.

Irkon answered, "If we stay in human form we shouldn't trip their alarm."

"How do you know that?" the taller male asked.

"I don't, but I'm starving. If it fails, we fall back and return to the lair."

"Easy as that." Pratt didn't seem convinced. "Should we fail, we will either be sent to the Ether by the fucking do-gooders or face you-know-who."

"We just need to cross the street and walk inside." Irkon wringed his hands. "Once in the club and out-of-sight from the flying feathered assholes, we've only two angels left to deal with. Then we can devour the human."

Azalian turned back from the window. "Actually there are three angels. You've forgotten the warrior with the woman. Plus, an alarm most likely will sound once we pass the barrier in human form or not."

A sphere of black flames the size of an SUV exploded behind them. They turned to it. When the dark fire winked out, their master, regal and wickedly handsome, stood before them. His eyes were invisible behind mirrored sunglasses, but they knew them to be steel blue. Though he wore an expensive Italian suit, the tailoring must've been difficult with his massive chest and bulging biceps. Even his legs looked like large beams of iron.

They fell to their knees and said in unison, "My lord, Vincorte."

"Azlian is correct," he voiced. The sound crashed like a waterfall with millions of gallons plunging to the pool below—not of water, but of blood.

"I am?" she asked weakly.

"Will you allow us a taste of the mortal, my lord?" Irkon asked nervously.

"You are so eager. I normally like that, but not tonight." Vincorte patted the top of Irkon's head like a human would pat a dog. "When we succeed, you will get all the human flesh you desire, but not Ms. Langley. I have big plans for her."

"Can we take her now for you, my lord?" Pratt asked.

"You must be patient, my dear ones. Micki Langley will be ours soon. Very soon." Then he vanished. The three darklings continued to tremble, both from excitement and fear.

* * * *

Bradley scanned Micki's slack body and sensed no bewitchment. Was she merely asleep? Or had she been infected with Jared's dark, poisoned with something beyond Bradley's ability to detect?

When Micki had slipped into unconsciousness, Bradley had been under her, dazed by the appearance of the portal, by the incredible joint climax, then by Jared's abrupt escape.

Bradley could've rolled Micki to the side and kept Jared from leaving, but he'd opted to stay with her, check on her, instead of apprehending the jinn. He'd been more concerned with Micki's well being than a potentially new ifrit—the evil equivalent of a jinn.

No justification existed for Bradley's failure to follow his training and capture Jared. No excuse, as David would be quick to point out.

Jared's parting words played again in his mind. *What have I done?*

Rage boiled inside Bradley. He'd deliver long overdue justice to the traitor if Micki—

She stirred beside him and then let out a long, relaxed sigh. Relief rushed him and all his muscles at attention fell at ease.

As he settled back, he became aware of the power spinning inside his chest. The largest sphere of blue light energy he'd ever received in a triad.

How the hell had that happened?

Still asleep, Micki snuggled into him, her body soft and inviting. The urge to stretch his wings and take to the sky became near irresistible. He imagined soaring with her in his arms, reveling in the most amazing exchange he'd ever experienced. That could not happen. She wasn't a human familiar of the Alliance. His duty demanded he follow the rules.

But he'd already broken them once and let his wings appear.

Though only for a second during their final climax, his lack of self-control shamed him.

Bradley glanced at the room, still bathed in candlelight. The smoky jinn's absence filled him with concern.

Did the same amount of power whirling inside him also reside in Jared? No longer jinn, but an ifrit—fallen. Would he use his new power from their tripling as a weapon against the Alliance and against Micki? More rage poured into his core. The sphere spun, ready for whatever Bradley called it to do.

Later, he *would* fly. When he did, he'd hunt Jared down and find out why the jinn had really left. If he didn't tell him, Bradley would send him to the immortal prison.

But what had happened at the end of their tripling troubled him. Had Jared learned the impossible—how to open the Ether, the place of void. Could he use it as a *get-out-of-jail-free* spell?

Bradley had seen the portal appear for a moment before disappearing. Could the balance be shifting to the other side? He tensed at the thought, knowing he'd have to inform David of his suspicions.

Later. Now he couldn't leave Micki. Not after seeing Connor. But Jared had told him about the Dark's familiar. Had that been a lie? Had the jinn's reluctance to triple been a fabrication, too?

He had to speak to David. His commander would also want a report, answers. What the hell could he say?

He would redeem himself, Bradley vowed. He'd bring Jared back to Zone Three to face justice. The jinn had deserted David's assignment—and Micki.

Bradley cast a mental search for Jared. Instead of locating him, an ache nearing physical pain boomed inside Bradley for another chance at tripling with Micki—and the jinn.

Why the hell should he despise Jared yet want to share Micki with him again? *So very strange!*

Leaning on one arm, he stroked her hair and tried to figure it out.

He'd never felt this way when a triad disbanded. He'd known immortals who formed longer-term triads, but humans died. Angels and jinn became bored.

Bradley had always discarded lovers like candy wrappers. After the orgasm, he quickly moved to the next conquest. He enjoyed the multitude and variety and hated feeling like he missed out on anything. With Micki, something changed inside him. He couldn't imagine touching another human again.

He tried to push the connection aside, but the power pulsing inside him would not let him disregard his link to her.

Micki shifted closer to him. His heat grew as he looked at her sleeping. The smell of their lovemaking filled the air and jolted him, reminders of their shared pleasure. Still, repeats never existed, not for him. Then why did he keep gazing down at her imagining—

Micki opened her eyes and he stared into their hazel-gold beauty fluttering to consciousness. His cock hardened.

"Good morning," she said.

"Good morning, sweetheart."

"So, it wasn't a dream." Micki yawned.

A dream—yes and no. Kissing. Tasting. Exploding. *The portal's appearance?*

"You are like a dream, Micki."

"I didn't think it was a dream. Not really." She looked around the room searching, no doubt, for Jared.

Bradley needed to distract her. "Do you feel okay? Any pain?"

"No. Are *you* okay, Bradley?"

The sheet fell away from her as she stretched out her arms with another long yawn. He fixed his gaze on her naked breasts sporting hardened berry-like nipples. He couldn't resist caressing one.

"Micki, being with you, I'm much more than okay."

Her thoughts shot into him. *He knows just what to say. God, he's glorious.* "Tell me about yourself. Where were you born?"

His gut tightened, and he guarded his thoughts from her. He didn't know and would never know what his human life had been. "Texas."

"Really? Dallas? Houston?"

She needed to stop. He couldn't bear lying to her anymore, even little things. "Just Texas."

"Love it there. The sun. Amazing." Luckily, her probing questions ended.

Bradley sensed her mind still floated in a state of afterglow from their tripling. Thoughts of her missing brother still far removed. That would change when she lost the orgasmic euphoria. He couldn't let that happen.

Bradley grazed his hands over Micki's hips.

"Where's Jared?"

Clearly, he hadn't distracted her well enough. "Gone."

She frowned. "Will he be coming back?"

"Maybe," Bradley lied. "Did you enjoy yourself?"

Enjoy? I didn't know sex could be like that. "Yes."

He cupped her chin, pulled her close, and pressed his lips against hers. Her fingers grazed the back of his shoulders and neck, flooding him with tingles, need.

He couldn't resist more of her and plunged his tongue into her wet, soft mouth. She tasted amazing. His dick swelled.

To go to the same well was foreign to him but having sampled Micki once—he wanted more of her. Much more.

She broke free from his kiss. "Shouldn't we wait for Jared?"

"Why? I'm perfectly capable of loving you all by myself. I'll be happy to prove it." Bradley smiled. A coupling with Micki would provide no power, just blazing hot sex and incredible pleasure.

She giggled. He loved that sound and wanted to hear more of it. He latched onto her breasts with his hands and began caressing them gently.

"That feels good." Her head tilted back. *His touch is amazing!*

Bradley leaned down and sucked hard on her left nipple, making her sigh.

He slid his hand down her naked abdomen to her clit. "Like that, Micki?"

"I do."

"Good. Then spread you legs wide for me and find out."

Micki gasped at his latest touch and parted her legs out under the sheet. He pulled the silk completely off of her and gazed down at her hot pussy.

"You getting wet for me?"

Her eyes widened. She bit her lip, nodded.

"Good."

Bradley wanted to taste every part of her. Another kiss, then he swept his tongue along her slender neck, inhaling her scent of jasmine and honey. He kissed his way down to her soft breasts, circling both of her raspberry nipples. Farther down he went to her taut stomach, lingering at her navel.

She trembled at his assault.

Down and down to her swollen clit. Bradley tongued it lightly.

"G-God!"

He flicked her bud of nerves with slow, steady pressure while he moved a finger into her tight slit, rubbing a spot high and inside her front wall.

No red power radiated out of her. Just amazing one-on-one sex. He felt almost human again.

Micki's body flushed with heat, matching his own lust.

Bradley used two fingers on her sensitive spot, rubbing, rubbing, driving up her pleasure. As she tightened around his hand and gripped the sheets, he knew he'd succeeded.

"Your pussy is white hot. You want to come for me, don't you?

"Y-Yes," she panted.

"Your body will surrender to me, right? I want your sex tight and convulsing around my dick."

He flicked her clit, then moved to slip his tongue deep into her pussy. She rewarded him with hot liquid release.

Micki rocked like a wild mustang underneath him, hips rising off the bed over and over. Then her legs wrapped around his head, pulling him tighter.

He lapped her juices up with delirious abandon. He loved giving her pleasure.

As he moved his hand to work over her clit and dined on her pussy, his cock stiffened and his balls filled up. He pulled Micki's legs off of his head and climbed up her torso until his dick touched her wet, swollen folds.

Bradley gazed into her hazel-gold eyes, half-closed in a lustful haze. "I'm going to plunge my cock deep into your pussy, and you're going to take every inch."

"Y-Yes!"

"Then I'm going to thrust hard and slow at first until you're clawing and calling my name."

"Get inside me. Please. I can't stand waiting any longer."

He loved hearing her beg for him. "You don't sound like you mean it to me. Make me believe you, Micki."

"P-Please, Bradley. I need you in me, now."

She writhed against his dick, tempting him to pound her fast and deep.

"Slow at first." He slipped the tip of his dick just inside her opening. It took all his will not to jackhammer his way inside her. "Like that?"

"O-Ohhhh! I-I love it. More!"

"Let me push into your pussy another inch." And he did.

"Y-Yes, G-God!"

Heat rolled through him. Lust urged him to go deeper, faster, but he resisted. He loved Micki's reaction to his slow advance.

"Want another inch of my cock inside you?"

"Please, I want all of it. Now!"

Instead, he only went forward another fraction. Her cunt convulsed tight around his dick, and he could no longer hesitate.

He plunged his whole cock deep into her pussy.

Her fingernails sank into his shoulders. "Y-Yesssssss!"

His passion flared and he accelerated, pounding Micki's sex relentlessly, one hungry thrust after another.

An upsurge of raw appetite spread over him ending at the base of his dick.

"You like that?" he asked.

"Y-Yesss!"

"I'm gonna leave you raw and satisfied."

"O-Ohh!"

In and out. Hard. Driving. Merciless.

Over and over.

"Squeeze my dick with your pussy, Micki!" Bradley shut his eyes as he felt her insides tighten around his cock. "That's it!"

His need to let go consumed him. No more holding back.

"Bradley!"

He loved when she said his name. Loved when she said anything. He couldn't get enough of her.

Their bodies rocked together, synchronized for their coming orgasms.

He opened his eyes. Micki's mouth opened slightly and her tears streamed. He felt her tremors, convulsions, as her orgasm rocketed through her. He came inside her, the explosion like an asteroid hitting a planet.

After several minutes, his body quieted. He relished holding her tight against him as they both shared their afterglow.

A sensual sleepiness spread over him. He listened to Micki's breathing elongate. The bliss that settled over him made no sense, but he wouldn't question the fact now that nothing on Earth or in heaven felt more right.

* * * *

Bradley's sleep ended when Micki's body jerked against him. Her breathing changed. *She's awake.*

Micki pulled free of his hold.

He asked, "What's the matter, sweetheart?"

She sat up on the side of the bed. "Jared. Where is he?"

"I don't know."

"I've got to go." Her voice trembled.

He wanted to console her, comfort her, make love to her again, but he didn't.

Damn it. Once she'd learned the jinn wasn't returning, she wanted to leave. The bastard's disappearance had hurt her, and Bradley knew that he couldn't ease the ache.

She's just human. Focus on your vow and your duty to the Alliance.

"I understand you're confused," he said, hoping to stall. He needed to come up with a plan—and fast.

"You think you do?" she challenged.

How he wished he could hear her thoughts like before, but now they came in whispers too soft to hear clearly.

"Do you want to talk about what happened?" he offered.

For a moment he thought she might. Instead, she placed an invisible boundary between them as she crossed her arms. Then even the whispers of her thoughts became silent.

"I have to go." She stood. Her dark hair fell to her soft shoulders, tantalizing him as it captured streams of the candlelight.

An idea came to him. "Micki, let me help you find your brother."

She studied him as if considering his offer. Would she stay with him? She had to. Leaving wasn't an option for her, not until he talked to David. Not until he knew she'd be safe.

A long sigh slipped past her full lips. "This is something I have to do on my own. Bradley, thank you for making the phone call, but I really have to go."

She wouldn't be safe out of the stronghold's walls. He wasn't ready to leave her.

He had to stop her. "You can't leave."

Her brow furrowed. "Can't?"

Bradley stood and grabbed up his clothes. He tried to enter her thoughts past the wall she created. He pushed a bit deeper.

Definitely not one of the guys from my dream, he heard Micki muse silently.

"You really can't leave, Micki."

"It has been fun, but I have to go."

As if handling a poisonous snake, she grabbed her panties off the floor. *I can't wear these. Never again.* And then silence.

No matter how hard he tried to read her thoughts anymore, he couldn't.

She shoved her panties into her purse. Her sweet curls disappeared when she pulled on her skirt. Her beautiful mounds he'd earlier tasted and caressed vanished when she buttoned up her silk shirt. A longing grew inside him to strip away the clothing and possess her all over again.

She bit her lip. His cock hardened at the sight of her.

Bradley pulled on his cargo shorts hiding his half-erection.

"Bye, Bradley."

"You are not going anywhere! It isn't safe."

Micki recoiled and gasped at his command. It pained him, but he couldn't let her go with the Dark looking for her, with Jared's whereabouts still unknown.

"What do you mean?" She slipped on her shoes and glanced to the door. He didn't want her to be afraid of him, but she must understand.

"You're in danger, Micki. I've been assigned to keep you safe."

"Assigned? But we just met." Her hands shook.

He wanted to tell her the whole truth. That he was an angel. That somehow her brother had caused her to be targeted by the Dark. That what they'd shared had been the most amazing experience of his existence. He couldn't. Damn rules.

Still, he *could* tell her part of the truth.

"Listen to me. You need my protection. David told me to find you."

"David? So you lied to me just to get me up here? So getting me into bed made me *safe*? You lying sack of shit!" She backed away, her face turned white hot. From fear or anger? He didn't know.

"You're staying put for your own good, sweetheart." Bradley clasped her shoulder to calm the brewing storm inside her. She jerked away.

"Don't call me sweetheart, asshole!" She shook off his hand.

Her words and reaction stung him.

"Okay. I won't. But I'm telling you the truth."

"That I'm in danger and David sent you?" Her words came out clipped tight and razor sharp. "What else do you know? Where to find my brother?"

"I really don't know any more than I told you," he lied, and swallowed back the guilt.

"And Jared? He in on this, too?"

Jared? The bastard had no concern for Micki.

"Yes, but he isn't to be trusted."

"And I'm supposed to trust you when you have sex with me to distract me and then try to keep me here against my will? Leave me the hell alone. I only want to find my brother." Her eyes glistened with unshed tears. "That is the only reason I came here."

"I know that. But you can't find him by yourself."

She snapped, "I can and I will."

"Micki, you've got to trust me."

Tears rolled down her cheeks. "Why? What on earth have you done to earn my trust?"

"Please," What else could he say? Or do? Break his vow and show his wings to a non-familiar?

David would definitely reprimand him if not string him up by the balls.

"Admit it, I'm just another lay for another notch on your bedpost." Her words stung him.

"That's not true. Not after last night."

Micki rolled her eyes. "Of course it is."

What could he say to make her believe him? She had no idea what waited for her outside these walls.

"Micki, try to calm down."

"Calm down? When it's clear I've been gullible? You and Jared have done this routine many times? How many women have you taken up here and—?"

"Stop." Nothing he said would change her mind at the moment. So he pulled from his training. Orders, direct and clear, might be the only way to make her stay. "You will not leave!"

"But I am leaving, Bradley!"

His gut went tight. He must convince her to stay without telling her everything. But how? He grabbed her arm.

With her free hand, Micki slapped him hard on the face. *"Get your fucking hands off of me!"*

Chapter 9

David seems very curious about me. He's an arrogant prick. I don't trust him, but unfortunately, I need his help.
Eric's Flash Drive: day 34—entry 2

* * * *

Jared forced his Harley to a speed that would've been considered unreasonable even if he'd been in rural Montana, which he wasn't, and here, an hour from Zone Three, seventy miles past illegal. No matter. Even at that speed it would take him twenty-four hours of driving to get back to his cabin. Away from Micki and the guilt.

No matter how full-tilt his flight, the image of her closed eyes continued to sting his psyche far more than the wind stung his face. He swallowed hard against the barrage inside his head.

Stop thinking about her!

The mental command went unheeded. The memory of his incredible embrace with Micki and Bradley swirled. A tripling for the ages. Though most of the current of power they'd created coalesced inside the ball in the center of his body, some continued to dance on his skin like static electricity—something he'd never experienced before and craved again.

He'd rationalized that their tripling became necessary to save her. Reason had abandoned him, leaving him with raw, aching need. He'd bedded Micki to satisfy a hunger for her he'd been unable to either explain or deny.

What about the portal?

His gut went tight. Had he done something to cause that?

"Fuck!" Jared screamed into the wind.

Suddenly, the sight of a white utility van pulling out from a side street directly ahead jerked him from his contemplation. It stopped in the middle of the intersection.

Trying to avoid a collision with the vehicle, he turned his bike to the left, spilling it onto the asphalt, keeping his head tilted away from the street. His leg hit the pavement first, then his leather jacket at the elbow. Pain spread from his thigh and arm. Sparks flew from the metal gas tank of his Panhead. He slid for an entire block. Finally, the skidding ended two feet from the white vehicle.

After a mere split-second, Jared stood, pulling his bike upright. He first inspected his ride. Except for a little paint, everything appeared to be okay. Then he examined his body. Blood flowed out of a hole on his jacket's left sleeve near his elbow and from a large laceration in his thigh. Many of the wounds from his days as an Alliance warrior had taken several hours to heal. One had even taken a full day and night. Though his arm and leg hurt terribly, he expected these two gashes would disappear in a couple minutes. The rip in his leather jacket would not. *Damn!*

"Asshole," he shouted to the van's tinted windows.

His Harley's headlight lit up the van's side with the words *Grafton Cleaning Service* and a phone number in blood red letters. The vehicle's sliding door opened. Eleven men and two women emerged, too many passengers even for such a large van. Though they looked mortal, Jared knew immediately that they weren't.

Darklings.

Black flames encircled ten of them, one woman and nine men—demons. Violet smoke surrounded the other three, two men and a woman—ifrit.

"You got insurance on that piece of shit?" Jared taunted aloud as he dismounted the Harley.

"You're the one who is gonna need insurance, jinn," one of the men taunted.

"Is that right?" The odds stacked up that he'd be getting his one-way ticket to the Ether from these pricks. Still, he would make sure to take some of them with him.

Jared felt the temperature rise several degrees. Then the thirteen discarded their human disguises. The demons' pointed horns and leathery wings appeared. The three ifrits' violet smoky bodies blazed, ready to fight alongside their brothers. They had a battery of automatic guns that could slow him down. Then the creatures conjured blades that could deliver an eternal deathblow.

They stood ready to attack.

Jared brought his spinning power ball to the forefront of his mind.

"Just like darklings, too scared to try a fair fight. I bet I could take on three of you at a time. How about it?"

"You'll never change, Jared." One of the females bathed in black fire sent him a smile, a smile he recognized from decades earlier.

Jared tried to hide his surprise. "Yassia? I thought you aligned with the Rogues."

"I did. Now, I'm with the winners."

The evil crowd laughed.

He'd met Yassia just after Gwyneth's death. She'd found him after his willing expulsion from the Alliance and brought him to the neutral faction of the immortals, the Rogues. He'd never joined them, but he admired their dispassionate ease.

"So, now you're a demon. Too bad."

When had he last seen her? *Eighty years ago.* The curvy, redheaded immortal had found his cabin in Montana. He swallowed hard at the image standing before him and remembering what she'd been before.

The demon prince's ancient words shoved to the front of his mind. *Count the bodies!*

"Why is being a demon a bad thing?" she questioned with the silky voice he remembered. "Wouldn't you love to triple with me,

Jared?"

"I'll never triple with you, Yassia." *Or anyone, ever again.*

He sent to the diabolic crowd, *This may be check out time, but I'm gonna take some of you bastards with me.*

One of them shot back, *Sure about that, jinn?*

If any human had been on the street, they would've seen him on his bike and then—as if by magic—would've seen him appear next to it. Jared didn't use his power but moved at speeds too fast for humans to detect, just like these immortals could.

"He's one of us. Don't you see it? Not fully re-born to the Dark, but he's tasted it," the one said holding an energy rope.

Energy rope? Did they plan on taking him prisoner? He could never let that happen. They'd have to kill him first.

"I'm *not* one of you," Jared said through clenched teeth, but he wasn't so sure. Micki's face, eyes closed, floated in his mind. Even though a whirlpool of guilt circled inside him, still his cock hardened at the thought of her. *Damn!*

Yassia said, "You say it with your mouth, but I feel your hunger for that little morsel you tasted tonight."

One of the other demons smiled at her words. "So sad you didn't take all of that bitch's life force."

He hadn't killed Micki? How did these monsters know that? He and Bradley must've been too late with their tripling to keep Micki off of the Dark's radar. Too late then, but now—

Jared's body turned to hot green smoke. The abundant power in him jumped from his opaque fist and pounded the last demon who spoke. The monster screamed and flashed out.

Lucky shot, one male ifrit sent.

The creature formed a fiery violet baton and charged toward him.

Where Jared had been fast before, now he moved like a blur of green—faster than he ever thought possible. He felt beyond powerful, his body buzzing with energy. He fashioned two daggers from the energy surging inside him and hurled them at the ifrit.

The creature's eyes went wide as he tried to duck but failed to escape Jared's blades. The ifrit's smoke turned dark and cold. When the violet fog extinguished completely, the fiend disappeared into the Ether.

Two down, eleven to go. Jared's odds improved, but not enough.

He avoided the fire arrows that Yassia and another demon shot at him, but a few of the bullets from their comrades' AK-47s ripped through him. He ignored the searing pain and charged two of the demons. Instantly, his mind fashioned two scimitars, both luminous and greenish silver. From mind to matter, they appeared in his hands.

Swoosh. Swoosh.

Their heads hit the pavement before disappearing with their bodies.

Swoosh. Swoosh.

Two more demons vanished after he sliced their chests wide open.

Then the power he'd used to make the magic scythes petered out leaving him weaponless.

"Get him!"

The remaining four male demons rushed him with the energy rope. Without thought, Jared grabbed his remaining power and torpedoed it on the attackers. A wave of green smoke spread through them and their horns melted on their heads, their skin turned ashy white, and then their bodies exploded, producing black smoke. The rope vanished with them.

Yassia and the other two darklings' jaws went wide in shock.

Jared grabbed the male ifrit by the throat and held the creature above the ground.

Yassia and the female ifrit jumped into the van. He smelled burning rubber as they sped away, abandoning their buddy. Jared took out his Glock with his free hand and fired a few rounds into the white metal, but that didn't slow its trek down the road.

Then he looked at this captive. The remaining darkling's eyes filled with hate, but the creature could not escape Jared's grip.

"That sweet little piece of ass really charged your batteries, both yours and the angel's," the darkling spat out.

An enormous rage churned inside Jared. He squeezed the creature's throat until he heard him choking. "What about the human and the angel?"

"The apocalypse is coming!"

A fucking fanatic.

"I didn't ask you about the end of the world, asshole." Jared applied more pressure, watching the ifrit's bravado change to fear.

Still, the darkling snarled, "Fuck you, jinn! You know the power. The taste of it. I know you do. You will join us again, and the woman will be devoured by you and my brothers."

Jared slammed the creature's head down to the pavement. Its entire body disintegrated on impact.

Jared fell to the ground bested by the depletion of his energy in the battle. Still, he was able to take on human form. Though the gashes on his elbow and leg disappeared, four hits from bullets remained. Those wounds bled like bubbling creeks. Unlike the previous lacerations, these would take a while to heal, at least an hour.

Still, he'd single-handedly defeated a Dark war party of thirteen—killing eleven of them. How? His precious battle record, taking out five alone, had been impressive to the Alliance when he still fought alongside them. Today, if they didn't hate and distrust him so much, he'd be a goddamned hero. Nine demons and two ifrit dead didn't seem possible, but it had happened. The only explanation—his tripling with Micki and Bradley had produced immortal voltage on a grand scale.

The avenue, illuminated by shop signs and streetlights, quieted with only traces of the battle—dark spots on the pavement.

When a trash truck rolled around the corner with two men hanging from the back, Jared dusted himself off and picked up his Harley.

Micki was alive, but his relief didn't last long. The Dark knew about her. His mouth went desert dry. No denying it now, she needed him.

The fact the monsters sensed the dark lust in him didn't fill him with a warm fuzzy, either. Because he sensed it, too.

He imagined the Fates saying, *Please pick up your baggage, sir.*

How had Micki's brother, Eric, gotten involved with the immortals? What angle did David play? Did the highest-ranking immortals in the Alliance and David's peers—the Seven—know about Micki's amazing energy? Even if they did, which he doubted, would her safety be important to their goals of winning the war against the Dark? Maybe, but maybe not. The bastions of light who promised to protect humanity would always twist their precious vow to suit their purposes. He knew that first hand.

Anger gripped him, tightening every muscle with fury.

He needed to get to David, demand he put more guards around Micki to protect her from the Dark—and from him.

Jared jumped on his Harley and headed back to Zone Three.

A single ball of green smoke, the size of a pinpoint, spun in his chest. That's all that remained of his enormous powers. The immortal hunger grew inside him, demanding his attention. A survival instinct, a need he must refuse.

An hour, maybe two, was all his remaining energy could give him to find David, ensure Micki's protection. Then all his power would be gone, and he would slip into the Ether. Forever.

So be it.

His fingers found Micki's bra in his back pocket. He closed his eyes, regret gouging him.

* * * *

Micki saw the bright red handprint appear on Bradley's cheek. He stepped back and released her arm. By his expression, she realized she'd shocked him. Something else showed in his face. Surprise? Hurt?

It didn't matter. If he tried to restrain her again, she'd scream her head off. How could she have been such an idiot? She'd given her trust to him and Jared. Why? What did she really know about him or the missing biker? They looked like the guys in her dreams, and they knew how to satisfy a woman. Beyond that, she knew nothing more.

Mustering as much calm as possible to her, she lowered her voice. "I'm leaving. Don't try to stop me."

Bradley didn't say a word. Her nerves felt like pinpricks on her skin.

She backed up to the door, ready for anything. He didn't move.

"Tell your friend David I'll be back tomorrow, and he better be here with some answers."

With that, she walked into the hallway and shut the door behind her. Then she ran like an Olympic gold medalist away from Bradley and his craziness. Her heart ran faster than her legs.

She half expected him to follow, but he didn't.

Micki flew down the stairs lost in her own thoughts as two men and a woman passed her heading up. The woman giggled as the men's hands wandered over her body. The three looked at her. Micki produced an artificial smile for them and continued down to the first floor.

One of the men said, "Carlie, you are such a tease."

"I know, and I love teasing you."

As they passed by Micki, the men touched every part of Carlie showing no discretion at all. She'd been like that woman just a few hours ago. Micki envied Carlie, but also wanted to scream at her, *Don't let them touch you! The pleasure clouds your mind.*

It's too much.

When Micki reached the club floor, the bartender from earlier watched her intently, but not just him. Others stared, too. Suddenly, they all turned to the top of the stairs. Micki looked back, expecting to see Bradley, but the upper landing held no one.

What are they all looking at?

Not wanting to be stopped, she hurried to the door and exited Zone Three. Light from the club's neon sign lit leaves blown down the street by a gentle breeze. Her gaze followed them, trying to hold back the tears that welled up.

Stupid, stupid, stupid.

Without a bra and panties, she stood on the uninhabited street. Vulnerability besieged her and the tears gushed. She needed a cab, but she didn't see a single one in sight. She could walk, but she didn't know exactly which direction to go. She looked for any store that might be open, but found only abandoned buildings. The one across the street held title as the worst of the lot as nearly all its windows were broken. When she'd arrived last night, she hadn't notice Zone Three's derelict surroundings.

Fear ran up her throat and threatened to choke her.

Everything she'd been through for the past few days had been madness.

What had happened to Jared? Was he as delusional as Bradley? Anger welled up in her stomach like a bubbling cauldron of lava fueled by her anxiety.

Casual sex, my ass! Her heart stung. There was nothing casual about the way they'd made her feel.

She suspected that Jared had left for good, never to come back, never to say goodbye. Pain reached to her very center, steamrolling her flat.

She pushed it aside. Her brother. That's all that mattered. Again, she wondered how he'd gotten mixed up at Zone Three. What kind of world had Eric gotten involved in?

Jared had left.

Bradley had tried to hold her against her will.

Both of them, assholes!

The night had brought to life a fantasy, nothing more. A dream turned into a damn nightmare.

What did she really expect from two men she'd known for a

handful of hours and all of their "quality time" spent in bed? Her mind swirled and her stomach went topsy-turvy.

What if they were con artists? What if Jared had taken her wallet? *Shit!*

Micki looked in her purse and pulled out her belongings. Wallet, credit cards, money—all still there. At the bottom of her purse sat Eric's flash drive.

She froze.

In her frenzy, she'd totally forgotten about Eric's errand. The wind howled. She couldn't swallow against her throat's tightening at the dread she felt for her brother.

After listening to Eric's voicemail, she'd found no book, no papers, only the silver portable data device. Still believing it all a gag, she'd placed the thing into the USB port on her laptop and had found the password-protected folders.

After all Micki had seen tonight, she realized that she had to get into those folders and try to piece together her brother's last days. If she couldn't figure out the passwords on her own, she'd ask Tom, the techie at the bank, to help her. He'd never failed her when it came to any data issue.

And what about Eric's voicemail? *Be safe.* It echoed Bradley's concerns. What did that mean? Safe from what?

Over the years, her brother often sent her cryptic messages, a game they'd played since childhood. He'd tried to shock her, and she would feign a reaction.

One of his notes, and one of her favorites, had said, *Held hostage, bring money to Harry's Pizzeria.* She'd showed up, and he'd surprised her with a birthday party. Year after year the notes had come. Sometimes they'd lead to big events, sometimes to blind dates, sometimes to remind her of something Eric thought important. But the notes had always come.

He had tried to be both a brother and a parent since their mother had died at the young age of twenty-nine.

Twenty-nine—the same age Eric would be on his next birthday. What if he didn't make it to his...? Her gut cramped and tears fled her eyes. She couldn't imagine being left all alone without her big brother.

Brooke might have heard something since their call.

Damn. She'd forgotten about promising to call Brooke back.

At one in the morning Micki had sent her a text message telling her not to worry. Then she'd turned the ringer to silent mode. *Another smart move by the brilliant Micki Langley.*

The phone's screen shined: *Four fifteen AM.*

Micki's legs shook and threatened to buckle. She steadied herself, fearing she might fall. That would be a fitting end to a crazy night.

She sat down on the curb and scrolled through the missed calls. Twenty-two, all from Brooke. Micki's hands trembled as she punched the buttons to call Eric's girlfriend.

"Micki, where-the hell-are you?" Brooke's voice blared from the cell.

Micki looked across the road and saw a green sign.

"I'm at the address I gave you." Tears flowed again.

"I came to that club. I looked everywhere for you. Do you know what kind of place it is?"

"You shouldn't have." Micki wasn't surprised that Brooke had done that.

Her grit matched and often surpassed Eric's mischievousness.

"I couldn't find you or Eric."

Micki felt despair seize her mind. "You still haven't heard from him?"

"No. I've checked every place I know he goes. Nothing. But I didn't know that he went to Zone Three."

Micki sensed Brooke's confusion and distress about the club. "And the police?"

"No luck. They said I'd have to come in and file a report."

What could've happened to him? Micki needed to find David.

Fast.

Shame hit her. How could she have let herself be so distracted by Jared and Bradley?

"Micki?" Brooke's voice sounded concerned. "Are you okay?"

"Yes and no."

"Stay put. I'm in my car now. I can be there in ten minutes."

Lost to her stupid fantasy, Micki had taken a risk that could have left her in trouble. With Jared and Bradley she hadn't cared, hadn't thought it through. Even now, she couldn't break free of the longing she felt for them. Longing for more of their embrace.

What did she really know about either of them? Bradley knew more than he told her, Micki was certain. He kept secrets, despite her fear for Eric. *You're an asshole, Mr—*

She gasped as she realized that she didn't even know either of their last names. The after-sex clarity disclosed the fact they were nearly strangers to her.

I'm a raving lunatic.

"Micki, are you there?"

"Yes."

"I'll be there in ten minutes," Brooke offered.

"I really appreciate it."

"Don't worry. Just hang on." The signal died.

Micki's entire body shook.

Had Eric been sucked into Zone Three's propensity to the erotic with its undertones of danger and mystery?

She'd bedded two strangers. With no protection. Groaning, she dropped her head into her hands. *Damn!* She'd been a complete fool.

She opened her purse to put her phone away and looked at the mocking panties and flash drive. She'd really fucked up. Her thoughts crumbled and despair with a nice side helping of shame threatened to do her in.

At least until she felt someone—or something—watching her.

She looked up and down the road. No one. Then she glanced back at Zone Three. Again, not a soul. She scanned the building across the street. A shiver of electricity shot through her. She couldn't see anyone in the abandoned building, but she feared that someone targeted her from there.

"I'm jumping at shadows now."

Chapter 10

Tonight, Brooke and I met Micki for dinner. We ate lobster, Brooke's favorite. My façade fooled them. Neither seemed to be aware of the storm brewing inside me.

I can't believe what I'm going to do tomorrow night, but if I don't there is no chance for Micki and me. I hope Brooke never finds out.

Eric's Flash Drive: day 39—entry 10

* * * *

Jared disfigured the street with black tire tracks from his Harley that squealed to a full stop at Zone Three's curb. He killed the engine and dismounted. For a moment, he thought he could smell Micki's scent. Involuntarily his cock hardened, and his body turned hot. His lust must've created the illusion of her fragrance. Like smoke from incense, images of Micki floated in his head.

Illusion or not, more heat, like the surface of the sun, spread to his groin. His immortal appetite, full-scale, assaulted every part of him at the very thought of her.

Fuck!

The club's non-descript door looked like a back entrance to a warehouse, not a front door to a nightspot for the in-crowd. Unlike his last visit, no parked BMWs or Porches lined the street. Not surprising since it was four thirty in the morning.

It took effort to get his legs moving, but he did. When he stumbled inside, just like the outside, he saw no evidence of the glamour of the earlier evening hours. The illusion had been completely consumed by the truth only impending daylight could bring, the former neon lights replaced by glaring fluorescents. A cleaning crew mopped, swept and emptied the grime working to resurrect the former glory of the club for the coming night. The speakers wailed a sad country song near the empty bar.

Jared hated mornings.

"Look what the cat dragged in at this hour," a booming voice shot at him.

He recognized David's voice and turned.

The archangel looked exactly as he had all those years ago. Behind narrow glasses, steel grey eyes peered out. Taller than Jared by a couple inches, his sinewy frame exuded elegance. He leaned against the wall smoking a cigarette. Forgotten, a blue backpack lay like a corpse on the ground at his feet. David's dashing good looks resembled the grad students attending the nearby university. Jared knew better. The eyes told of the ages David had lived. How ancient, Jared didn't know, but much more than his own four hundred and ten years.

The two of them had fought together, side by side, in many battles with the Dark. The last time had been London, 1808, when the darklings tried to burn the city. They'd gone there on a lark, wanting some respite from their battles in North America. A vacation of sorts. But if it hadn't been for David and Jared, tens of thousands of humans would've lost their lives that night. That would've been a major Alliance defeat. Parkor, the archangel who led the Alliance forces in Europe had been absent when the demons attacked.

Jared and David had kept the carnage to a minimum. Only the original Theatre Royal had been destroyed. Did Parkor care to thank them? No.

A year later, Jared had seen David at the scene of the crime, then not again, until now.

"You look like the plague," David stated.

His wavy brown haircut revealed he still yielded to the latest trends. Jared had stopped imitating human fads in the later half of the last century. *Fuck fashion.*

"I am," Jared said with anger and irritability. He walked to the table next to the angel. *A mess and more. And I bet you know why.*

Maybe I do.

Where is she?

She's safe, David offered with a tight smile

Not true. The Dark wanted her. He needed to make sure Micki was truly safe. Bradley, too. If he let his power wink out, he'd never see them again. Jared opened his eyes. His throat went dry, but he must make David understand.

We have a problem, Jared sent back. He looked around the room. A few regulars entered. He knew more than most that other eyes and ears might be present.

A problem for the Alliance, or for you?

Sending thoughts became more difficult as his power shrank back, so Jared leaned in. "Both. Thirty minutes ago I knocked off eleven darklings, ten demons and an ifrit. Two got away."

David took off his glasses with a grace that would've been lost on most but not on Jared. *Glasses?* Jared knew well the archangel didn't need them. Subtle or not, his charms snared many.

"Impossible," David said aloud.

"Not only possible but real."

"You defeated that many darklings by yourself?"

"The power Micki gave me... I can't explain it." Jared struggled to push out his breathy words, "but... Yeah."

"Interesting."

"W-Why did you pick me to g-guard her?" Now his energy waned, and he struggled with speaking.

"You were available."

"For b-being as old as... you must be you sure are a d-dumb ass." Jared pulled in the tiniest sliver of his power. "Don't fucking lie to me, David!"

The calm exterior of the ancient angel belied the quiet rage bubbling up. The charge in the air heated the temperature several degrees. Jared had seen David burn enemies from the inside out like a microwave cooked a hot dog. The last thing he needed now was to piss David off, at least not before he'd ensured Micki's safety.

That's right, jinn. Don't piss me off.

Fuck you.

Jared had let his thoughts float freely. Not only weak but also careless. He knew to guard his mind—even in the company of angels. With someone as powerful and old as David, Jared wasn't sure he could keep him from entering his thoughts, but he had to try.

Jared imagined great steel walls circling his thoughts. Then he took a fleck of the little power left in him and created the invisible border around his mind.

David sent, *The woman is being guarded.*

His green sphere shrunk to less than the size of a pinpoint. "Guarded by Bradley? I'm...n-not impressed."

"Not just Bradley. Rafiq and Trey, too."

"Did you have them guard her brother, too?"

"You know you are very funny."

"That's something no one has ever accused me of."

"Pity. It's true, though."

The nuances of immortals of David's age—not that there were many of them—were difficult to follow. *Immortal generation gap.* He had to keep David on topic. Fuck the small talk.

"What do the d-darklings want with Micki?"

"Who can know with the Dark?"

"Y-You do, I-I *know* y-you d-do..." Unable to say more, Jared fell to the table, his smoke body appearing.

The little energy left from his battle neared extinction. He felt the pull of the Ether.

Jared felt wings surround him—David's. The archangel must tell him what he knew. The only way he could be sure that Micki would stay safe. He didn't want to be so attached to her, to care for her, but he did. Panic spread through him as he tried but failed to lift his head up.

A feeling of calm pushed out the hysteria as David easily removed the mental walls he'd just raised.

David ordered, "Concentrate. You have enough life in you to maintain—for now."

I don't.

Jared, you were foolish to waste energy to block your mind from me. You are too drained.

David pulled him up.

"Must keep you out of my head."

You'll never have enough power to keep me out if I choose to enter.

"With the power from earlier, I could have."

David hesitated. "You might be correct."

Jared took a deep breath and consumed a fragment of green energy, leaving only a fraction of a speck to keep him in the world. He closed his eyes and concentrated on his hips, waist, then his chest and shoulders. He imagined the green smoke growing more solid until it became flesh. Jared opened his eyes and saw his human form. The effort left him exhausted.

"Excellent," David said, tucking away his wings.

Jared's teeth clenched as pain exploded in both his temples and he fell to his knees.

"We better get you up on your feet." David's large hands helped him up.

The angel motioned to another immortal. Jared struggled to speak, but David held up an index finger to his lips.

We'll talk later, Jared.

Turning to the young angel, David instructed, "Take him upstairs. You and Eve take care of him."

Jared shook his head 'no'. He would never triple again. Never.

David had to already know that.

He couldn't speak.

Don't worry, Jared.

"Bind him before you triple," David added.

Fury and resignation assailed Jared, but he had no energy to lash out. He'll it took all of the green smoky speck left him to not to pass out.

Images of Micki and Bradley appeared when he closed his eyes.

That sweet little piece of ass last night really charged your batteries--both yours and the angel's.

His desire to feel Micki's soft skin consumed him, but he could never let that happen again. Micki had been lucky to escape their tripling with her life.

The young angel David had just assigned to Jared put his arm around him, helping him up. Jared wanted to resist but didn't. With his strength gone, he felt like a sack of potatoes as they shuffled along. He didn't want to be with this young angel or the human woman that David offered. At least the archangel had sense enough to tell the angel to tie him up.

"Make sure I don't hurt anyone," Jared choked out.

The angel scowled. "You bet I will."

* * * *

The clothes on Micki's bed looked like a burial mound of skirts, pants, jeans, blouses, tanks, and jackets. She finally decided. No leather skirt tonight.

Looking in the mirror, she smiled at her choice. Not too sexy but not nun-like either. She sported low-rise jeans and a top that didn't reveal any cleavage whatsoever. She also planned on wearing her denim jacket.

Lipstick color?

She walked into her bathroom that mirrored the disaster on the bed. Makeup and jewelry covered every inch of the counter. She selected a pinkish shade with some shine. Looking in the mirror after applying it to her mouth, she shook her head. No way. Too pale. It washed out her out.

She tossed the tube into the trash then wiped her lips clean.

She picked up her favorite red. Much better. *Better to kiss Jared and Bradley.*

No, she couldn't think about kissing them--or anything else. Still, she replayed every second of their amazing night together, every touch, every caress, and kiss, over and over since leaving Zone Three.

Wings. Smoke. Rainbow. Micki went over everything again, especially those puzzling parts, in her mind from every angle and still couldn't make any sense of the visions she'd experienced during that last stunning dream-like orgasm. Best to forget it.

No trips upstairs for her—to unwind.

Her phone beeped. A message from Brooke popped on the screen.

B N UR DRIVE 5Min.

Micki looked at herself in the mirror one last time. For an instant, she thought she saw Bradley standing behind her. She jerked around. No Bradley. Tingles spread over her skin.

Boy, I'm so jumpy.

With Brooke as her backup, Micki would stay on task. No sidetracks. No trips *upstairs.* No Jared. No Bradley. Only Brooke, the safety net she'd needed last night.

Micki headed out the door to wait for Eric's girlfriend in her driveway.

They would go to Zone Three. Together, they would find this David-person and ask him if he knew anything about Eric's disappearance and where they could find him.

Then she and Brooke could leave together—alone.

Once again, Micki opened her purse to make sure it didn't hold Eric's flash drive. Did she expect it to magically transport out of her safety deposit box and back into her purse?

Tom, the techie, had been able to open one of the files, but only one: *day 9—entry 3*. Reading it had jolted her.

I've read until my eyes burned. It seems that immortals need humans for life essence. But it takes a triad, similar to the laws of electricity and the flow between positive, negative, and conduit. In this case, an angel, a jinn, and a human. If I try to tell anyone this, will they believe me?

Had Eric really written that?

Did Jared and Bradley believe they were some kind of eternal beings? Had her brother stumbled into some erotic cult?

Thankfully, the police finally had filed the report about Eric's disappearance, but past that they'd been less than helpful, even discouraging. Micki had told them about the voicemail. They said they'd follow up, but both she and Brooke didn't believe they'd do much of anything since he was a grown man with a long history of roaming the road.

So they'd decided that rather than give away the only bargaining chip she had, she'd meet with David first. If he knew anyway to help them find Eric, she'd set up a time—away from the crowd—to give the flash drive to him.

When Micki got to the street, Brooke's silver Mustang squealed to a stop in front of her. Brooke waved her into the car. She wore a camouflage print top and jeans. She looked like a female Rambo with her hair pulled back into a ponytail. Even with the military-like outfit, Brooke was stunning.

"So, did Eric's voicemail give a last name for this David person?" Brooke asked.

Eric's girlfriend had figured out quickly what kind of appetites flocked to Zone Three for satiation when she'd gone looking for Micki. A place Eric had gone to often, unbeknownst to his girlfriend. Brooke's anger pegged the needle, only to be exceeded by her worry.

"No. Only that David goes to Zone Three most weekends," Micki informed her.

Like her, Brooke probably wondered if Eric had gone to Zone Three for research--or hooking up for threeways.

Brooke and Eric had always had an on-again, off-again relationship. They currently resided in the on-again phase. No one could blame Brooke for any of the breakups with Eric. Micki wasn't sure how long this latest on-again phase would last. Typically, they would break up once or twice a year. If they didn't find Eric soon they might never...

Micki refused to finish the thought.

Part of Micki hoped Jared and Bradley wouldn't be at Zone Three tonight. Another part hoped they would. If she saw them, she wasn't sure what she would do. They'd fulfilled her fantasy, but she couldn't afford to look back. Micki had a life, a familiar life without risk and danger—real or imagined.

"Brooke, thank you for going with me."

"No worries." Brooke turned left. "This shouldn't take too long."

"I hope not."

"First, we go to Zone Three. Ask for David. Find out what he knows about Eric." Brooke turned right. "Then we're out of there."

"And if he wants us to come back with the flash drive, too bad. He can come and get it."

Brooke nodded. "After tonight, I, for one, won't be going back to that club."

Micki wondered once again if she would find Bradley and Jared back at Zone Three. Deep inside, she wanted to be alone with them. Entwined with them. Bradley might choose her again for a tumble, but Jared would move on to someone else like—

Brooke!

Shit!

She couldn't bear seeing them with anyone else.

Then Micki shook her head. What was she thinking? She had no hold on them. They owed her nothing.

"Five minutes. That's all it will take," Brooke continued.

"In and out," Micki said.

She visualized Jared and Bradley's muscled bodies pressed against hers. She bit her lower lip until she felt pain.

In and out. Heaven.

* * * *

The young angel, at least two inches taller than Jared, supported him up the stairs. Jared's weakness grew, and the green in his chest withered. Not much time left.

"I'm Kronos."

"Great," Jared said with effort. The Ether's nothingness called to him, reached out to him.

Images of Micki and Bradley swam in the abyss of his mind.

Micki and Bradley's naked bodies chained to a stone altar. Demons surrounded them, slicing their skin with their claws. Jared looked at his former lovers' faces as they writhed in pain.

Was it a vision of their future? It might have a clue on how to protect them.

Then their faces blurred.

He concentrated on the image trying to bring it back.

It cleared, no longer of Micki and Bradley, instead it held the face of his victim staring back at him just like that awful night.

Nash's love, Gwyneth.

"You better not try anything, jinn."

"You make sure of it," Jared said.

Kronos looked puzzled.

"You really aren't a normal jinn, are you?"

Struggling to speak, Jared choked out, "N-Not the Persian room." *He couldn't bear seeing the place he'd tripled with Micki and Bradley, couldn't stand the thought of being with others in there.*

"Eve likes the Pirate room."

"Fine."

The place revolted Jared with its fucking theme park motifs. His kind usually liked erotic games, but as Kronos noted, he wasn't normal.

When they topped the stairs, the angel led them to the closest door in the hallway. Like Bradley the night before, Kronos disarmed the traps meant for darklings.

The angel opened the door to the room. A black flag with a skull and cross bones hung on the back wall. An angry sea had been painted on all the other walls. A large telephone pole stood in the center of the floor rising up to the ceiling with sheets and ropes attached to it, a poor imitation of a central mast. The sounds of crashing waves came from the hidden speakers.

The large wool blanket in the middle of the floor contradicted the illusion.

This place is fucking comical!

In the center of the room, with bucket by her side and mop in her hand, a young woman swabbed the floor.

Jared blinked. The woman looked so much like—*Micki.*

Did dark lust cloud his sight?

"Ahoy, captains," her voice silky and inviting shot out.

"Yo ho, Eve," Kronos answered back.

Jared stared closer. Though she resembled Micki, Eve was no twin. Auburn hair hung down in twisting curls. She stood a couple inches taller than Micki, but their eyes—an exact match.

Earlier, Jared had missed the fact the young angel wore black pantaloons. *Immortals and their games.*

"Forget the role play," Jared barked.

Kronos turned, ready to pounce.

Eve asked, "Why? That's the fun."

"Just for tonight," Kronos said to her.

"Yessir," she answered, smiling.

Jared collapsed to the ground.

"Is he okay?" Eve asked, rushing to his side.

"He's fine."

Kronos tied him with invisible power ropes. Good soldiering. Much better than that idiot Bradley had done.

"Should we get him to a doctor?"

"No. He's just playing the captured buccaneer bit."

"Oh."

Clothes dropped to the floor as the two teased each other and stripped, but he could only see their feet given his position.

Kronos gave a staged whispered, "The tiniest wrong move and you're dead."

Jared mustered a nod that he hoped the angel understood as agreement.

"Yeah." Eve giggled. "You better not try anything or else my captain will make you food for the fishes."

Kronos and Eve knelt down on either side of him. Kronos rolled him on his side to face Eve. Jared felt a dagger point in his back, its steel magical and sharp. The guy had common sense.

Jared's head swam. He wanted to say something, but he couldn't clear his mind.

When Eve's flushing face, so much like Micki's, came into view, his cock stirred. Kronos' quick breaths on his neck let Jared know they could get to the tripling in minutes.

"Eve, don't do anything without my approval," Kronos commanded.

Jared wondered if the air would crackle with power like it had done with Micki and Bradley. All he could think of was how great it had felt devouring her ripe nipples, tasting her hot pussy, popping her anal sex cherry. Keeping thoughts of Micki front and center would be the only way he could get through this tripling with Eve and Kronos.

"I think I like this game." Eve laughed.

Jared's gut wrenched, remembering the demon's words: *That sweet little piece of ass last night really charged your batteries—both yours and the angel's.*

The Dark wanted Micki and maybe Bradley, too. He knew firsthand what that meant. He needed just enough power, only a bit, to make sure they would be safe. He needed life force from Eve and Kronos—for Micki and Bradley. Jared barely held onto consciousness. They needed to act quickly.

Eve leaned within an inch of his face and pursed her lips to kiss him. Kronos reached out to stop her, but she moved too fast as her lips touched Jared's cheek. Simultaneously, the angel grabbed Jared's arm.

A detonation of pain ignited inside him. Jared heard screams, both Eve's and Kronos'. He wanted to scream as well, but couldn't muster the energy. The smell of burning flesh filled his nose.

Again, the voice from his terrible past filled his head. *Count the bodies as they fall!*

Chapter 11

1) Now behold, I, Timu, write, so that the truth of The Children of the Divine and The Children of The Damned may be known to those who seek. 2) It came to pass, at the time of harvest, that I, Timu, came upon a wounded angel in the midst of my field. 3) My wife and I welcomed the angel to our house. Showing mercy on the creature, we offered our best incense and balm, and the Divine showed mercy, and the angel was healed. 4) The angel told me his name was Rajiah, and He spoke unto me, saying: Listen! And I listened. 5) These are Rajiah's words, about the nations of man and the kingdoms of the Everlasting. 6) And the prophecy he imparted unto me.

The Book of Timu: Verses 1 through 6—Chapter 1

* * * *

When Jared opened his eyes, he saw that Kronos and Eve had been flung across the floor by whatever force they'd ignited. Eve crawled to the farthest corner of the room, putting more distance between her and Jared.

"What the hell is going on?" she demanded.

Kronos leapt to his feet and rushed to her. When the angel reached her, he took Eve in his arms. Jared saw her eyes fill with tears. She shook, clearly from pain. Kronos glared at him, his eyes filled with hate— and fear.

Tremors of agony erupted in Jared everywhere Eve had touched him. His power dimmed to darkness. He'd been excruciatingly weak before, but now he neared oblivion. Whatever had happened with

Micki and Bradley had sealed them together. No exchange of power would come from any other triad ever again.

Anger tasted bitter on his tongue. Like always, anyone who got close to him suffered. Now that it seemed Micki and Bradley were linked to him if he didn't triple with them, if he blinked out, would they be doomed, too?

Now that's real baggage. Fuck.

An image of Micki being stalked by demons filled his mind. And Bradley? He needed to contact the angel. Warn him to guard Micki.

Pain rolled through Jared like a hurricane.

The angel growled, "What the fuck did you do to us?"

Eve stood crying with the young immortal's arms protectively around her.

Jared's would-be lovers looked to be recovering, but he knew he couldn't convince them to touch him again, not that he let them.

He must do something to save Micki, but how could he? He had no energy left to escape the Ether that kept pulling at him. He searched inside himself and dug out every last bit of his power.

He sat up on his elbows, "Kronos, go get David."

"Fuck you!"

Tell him that the woman he assigned me to guard last night is in trouble. She's close. I can feel her.

The angel glared at him.

The Alliance can sentence me later. Follow your vow. David sent you here with me. He needs to know about this and about the woman.

"What woman?"

Though sending mental messages was less taxing, Jared needed to get his point across to Kronos. So he spoke aloud. "David knows."

The angel didn't move. He continued to hold Eve, tears still running down her face.

Jared choked out, "This is critical for the Alliance."

He saw surrender in the immortal's face. He'd won, but he didn't savor the victory. He liked Kronos' temperament and his judgment.

Unlike David, this angel knew not to trust Jared.

Jared closed his eyes. Nothingness. No images.

"What's he doing?" Eve asked.

Jared concentrated.

"Sweetheart, go downstairs," Kronos gently demanded of Eve.

"I'll leave when you do," she informed him.

Jared had only moments before he would be gone. An image of Micki floated like a spirit in the fog. When it cleared he could see fear in her eyes. A gun. It made his blood run cold. He sent the terrible image toward Kronos.

The angel nodded and led Eve out of the Pirate room. Jared sensed him rearming a magical trap. That would keep darklings out and Jared in.

In the empty room, Jared listened to his own breathing. It sounded like waves crashing on the hull of a large ship. He put his head back on the floor. He listened to his breathing. Inhale. Exhale. Crashing waves. Drifting. Silence.

There must be enough time to save her. He wished that he had enough life force to send a message to Bradley, but he didn't. If the angel possessed any of the power from last night, Jared knew he could save her.

Wings. Rainbow. Smoke.

He smiled remembering how amazing the tripling with Micki and Bradley had been—her body welcoming with heat and desire as he and the angel plunged their cocks deep into her warm body.

Unbidden, his smoky body emerged as the last of his power blinked out to blackness of the Ether.

* * * *

After fifteen minutes of trying to locate a parking spot close to Zone Three, Brooke pulled into a pay-garage twelve blocks from the club and killed the engine. Micki's body shook.

Paranoia tugged at her. Just like when she'd left Bradley early this morning, she felt invisible eyes watching.

She didn't like the thought of walking to the parking barn in the dark, but perhaps they would find someone at the club to escort them back. Maybe Jared or Bradley.

"You ready?" Brooke asked.

"As ready as I can be."

Without another word, they left the car and the garage for the sidewalk.

The warm air hit Micki's skin. Being summertime, the late sun slipped down behind some tall buildings and several clouds floated in the darkening sky.

After only a block, Micki doubled over in agony.

Brooke stopped with her. "What's the matter?"

The pain rolled from her chest through her gut. She closed her eyes.

"Damn it! I-I—."

"Micki? What can I do?" Brooke pulled out her cell. "Do you need me to call an ambulance?"

"No. Just give me a minute." Micki steadied herself. She opened her eyes, and the hurt eased a bit.

"Are you sure?"

"Yes. It seems to be going away. I just need to sit for a minute or two."

Brooke pointed to a bench ahead. "Let's sit there."

Suddenly, Jared materialized right before Micki.

Her jaw dropped. "Jared?"

"Who?"

He faded into a green smoke, and then even that was gone.

"Nothing." A longing for him shook her to her core. How could she miss him so much after only one night? But she did.

"I think we should try coming back to this club another time," Brooke suggested.

Micki took a seat on the bench. "No. The hurt is gone now."

Brooke sat beside her. "Have you ever experienced something like this before?"

"No."

"What did it feel like?"

"Cold." It felt like utter emptiness, loss, which made no sense. Did it have anything to do with Jared?

I wish he were here.

"You sure it's over?"

Micki wasn't sure. Then she saw Jared materialize in a haze before her, there more in spirit than in body. Odd... She stopped thinking about how and why when he grazed his hands on her thighs straight to where she needed him most. His touch was very real. Lust sprang like a living thing in her, and she sucked in a breath.

"Micki?" Brooke's voice sounded far away.

As she looked up, Micki's surroundings dissolved, leaving only her and Jared, floating in a fog of rising pleasure. He kissed her, his hands gripping her thighs, spreading them. She trembled as the desire quickly became an inferno.

Micki closed her eyes, and the image of Jared's muscular body and erect cock came into view. *Is this real or a dream?* She reached to touch his chest.

He grabbed her and pulled her close. *He feels so real.* His tongue slipped into her mouth like an intruder, then guest, then resident. Long, deep, delicious. Their kiss broke.

Micki, I missed you.

Her skin tingled. Then his wolfish eyes darkened and showed an insatiable appetite. *Oh God!*

Jared's thought barged into her, *I can't wait to spread your ass for my tongue and dick.*

Something tugged at her chest. She looked down and spotted two ropes jutting out of her, one connected to Jared. She looked at Jared's other cord that twisted with hers heading out into the distance. To where? Or whom? Bradley? Something they'd done last night had forged a bond. She'd felt it then and she felt it now.

Micki stared at her biker. *Why did you leave without saying goodbye?*

I didn't want to hurt you anymore than I already had.

You should've told me.

I know.

The rope to Bradley vibrated and contracted. Instantly, he came into view. A look of surprise that quickly turned to lust.

Micki opened her arms. *I'm glad you're here, Bradley.*

What's going on? Bradley glared at Jared.

Micki spat back, *This is a crazy dream where you both are going to pleasure me again, I hope.*

They both turned, their eyes showing totally carnality rousing wantonness inside her. She glanced down at her body. No clothes.

She trembled with anticipation for their hard dicks.

Four hands danced over her skin. A thundering of desire spread through her.

Micki willingly succumbed to the crazy vision.

Bradley dove down between her thighs. A shiver run up her spine. His tongue pressed against her clit.

Ohmigod!

He looked up, eyes blazing hot. *Your pussy is so juicy.*

Jared stepped over to her and latched on to her left breast with his mouth. Still feeling a bit sore from last night, her nipples hardened quickly as he sucked and nipped at them. An onslaught of flutters danced in her belly.

Desire washed over her, imagining the men entering her with their massive dicks. Her insides heated.

Jared's thought shot into her like a jackhammer, *That's it, sweetheart! Get ready for us to fuck you.* Then he moved behind her.

Bradley's fingers danced across her clit as he drove his tongue up her channel.

Ohmigod! Y-Yes!

Jared cupped her ass. He spread the cheeks apart, and she felt the head of his cock knock for entrance.

Micki screamed silently, *Do it, please!*

I love when you beg, sweetheart!

Bradley continued his oral assault on her pussy, and Jared's cock slipped inside her ass stretching and filling her insides, igniting her lust—a lust that had been hibernating her entire life. These men made her feel like a woman, a real woman, and she loved them for it.

O-Ohh!

Jared's large hands rubbed her shoulders as he picked up his pace inside her from behind. Earthquake like tremors came fast, deepening quickly as she responded to their handling.

I've got to get into your tight little cunt. Bradley stood. Blue light surrounded him.

Before plowing into her pussy, he kissed her hard on the lips, as if branding her mouth with his. Then she felt his cock slide up and down the outside of her mound.

Ready to beg? Jared snarled.

She nodded. *I want you both.*

To do what, exactly?

More moisture and want poured out of her. *To get inside me.*

Say it! Jared commanded. She wanted to please him.

Fuck me! Please!

She watched Bradley's eyes gaze into hers. *That's it. That's our girl!*

And then he pushed his cock into her channel. Pleasure shot through the roof. Vibrations of excitement joined to the rhythm of the two men working their dicks inside her.

In and out.

She felt so filled, so cared for.

Jared slammed her backside. Bradley pounded her pussy.

In and out. In and out.

She cried out, *Ohh!*

Blistering heat built up. Rising. Higher.

She burned and couldn't hold back.

G-God! I'm going to—

Bradley agreed. *So, am I!*

Let go! Jared commanded.

The two studs' bodies went rock-solid still as they shot their loads into her. Her inner muscles contracted around them, and her climax took her higher, and higher.

No door appeared, but she did see the cord that connected Bradley and Jared vibrate. Blue light shot down it from Bradley to Jared.

Micki felt flipped inside out. She flew high, floated high. Laughed. Cried. Orgasms had never been so powerful before these two.

As soon as she took a deep breath, Jared and Bradley disappeared.

She opened her eyes, then slumped across the bench Brooke had led her to. The evening sky and Brooke's concerned face filled her vision.

"Micki! Can you hear me?"

"Yes."

"You seemed to be having some kind of seizure. Are you all right?"

Was she? Or had that dream been real. Suddenly, she felt energetic and alive. The pain was all gone. And she ached to see Bradley and Jared.

"I haven't eaten much today. I'm fine now," Micki lied and stood. What else could she say to Brooke without the woman thinking she was insane? "Let's get to the club and get this over with."

"You sure."

"Totally sure. I'm okay now."

"I'm not a doctor, but my mom is. She would say that wasn't normal. So, let me know if it starts up again. Because, like it or not, I'll be taking you to the hospital."

"I don't think I could hide it from you anyway. I'm much better now." *Better?* Her panties dripped and her body hummed from her mind trip.

Before they stood up, Micki noticed five men in black trench coats a few blocks up between them and Zone Three. Thankfully, they were on the opposite side of the street, leaning against a building.

"We better go now, Brooke. We still have ten blocks to cover."

Brooke nodded. "Let's go, then."

Micki jumped to her feet, and she and Brooke headed to the club.

Micki looked over at the men. Panic scratched the inside of her head like a cat's claws. One of them carried a weapon. A sword? Then it disappeared as if by magic.

"Did you see that?" she asked Brooke.

"Yes, I see them."

"But the sword?" In the past few days, dreams and visions came to her regularly. This one, she'd gladly do without. Her body shivered.

"What?"

"The guy in the front has a sword."

"I don't see any sword. It's probably just some guys partying," Brooke's hand disappeared into her bag. "But just in case, I've got a pistol."

"What!" Micki's shoulders tensed. "Please, don't pull it out."

Her heart slammed against her rib cage faster and faster. She expected to hear footsteps as the men got closer, but she heard nothing.

"I won't unless I need to."

Less than half a block away the men crossed to Micki and Brooke's side of the street, then the lined up across the sidewalk blocking their passage to Zone Three or anywhere else.

Ohmigod! We're in real trouble.

Brooke's voice quivered. "I guess I might need to use it."

Micki needed Jared and Bradley. The strength they had in those massive biceps could easily take these guys. Danger averted. But they weren't here. Only Brooke with her gun. Nausea whirled in Micki's stomach.

"Let's cross the street."

Brooke nodded.

Micki looked for a police officer or anyone that might help. She found none as she crossed the street.

Brooke followed.

When Micki looked up, she saw two of the men crossing as well. No, they weren't party boys; they were criminals.

"Back to the car," she told Brooke, but before they could turn around, the men started walking directly toward them.

"Yes," Brooke agreed.

Micki and Brooke whirled to retreat and found more danger. Two men and a woman had been behind them all along. They stood six feet away staring back at them with dead-black eyes—*and horns.*

* * * *

Waves of agony jerked Bradley from his wicked thoughts of tripling with Micki and Jared. The sex had felt so real, as if he'd really been inside her.

His wings folded in as agony drove him to the ground, a hundred feet below.

Pain. Not my pain.

Micki's? No. Not hers.

Jared's.

Bradley pulled up before hitting the pavement. It wouldn't have killed him, but it would've taken a long time to heal.

A weak thought from the jinn floated to him, *Micki isn't safe.*

Not true! I'm protecting her, along with Raf and Trey. Though for the past half hour he'd been perched on the top of a building consumed by the lusty dream, trusting his buddies to guard her.

Jared's pangs of guilt and loneliness blasted Bradley, accompanied by the warning.

Bradley spread his wings out, and rose higher into the sky.

More tides of Jared's suffering shot into him.

So, the vision of fucking Micki again with Jared had been more than fantasy. He'd never heard of anything like that happening before. Never experienced anything close.

Alarm and anger clutched him. He closed his eyes trying to magically bring up Micki's location. The attempt failed. Had the jinn done something to her? Led her into a trap?

She's in danger, angel. Help her.

He sensed Jared had almost no power. That confused him. The jinn should be feeling the same amount of energy from their earlier physical tripling as whirled inside of Bradley. What had happened to the jinn's portion?

Bradley scanned the center of his own power he'd created with Jared and Micki. A basketball-sized orb of blue burned hot inside him.

Where are you, Jared? What happened to all that voltage?

No answer.

If you or any of your darkling buddies hurt her, you're gonna learn exactly what being fucked up really means from me.

Jared appeared again. The stillness ended, replaced by the jinn's extreme concern for Micki, and his incredible agony. What had caused him such pain?

Jared slipped into the Ether, weakened as the last of his power blinked out. Good. The bastard should die.

Though Bradley should have felt relief and satisfaction at a fitting end to a betrayer of the Alliance, he didn't. Instead, what assailed him was a sense of loss, like he'd forever miss someone close. That was crazy, especially to feel for Jared.

Go to her, Bradley.

Jared's anguish and concern nearly knocked him from the sky.

Bradley landed on top of a building afraid him might fall from the empathetic pain.

He looked down and saw his blue sphere shrink in half. He wasn't using any of it. Bradley closed his eyes and concentrated on the jinn.

Two threads of light came into view. They shot out in opposite directions from inside his chest into his core of power. One went to the west, and one to the east toward Zone Three—that one siphoned energy from him. It must've terminated where Jared lie. In the Alliance stronghold?

Jared, what the fuck are you doing?

Bradley opened his eyes. He'd find the bastard and do what should have been done all those years ago when David had given him an underserved pardon.

Stop thinking about me and what I deserve and get to Micki, you stupid angel.

The power drain stopped, and Jared's image disappeared.

Then Braldey heard Raf send the alarm, *It's an ambush!*

He folded his wings in tight, heading straight to Micki.

Chapter 12

Brooke came home from work and I kissed her though I was filled with incredible guilt for what I did last night at Zone Three. She doesn't seem to suspect anything. What a fucking good liar I've become.

David set me with two immortals. I'd hoped it would work, but I didn't feel much. So I don't think it did. What did I do wrong?

Damn it, I must try again, for myself, for Micki—and yes, even for Brooke. Because I'm still dying, and so is my sister.

Eric's Flash Drive: day 41—entry 1

* * * *

Micki didn't know whether to scream or run. Instead, she froze. Beside her, Brooke held her breath.

The trio between them and where they'd left Brooke's car stared at them, daring them to run. Micki didn't look back, but knew the five men in trench coats worked with these three.

Both men sported black leather coats and military-style boots. The violet-eyed woman wore six daggers sheathed in a criss-cross harness around her full chest. Every last one of their attackers was imposing as hell. None looked entirely human.

"What the fuck do you want?" Brooke shouted.

The horns dissolved.

Had Brooke seen the horns, too? Or had Micki just imagined them? Though the air around them grew hot, a shiver continued up her back.

"Your friend knows," the woman chimed in a malevolent voice.

The flash drive! *Eric, what have you gotten us into?*

If she had the flash drive with her, they could force her to give it over, the only clue to his whereabouts. She was glad that she'd put Eric's drive in her safety deposit box, away from these villains' reach.

Thinking about her brother filled her with unease. He'd gotten himself into major trouble. She hoped he hid somewhere these creatures couldn't find him. Somewhere safe.

Unlike she and Brooke.

All of the assailants glared murderously at them. She and Brooke could try to scream, but she doubted anyone would hear since the street looked deserted.

The tall bald man growled, "What's it gonna be, ladies?"

Micki glared back at the man. "Where is Eric Langley?"

The woman shrugged. "Should we tell them, Irkon?"

Micki's heartbeat pounded fast and hard. *Did they know where Eric was?*

The short man winked, "Naw, Azlian. Let's not. What do you think, Pratt?"

"I think I'd like to fuck the blonde." The tall man sent an evil nod to Brooke.

She pulled out the gun from her purse and pointed it at the assailants. "Then I'm glad I brought lil' Miss Pistol Sally."

The woman creature and her companions appeared unconcerned. For a split-second, blurs of blue light and green smoke materialized in the corner of Micki's eyes. She felt cool wind blow around them. Their would-be attackers' gazes moved from Brooke and her to the shadows and the sky.

Then Micki spotted wings, black flames, and violet smoke.

She watched the group shift, tighten, and look to each other. They communicated but without words—just as she'd done with Bradley and Jared last night.

Azlian glared at Micki.

The woman's words floated into her. *Another time then, Ms. Langley.*

The group ran into the alley, they seemed to battle something invisible as they left. Micki looked back over her shoulder. The others behind them had vanished also.

Brooke patted her pistol. "Guess Sally scared them off." Micki noticed Brooke's hands shaking when she put the weapon back in her purse. Had the entire dangerous event appear to Brooke as ordinary, instead of supernatural?

"I suppose so," Micki replied. She didn't believe it, though. Something about the lights and smoke had scared them away. Lights and smoke eerily similar to those she had seen when she'd been with Bradley and Jared. Had they only been her imagination? Another dream?

The air calmed, but Mick couldn't relax. Though the threat had ended—at least for now—she vibrated with fear.

Had Azlian spoken to her aloud with her threat or had she thought it?

Suddenly, I can read minds. I'm well on my way to the men with straight jackets.

Brooke turned back the direction of Zone Three. Her eyes widened. "Someone's coming."

Ohmigod! Micki tensed.

Then she saw Bradley running toward them. Her knees went weak. *He tried to warn me, and I didn't listen.*

Brooke opened her purse.

"I know him." She wanted to run to him.

Eric's girlfriend nodded and closed her purse again just as Bradley stepped up to them.

He swept her up in his arms and hugged her tight. His breathing labored. "A-Are you okay?"

Before she could answer, his kissed her desperately.

Overwhelmed by his concern for her and blown away by his

tenderness, Micki melted into the man who'd tried to warn her, tried to keep her with him, to keep her safe.

Micki couldn't speak. She wanted to say something. Those monsters wanted to hurt her and Brooke. More than hurt—until Bradley showed up. Her knight in camo.

Slowly, he pulled back, looked her over with a concerned stare. "Really, are you all right?"

Other than nearly being attacked by supernatural beings with horns—and would ever believe that? "Yes."

"Thank God," he breathed, then kissed her softly.

When he released Micki, he extended his hand to Brooke. "I'm Bradley."

"Brooke Caldwell." She took his hand, though her eyes showed distrust. "I've heard about you."

Bradley ignored her pointed comment. "Looking for David I assume."

"We are, but how did you know we would be here?" Micki blurted.

Bradley shrugged. "Good guesser."

Micki spotted a drop of blood at the corner of his mouth. "Your mouth is bleeding. How did that happen?"

Bradley wiped the drop away with his index finger. "I must've bit the inside of my cheek."

She doubted that had caused the injury. Something more ominous, deadly even, seemed more likely. "Did you see those men in trench coats?"

"I saw some people."

"Did you do something to make them leave us alone?"

"What could I have done? I was blocks away." Bradley's eyes betrayed him. "You still want to go to Zone Three to see if David is there?"

"We do," Micki said.

"Maybe we should go to the police," Brooke said.

"Zone Three will be fine," Micki stated.

Bradley extended his arm to her.

She placed her arm in his.

Micki loved the feel of him next to her. His manner seemed to be from a different age—an age of knights and maidens in distress. Tonight, he'd been her *Sir Bradley*. With him, she felt safe, protected.

Now she just hoped David would be at the club and would have information about Eric. If so, she would set up a time to deliver the flash drive to him. Micki didn't want to have anything those people on the street might want.

* * * *

Jared lifted his head from the wool blanket. The sounds of crashing waves from the hidden speakers changed to gentle calls of sea gulls. Immense power pulsed inside him. How? From where? The pain derived from touching Eve and Kronos had vanished.

Bewildered at the strength of his current energy, Jared shook his head. It should've been used up. Gone. He should've been trapped in the Ether.

That he wasn't seemed impossible. Still, he couldn't deny the ball of green spinning inside him. Not as large as the power he'd gotten last night with Bradley and Micki, about half as much, but still impressive. Familiar.

Had the sexual dream of Micki and Bradley not been a dream after all? Recalling the previous images of Micki stalked by demons jolted him. Jared jumped up. Had that been real, too? He brought forth his smoky body. He needed speed.

He magically transported out of the building. He'd only used sight magic once before. Immortals could use the spell to locate any human they'd tripled with.

Not sure it would work, he guided a portion of his power to invoke the spell and pushed his mind to search for Micki.

Nothing.

Then slowly an image formed. Concentrating, he brought it into clearer focus. A rainbow and wings.

Micki's vitality shot through him. An image of Bradley walking beside her came into his magical view. They were close. *She's safe, thank God!*

The urge to go to her, wrap her up in his arms, tell her why he left. *Why I left?*

Jared checked himself. No matter how badly he wanted to be with her, he couldn't. His gut tightened and his jaw clenched.

Best for her not to see him—though he ached to see her, hear her intoxicating voice—he couldn't, for her sake.

Instead, he would protect Micki from the shadows. Forever.

Before he could continue using his magic to locate her, a very different voice called him, the voice of an immortal he knew too well.

Jared. David called.

Jared looked around but saw no one. *Where are you?*

"Over here."

David shimmered into sight, shaking off the invisibility he'd been cloaked in. He stood in an alley by a large gray dumpster. The only other occupant of the place, a cat, jumped when the archangel materialized.

Jared reshaped his body into flesh and walked over to the the Alliance leader. As he got closer, he could see that he'd been in a battle. Then Nash suddenly appeared next to his commander, on guard. A giant gash covered his left arm.

Jared readied himself for whatever they had in mind for him. Surely Kronos had told them about what had happened in the Pirate room.

Relax, Jared, David sent.

Jared stayed alert. *By the looks of you both, you haven't been relaxing much.*

The archangel shrugged. "That's true."

"Is Micki safe?"

"She is, for now."

"What's going on?" Jared balled up his hands into fists.

The archangel didn't answer his question but turned to Nash and said, "Keep searching for the Dark's lair."

Nash bowed. "Yes, my lord."

The jinn commander nodded and vanished in green smoke.

Jared spotted Kronos glaring at him from across the street and grimaced. He hated the pain he'd caused in the young angel and Eve. No doubt David would be pissed off.

David sent to the angel, *Circle the perimeter, Kronos.*

The angel bowed and disappeared.

"I can see the energy in you." David peered down at Jared's chest. "Quite amazing."

"Yeah. What the hell is going on?"

Instead of answering, David asked, "Can you tell me how you got the power you have now?"

"No."

"Are you going to go to Micki Langley?"

"Why should I?" If he went to her, it wouldn't be because David wanted it, but to ensure her safety.

"If you really want to know what is happening to you, Bradley and to Ms. Langley, follow me."

Riddles and games, David's typical M.O. He hated it, but decided he better follow the tricky archangel. If it took going with David to gain more insight to Micki and his current situation, so be it.

David walked deeper into the alley to a blank wall. He waved his hand and a shimmering portal appeared. He walked through it.

Jared followed.

They entered a room in the shape of a heptagon, seven walls of dull gray rock. Each wall held its own insignia and inscriptions. A wooden table with seven chairs sat centered in the room. *Seven?* David had taken him where the Alliance's highest nobility met, the

Secret Room? Not a physical place but a magical one. Only a member of the Seven could conjure it.

Why had David brought him? Wasn't it forbidden? Would they actually convene a quorum with him present?

Astounded, Jared watched the remaining six highest nobles in the Alliance enter the room through doors that magically appeared on each of the other walls. They joined David. *The entire Council of Seven, together?* A quorum consisted of six of the Seven. No more, no less. One chair always remained empty representing the absent member.

"David, you do know what you risk bringing us *all* here?" the female jinn intoned.

"I know, Jezzel." David nodded.

Though Jared had only met David and Parkor before, like all immortals, he knew their names, descriptions and reputations. Each oversaw a single continent on the earth—even Antarctica—to ensure that the Dark remained in check and that humanity stayed safe.

"It is necessary," David offered.

The ancients each took a seat at the table. First, Jezzel an archjinn. She ruled Africa. She looked to be in her late twenties, but Jared knew better. Her dark skin glistened as if the green power inside her couldn't be contained in her body. A leather cord bound her hair. Priceless emeralds encircled her slender neck. Her eyes burned fierce, the color of dark earth.

The next to sit was the archangel who ruled Asia, Gravian the only one of the ancients older than David. Gravian walked with a cane and appeared feeble, but underneath lived something more—deep blue power. Jared admired Gravian's ruse of frailty. It would fool most.

Next, Europe's commander, the thankless Parkor, a muscular man that reminded him of Bradley, though he wore his hair long and sported a beard.

The others followed ceremoniously, one by one. The archjinn,

Samson, ruled Australia. Ramon, an archangel, governed South America. Finally, Mavin, her skin and hair white as the snow continent she oversaw. Jared could not tell if she was jinn or angel, but whichever, her white power chilled absolutely.

Finally, David representing North America, took his seat.

Jared stood back from the table.

He suspected that whatever was going on had something to do with him, Micki and Bradley. Why else would David have brought him? He would wait and find out.

"Get on with it," Ramon spoke.

"Yes. The quicker the better," Samson added.

"I beg my esteemed colleagues' forgiveness for the unusual summoning," David had adopted some bullshit elevated speech pattern for the meeting. "But I have brought us together because the Dark is attempting to release Prince Terrok."

"Impossible!"

"That cannot be done."

Though the great ones expressed disbelief, Jared saw fear in their eyes. Terrok had orchestrated the killing of their predecessors, the previous Seven.

Whatever information David had about Terrok was probably a ruse of some Dark master wanting to elevate himself. It had happened before. Other demons had tried to consolidate power under the guise of a resurrected Terrok, fooling young demons into following them. That would explain the attack from the van.

Jared had seen Terrok cast into the Ether. But so had David. What about the portal he'd seen last night? Did that play a role? His gut seized at the possibility and what that would mean.

David began, "I will explain as much as I know."

"Start with why this disgraced jinn is here," Jezzel demanded, staring at Jared.

Apparently his reputation reached the highest levels of the immortal world. Jared's anger swelled to the shores of his smoky power. Foolish as it would be, he wanted to introduce these arrogant upper-class assholes to his fists. They played games with mortals and immortals alike for some inexplicable "higher calling." Not him. Not anymore. He wasn't buying into their fucking bullshit.

"Jared nearly blinked out mere hours ago." David informed them.

"Good riddance," Jezzel interjected.

"Ah, but listen. Now he is full of power, and he has not tripled."

"Power without tripling? Preposterous," Parkor mocked.

"That is not all." David stared back at the bearded archangel. "The three of them opened a portal to the Ether last night. It didn't last, but it proves opening the Eternal Prison is possible."

David already knew they'd breached the Ether. *Shit!* Was that his game? Get to Terrok before the Dark? By using Micki and his connection, along with Bradley's to her?

Jared's anger swelled. The photo of Micki that David had sent to him so resembled Gwyneth, her ancestor. Why had the archangel involved him? To force him to protect her? Or, as this meeting suggested, more?

"That dare not be true," Mavin whispered, her voice sounding like ice melting.

"We all know the myth," Jezzel said.

David said, "Once a myth, but I now know it to be real."

Jared couldn't stay quiet one more second. "Cut the crap. What's happening?"

"Tell us about last night," Ramon asked, his finger pointing straight at Jared. *About being with Micki and Bradley, one physical, the other magical, and the excitement of tripling with them?*

Thoughts, memories, images flooded into Jared's mind. Ramon pulled those out of him. Jared resisted, wanting them for himself and him alone. Ramon was too strong to deny. So the ruler of South America saw it all, including the Ether portal opening. *But who had opened it?*

"More," Ramon commanded.

A vision of Micki's rainbow crashed through his head. He tried to shove it aside.

"Stay out of my head, you bastards."

I wish we could, but this is too important, Parkor sent to him.

"About last night." Jezzel raised her finger.

They pulled his thoughts like puppets on string. These fuckers were no different than the Dark Masters, or even Terrok.

Words ran freely in Jared's mind, and though he resisted, he spoke them. "Yes. Very different. Like I told David. Very different."

"See the power in him. It is not from a normal tripling," Parkor called out.

The power inside him? He could use it against these assholes, no matter their strength and elevation. He would make sure they knew how his power felt slicing into them.

He grabbed at his energy sphere and sent over half of it out like a grenade. Instantly, his mind jolted free from Ramon's invasion.

When he opened his eyes and looked around the room, he saw all the chairs askew on the floor with the Seven in various states of distress against the walls—except Gravian.

"You will pay for that, you half-ifrit!" Ramon shouted.

"Silence!" Gravian ordered.

The others quieted and Ramon sat back down.

Jared watched Gravian walk toward him, this time with no limp. The old angel patted him on the back. Jared didn't stop him, but he didn't know why. The old man's apparent weakness fell away like a discarded mask at the end of a masquerade party.

Forgive us, Jared. We are not like the Dark. If we were, you would be in a much worse condition. But you already know that.

Jared wasn't so sure.

"Clearly we must consider the possibility that what David has told us is both possible and true," the old angel said.

"But Gravian, the bloodline is no more." Ramon glared at Jared.

Bloodline? As in *the* bloodline? "Come on. That's a myth. All the bloodliners have been dead for more than a millennia."

Worse, David thought Micki was a bloodliner. Oh, good God, what sorts of experiments would the archangel want to try on her if he believed that? Even trying to imagine chilled Jared's blood. Had the Dark learned about Micki when her red power flared last night?

"Is that why the darklings are after her, David?"

Jezzel's eyes darkened. "The Dark knows about her. And the new triad?"

David nodded.

"Ramon, apparently, we were mistaken about the bloodline's demise." Gravian waved his hand, and the chairs went back neatly under the table. "But we must not be hasty else we make a mistake that would tip the scale in the Dark's favor."

"If Terrok is free, what can we do?" Mavin asked.

Closing his eyes the old man said, "I do not sense that he has escaped the Ether."

The others closed their eyes as well. After a few seconds they all nodded.

"You are correct. He is not in our world," Jezzel responded.

"What has happened to me? To Micki and Bradley?" Jared's jaw clenched.

The Seven knew, and they'd fucking tell him—or else they'd taste more of his anger.

"You, the woman and the young angel formed something different. Something we did not believe possible," Gravian answered.

What the hell did that mean? Jared felt his gut tighten.

"A perfect triad," the old man said.

"I've never heard of that. Another myth?"

"No, Jared, not a myth." David stepped up. "According to the lost book of Timu, a perfect triad consists of two immortals and a bloodliner that are bound together in an unbreakable union. The power from such a merging is unfathomable."

Jared glared at David. "You think Micki Langley is a bloodliner?"

"Yes," David answered.

Gravian sat down in a chair. "Do you know who Ms. Langley's ancestor is?"

David looked directly at the old man. "Gwyneth."

The woman who had died by Jared's hand, by his body. His knees weakened, his breath rushed out.

The Seven shot him accusing stares, and Jared closed his eyes. *Motherfucking hell!* Was David right? Had Gwyneth been a bloodliner?

The reality sank into Jared, and memories of Micki's ancestor flooded into him. How had he been so blinded? The Dark wouldn't have placed him with just any human. No. They had placed him with a bloodliner to consume her, fill him with her incredible power, power that became his dark lust as her life slipped away. No wonder it had kept him alive for two centuries.

"But I didn't form a perfect triad with Gwyneth."

"No, you didn't. Her bloodline power did not bind with you." David stare fixed on him. "We only have some of the pages of the book of Timu. Not every tripling with a bloodliner forms a perfect triad. Why, I don't know."

"You knew when you assigned me and Bradley to guard Micki. You hoped to turn us into some kind of weapon for the Alliance!" Jared shouted. "Gwyneth you knew and did nothing to save her? You fucking bastard!"

"Such are the casualties of this war," David intoned. "After careful research, I believe the bloodline went into hiding a millennia ago. The Dark had eradicated most of them. From time to time, one of the bloodline emerges. Terrok found out about Gwyneth before we did."

"Did Nash know about her bloodline?"

"No. None of us did."

Gravian nodded. "So, Gwyneth's death backfired on Terrok. She caused him to fall into the Ether. It wasn't by your doing."

"Correct." David nodded.

Samson added, "Then Micki Langley's brother is a bloodliner as well."

David nodded. "Do you see why I insisted upon this meeting?"

"The existence of Micki Langley and her brother, Eric, proves that bloodliners are still in the world." The ancient archangel's false feebleness returned. "And the Dark knows about them."

The truth of Gravian's words washed over Jared with dark horror and gnawed at his gut. He could never let Micki fall into the clutches of demons and ifrit. Whatever it took to keep her away from them, he'd do it.

"Is the bloodline strong in this Eric, too?" Jezzel asked.

"I do not know." David looked weary. "I assigned multiple immortals to him to no avail. Eric's bloodline power never fully awakened."

Jared turned to David, anger swelling up inside him. "But how, damn it? How did we do that?"

"We do not know," David answered flatly.

"So, did you enjoy your fucking experiment? Why me? Why not another jinn? I understand your choice of Bradley, but not me."

"You orchestrated this?" Jezzel glared at David.

The archangel shuffled.

"How did you locate Micki and Eric? How did you know of their bloodline?" Gravian questioned.

"Her brother, Eric, came to see me several weeks ago. He claimed to have the writings of Timu."

"What the fuck are the writings of Timu?"

Silent communication between the Seven began.

"Stop fucking with me! And with Micki and Bradley! Tell me what the fuck is going on, or I'll blast all of your asses again. And this time, I won't hold back any of my new perfect triad power."

Gravian patted him on the back. "Calm yourself, jinn. The book of Timu, once thought lost or destroyed, holds a wealth of information about the bloodline, the Dark, and the Alliance. In the wrong hands it would be very dangerous."

"And the power he now has, how could he get it without tripling?" Jezzel asked.

"I believe that since they have formed a perfect triad with their tripling last night, they now can transfer energy between them without a sexual connection," David informed them.

"Perhaps," Gravian spoke. "But if true, that is something forgotten from the past."

"We need Timu's writings," Ramon added. "It would have more about such things."

"That is true," David agreed.

"I must go." Parkor clapped his hands together, and vanished.

"Whatever you do, keep this new triad out of the hands of the dark." Ramon rose and disappeared through his door.

"They may be our only hope," Mavin breathed. Her exit consisted of a whirlwind of snow and ice.

"David, assign Jared and Bradley to guard this female bloodliner. The rest of your troops should try to locate the lair of the demon trying to release Terrok." The old angel gave his final words then disappeared in a flash of light.

Samson vanished without a word.

Only Jezzel stayed behind.

Her stare pissed Jared off. He spat, "I don't give a damn about the war. Nor do I care about this myth. It means nothing to me."

"Maybe not," Jezzel answered, "but I will make sure that whatever needs to be done is done."

Not waiting for a response, she waved her hands, clapped them together, and vanished in flash of green smoke.

Jared's anger boiled. "So David, shall we try the easy way and you tell me everything? Or the hard way?"

Chapter 13

A month ago, I learned from the bloodline genealogical pages in the book that our mother had a sister that neither Micki nor I ever knew. Our aunt is dead. But she had a daughter. I found her with the help of the book. She'd been living on the streets in Los Angeles. She hadn't eaten in several days. She was only three when her mother died. No siblings. I'm so glad I had Micki growing up. I can't imagine how my cousin survived.

David agreed to place her under the Alliance's protection.

She's only a year younger than Micki, but she, too, will die unless I can figure out how to fix the Bloodline's genetic time bomb.

I can't believe that I'm tired of sex, but I am.

Eric's Flash Drive: day 55—entry 6

* * * *

David raised an eyebrow. "You think you can take me?"

Jared imagined tearing off the archangel's wings and feeding them to him, one bloody feather at a time. David had experimented with Micki, Bradley and him, and now the Dark wanted them. For himself, he didn't care. But he'd make damn sure they never touched her.

"I just knocked all of the Seven on their asses. Yes, I think I can."

"Are you not curious about what happened with Kronos and Eve?" David asked.

"Sure I am, but what has that got to do with this perfect triad bullshit?"

"Everything. According to legend a perfect triad has only three members—forever."

"Damn it."

"They cannot drift outside of their bonding. Ever."

Fuck, fuck, fuck!

"I picked you because you are the most powerful jinn I know outside of the Seven."

"And Bradley?"

"Powerful. A loyal soldier."

"How did you know she would respond to us?"

"I didn't, but I hoped. I provided her with sexual dreams of you and Bradley to get her ready to join you two in a tripling."

"You're a goddamn son-of-a-bitch!"

David shrugged.

Jared hoped he could dismantle their triad, David's would-be super weapon. It might be the only thing that could save Micki from the Dark.

"So, how do I undo this thing?"

David patted him on the back. "You do not. It is eternal."

Jared turned and grabbed David's arm crushing with all his strength. "Micki is not your plaything; she's human."

The archangel shook off Jared's hold and stepped back. "True, but remember how she looked when you last saw her. Had she changed somehow? Is it not possible that the tripling with you and Bradley—"

"—made her immortal," Jared finished. His gut tightened. Not an angel or jinn, but something different. *A human immortal.*

"Yes. If the Dark is able to tap into her brother's bloodline power, the first thing they'll do is to try to open the Ether."

"They might succeed. They almost did with Gwyneth."

David agreed. "Yes, they almost did."

"You also picked me for another reason."

"I did."

"Other than Nash, I'm the only immortal you know that has been with a bloodliner."

"True."

"Then why not Nash for your first choice?"

"One, he never awakened Gwyneth's power. That night in the cave, hers almost sparked to life, but then she died. Two, if the attempt didn't work, losing you would do no real harm to the Alliance."

"Losing me?"

"I planned for the possibility, Jared. But we can continue talking while the Dark continues looking for Micki Langley, or we can make sure she is safe, cared for. You know better than any the danger she is in."

Jared clenched his jaw.

"I'm going to meet with Ms. Langley to see what she has for me. She is arriving at Zone Three in a few minutes with Bradley."

"What does Micki have for you? The book?"

"Her brother had it and may have hidden it away for her. Timu's writings are too dangerous to be in the hands of mortals, even if they are bloodliners. That's why I have Bradley and some other warriors guarding her. If I can locate the lair and Eric, I can spare Ms. Langley from harm."

"Just like you did before with Gwyneth?"

David's wings spread wide and blue energy filled the room. Jared could not breathe. Anger swirled around him. David's anger.

Jared choked out, "So, you're willing to let her be captured, or worse?"

"Are you?" David's power grip over Jared eased up.

"No."

"Then forget both of our past failings."

Jared choked out, "I will never forget."

"Go to Micki and protect her." David flew up and disappeared through the ceiling.

Jared stood alone in the room. The magic faded seconds later, and he found himself standing in the same empty alley.

* * * *

Bradley stayed alert. Until he got Micki and Brooke inside Zone Three, risks still existed. No darkling would touch her, not on his watch, and he planned on that being for a very long time.

Jared's message about the danger around Micki had been true, but there was no sign of the jinn anywhere. Where could he be? If he gave one damn for Micki, he'd be here.

Guess he didn't.

"Bradley, I'm sorry for slapping you." Micki whispered.

Heat rolled into him. No other woman could be more heroic or incredible. She ensnared him completely.

"Sweetheart, you don't have anything to apologize for."

As they walked to the club, she continued to shiver, clearly frightened by what had happened outside.

Bradley sent out, *Raf, you still with us?*

Still here. Trey, too. The others are still pursuing the coward darkling bastards. Our orders are to stay with you and the women until you enter the club.

Bradley's anger boiled thinking about the Dark's attempt to abduct Micki and Brooke just blocks from Zone Three, one of the top Alliance strongholds in the world. David's grade as commander? A big red F.

They'd won the battle, but they'd been lucky. Though Micki and Brooke had only seen a total of eight darklings, there had been another hundred cloaked in invisibility. Bradley had taken two of the invisible bastards out before the rest fled. They'd been outnumbered and outgunned by more than double.

Why had the darklings retreated with such an advantage?

He scanned Micki. He'd noticed her red power when he first saw her. Now it grew. Had the darklings sensed it, too?

Her red seduction pulled at him. He wanted to take her right there in the street, ravish her. His cock stiffened.

Must keep my head clear.

He would not let what happened last night happen again. Bradley surveyed the street for any more demons but saw none.

Finally, they made it to the velvet rope and Stone.

Stone turned to Bradley. "Welcome. Please come in." *David will be here soon.*

* * * *

Micki gasped as she entered the club with Brooke and Bradley. Instead of a hot spot, Zone Three seemed like a morgue.

"What's going on?" she squeezed Bradley's arm. "Where is everybody?"

He shrugged.

She looked around the nearly empty room. No sign of Jared. She did recognize the bartender from last night. Less than ten people inhabited the inside of the club.

"Is one of those guys David?" Micki asked Bradley. "I don't know what he looks like. That bartender I remember from last night."

Her champion kept moving her and Brooke forward. "I don't see him, but it is early."

"Shall we go over there to the sofas?" She wanted as far away from the door as possible and the men in trench coats.

He smiled. "Great idea."

They sat on a large overstuffed sofa. Micki took the middle spot. Bradley sat on one side of her, Brooke on the other.

Her fear thundered to the surface with each of her heartbeats. He pulled her in closer. Bradley seemed to want to console her, to let her know he would make sure nothing like that ever happened to her again. She wanted him to hold her tight and make all her worries fade away.

Bradley squeezed her hand. "You're safe. You're with me now."

"Just a bunch of troublemakers," Brooke spat. "That's all."

Micki wanted to ask about the blue lights and green smoke that swirled on the street around her and Brooke. About the wings. She could no longer deny that Eric's research and disappearance had uncovered a hidden world of monsters?

Would Bradley think she'd totally lost it? She didn't think so.

Micki gazed at his blue eyes. "What about the horns?"

Brooke turned toward her with a look of totally surprise. "Horns? Like trumpets?"

"No. Like demons." She could see through the masks the monsters had created, but how?

Bradley shrugged. "No, I didn't see horns."

She sensed the dishonesty in his tone. Was he lying for Brooke's sake?

"I guess I was more scared than I thought." She didn't believe her own words. "Just my imagination I suppose."

Brooke turned to Bradley. "So, you know David. Do you know Eric, too?"

"I know of him. That's all, though."

The bartender walked up and asked, "What can I get you?"

"Nothing," Micki answered.

"Same," Brooke agreed.

Bradley turned to the man. "Make it three, Greg."

"Greg, is it?" Micki glared at him. "I know David keeps his own calendar, as you stated last night, but do you have any idea if he will be here tonight?"

Greg smiled at her. "He knows you're here."

The man turned and headed back to the bar, leaving the three of them alone.

Thank God! David had to know where Eric was. She couldn't bear another night without knowing.

She felt a single tear slide down her cheek. She wiped it away quickly. She wanted Bradley to sweep her up and hold her tight against him until her fears subsided.

She looked up at him. "You think David might know where my brother is?"

Brooke blurted, "What the fuck was Eric doing in a place like this in the first place?"

"Are you his sister, too?" Bradley asked.

Micki felt certain he already knew the answer.

"No. Not his sister."

Bradley continued, "But someone special to him, I suspect."

"That's right," she shot back.

Micki patted Brooke's hand. Eric's girlfriend needed answers, maybe even more than she did.

Bradley turned to Brooke, but kept squeezing Micki's hand. "You'll get some answers soon."

"Thank you." Brooke's hardness melted some.

Micki shifted beside him. She flicked open her purse and peered into it. "Eric left me a voicemail. He also had a flash drive with some research on it. He wanted me to give it to David."

"You really do know David, right?" Brooke's words came out more softly.

Bradley nodded.

"I knew something was up a while back, but I had no idea that Eric was in trouble." Brooke's eyes welled up.

"You knew?" Micki asked. "How?"

"Before I left for my mother's we had a big fight. He'd been coming in late, smelling of whiskey. I thought he was cheating."

"Oh, Brooke. I didn't know." She put her arm around Eric's girlfriend.

"I know. What an idiot." Tears rolled down Brooke's cheeks. "Now that I know he was coming here it all makes sense."

Micki hated herself for pressing Brooke, but she had to. "What did he say when you confronted him?"

"Eric told me that he was working with someone on a top secret project. I thought it was another one of his silly scams, but now…"

"What did he tell you about the project?" Micki's gut tightened against her growing panic.

"Eric got something from your mother. A package."

"From our mother? But she's been dead for over twenty years."

"I know, but that is what he said. Some woman named Lily, I think, gave it to him. When I tried to ask more questions about it, he clammed up."

Micki asked, "Why didn't he tell me about all of this?"

"You know Eric. He didn't let me ever see any of it. But I did see him studying an old book one night."

A book? She'd forgotten all about that part of Eric's voicemail. She hadn't told Brooke about it, or the police. *Damn!*

A handsome man with steel grey eyes and wavy dark hair walked up to them. His gaze fixed on Brooke. "Where is the book now?"

"Ladies, let me introduce you to David," Bradley said, his arm pulling Micki in tighter.

The out-of-control sensation she experienced at Zone Three less than twenty-four hours ago rolled in her. Still red-hot, but unlike last night's passion—now, she could only feel fury.

"Where the fuck is Eric!" Micki shouted, standing up.

"I honestly don't know, madam" David took a chair that faced the sofa. "Bradley, introductions are in order."

Again, his stare turned back to Brooke, his attraction to her obvious.

Bradley glared at the man. "This is Micki Langley and Brooke Caldwell."

"A pleasure." David offered his hand, but neither she nor Brooke took it. "Bradley, can you get these beautiful women some refreshments?"

"They already told Greg they didn't want any." Bradley seemed uneasy defying the man.

She squeezed his bicep. It made her feel better.

David looked younger than most in the bar, but respect and a sense of awe poured out toward him from a majority of the crowd.

"Is that right? Ladies, you don't want a drink?"

Like Jared the night before, Micki felt Bradley's fist on her thigh, just waiting. Though Bradley and David looked equally matched, she sensed that wasn't totally true. He'd need Jared if a real fight ensued. Again, she looked around the room for her biker.

Best to ease the tension right now.

"We'd like margaritas," Micki leaned into her champion. "Would you mind going with him? I want to talk with Brooke for a second."

Bradley hesitated, then nodded. He didn't want to leave her, even for a minute? "I'll go with David to help with the drinks."

Micki hated sending him away, but she needed to ask Brooke something. Alone.

"Thanks, Bradley."

After they left, she could see that the bravado Eric's girlfriend had shown with the gun earlier melt away as she dabbed her eyes with a tissue.

"Tell me more about this book and the woman Lily," Micki urged.

"I really don't know anymore than I told you. I saw it just once. Lily, I never met. But after Eric met her, his mood changed. He seemed…obsessed."

"That isn't like him." Eric had a secret life Micki knew nothing about.

Brooke turned toward her. "Not like the Eric we thought we knew. Look where we are, Micki. He came here for several weeks. You trust this Bradley guy?"

"I do." Micki did trust him, but she wasn't sure why.

"Do you know what we should do now?" Brooke asked.

"No." Micki trembled filled with anxiety.

Fear shackled her thoughts. *Eric, please be okay.* An image of Eric bleeding filled her mind. She shook her head and closed her eyes trying to shut out the terror.

Thankfully, Bradley's voice ended the painful illusion. "Micki?"

There he stood, utterly manly, menacing, ready to leap to her defense at any threat.

He sat the two drinks down he carried and he took her in his arms, lifting her from the sofa.

"I'm here for you," Bradley offered.

"I'm glad you are." Micki couldn't keep back the words.

Bradley embraced her. "I'll help you find your brother, I promise."

Chapter 14

Brooke and I had sex. I loved it because I love her. It's nothing like the crap upstairs at Zone Three. I hate the deception and the guilt, but this is literally life or death.

Afterwards, Brooke asked me to go with her to visit her mother in two weeks. I made up an excuse, and she seemed to buy it. I'm a damn good actor. I don't think she suspects anything. I hate lying to her, but I can't imagine telling her about all this.

Why the fuck isn't it working? I don't give a damn about the little magic I can now perform. The passage in the book says bloodliners have to form a perfect triad in order to live. What's the use of tripling if it doesn't save my life?

Eric's Flash Drive: day 62—entry 3

* * * *

Bradley kept his arm around Micki's waist. She felt protected—safe.

She pressed into his chest. "Will David help us find Eric?"

He hesitated. "I think he will."

She sighed.

The music gained intensity as David walked back with the rest of their drinks, then he sat in the sofa facing theirs.

Micki trembled, her mind moving at lightning speed. "I have something that Eric wanted me to give to you."

"And what would that be, Ms. Langley?"

Brooke glared back at him. "First, tell us how long Eric has been coming to this place."

The man turned back to Brooke, his eyes filled with lust for her. "A few months."

She spat back, "Are you the one who got him involved in this crap?"

"Ms. Caldwell, there are bigger things afoot that demand my attention other than your jealousy." His gaze turned back to Micki. "Ms. Langley, about this book—"

"Don't give me that! You know something, and you if you know what's good for you."

David cocked an eyebrow. "What's good for me, Ms. Caldwell?"

"I don't know anything about a book." Micki felt the panic grow inside her. "Will you help us or not?"

"But first, you must help me find the book Eric had."

"What do you know about it?" Her bottled-up worry crowded her stomach.

"A veritable Rosetta Stone for those looking at ancient secrets. At least a thousand years old, but the text is actually much older. Several monks wrote down oral traditions that had been brought up through Northern Africa by the conquering Moors into Spain."

"History buff?" Brooke asked.

"You might say that, Ms. Caldwell. Or may I call you Brooke?"

"No, you may not."

Micki asked, "So, what is the book called?"

"The *Book of Timu*. All the copies were thought to have been lost during the *Battle of Las Navas de Tolosa in 1212.*"

Micki wasn't sure the man told the truth, but he'd been passionate during his history lesson about Eric's ancient book.

The discussion alarmed her, producing more questions than it answered.

Micki glared at the man. "Pretty valuable?"

"Priceless."

So many people wanted Eric's book and flash drive—the men on the street, David, only heaven knew who else. Micki believed that more than money tempted the secretive and dangerous crowd.

"Then tell me the truth about what is going on here. Do you think immortals are involved?"

Brooke's face showed more puzzlement.

Micki, can you hear my thoughts? David's words floated into her mind.

"I think I can," Micki said.

Don't speak. Think.

Micki sent a thought, *This isn't possible. I'm only imagining we're reading each other's minds.*

You know that is not true, Micki. Amazing. I didn't know it possible with humans, but given what you are I shouldn't be surprised.

What am I? What is Eric?

As you surmised, there is an immortal world. You and your brother are part of it, in a way. You are both part of a bloodline thought lost ages ago. Human, but not like any other humans.

"You think what?" Brooke asked.

"Nothing. Just thinking." Micki's eyes burned with tears. *Is Eric okay?*

An image of Eric being abducted by horned creatures, like the ones on the street earlier, entered her thoughts. She realized it came from David. Frenzy and panic knocked on the door to her mind.

Micki, he's still alive.

Bradley squeezed her hand. Could he hear the exchange as well? Could Brooke?

Brooke is human and cannot hear. I'm blocking out Bradley.

Why?

He and I are having a private conversation, just as you and I are.

If Brooke was human and couldn't hear, but David had to block out Bradley, then what *was* Bradley?

Micki, you are correct, he's not human.

Her head swam from the flow of crazy information David sent her. Ever since she'd first met Bradley and Jared, she'd suspected they were extraordinary men in her extraordinary situation. Perhaps she should've been shaken by the fact she'd been having sex with powerful immortal creatures, but they were just Bradley and Jared to her, fortresses of strength.

What exactly is he?

Best to ask Bradley yourself. Micki, you better figure out if you're willing to do whatever it takes to find your brother. You do remember the creatures on the street. Well, their kind, demons and ifrit, have your brother.

Oh God, no! I'll do whatever you want. "I have Eric's flash drive. That might have a clue about the book."

She couldn't be safe with the flash drive in her possession whether at the bank or not. She didn't have anyone to keep the thugs away, like the ones on the street.

She needed a bodyguard. Micki felt Bradley squeeze her hand as if he'd heard her request.

Bradley didn't hear your thoughts, but he will go with you to your bank. David's eyes darkened to a deeper blue. "Eric's flash drive would be helpful."

Brooke shifted next to her.

Micki reached out and grabbed her hand. "David, do you have a number where we can reach you?"

"You will be back here shortly, Ms. Langley."

Brooke glared at him. "Are you hoping to get her upstairs?"

David sent a wide smile to Eric's girlfriend, "Brooke, would you like to join me upstairs?"

Brooke's face flushed, then she crossed her arms. "Hell no."

"Too bad." He shot Brooke a wicked grin. "Until we meet again.

He waved and walked away, headed to the stairs with the velvet rope.

"He's an arrogant asshole." Brooke turned back to her. "So,

what's next?"

* * * *

Micki, Bradley, and the blonde woman exited Zone Three.

Jared concealed himself with energy so that they would not see or sense him.

"I'm going back to mine and Eric's place," the other woman said. "Maybe I can find that book."

"That's a great idea, Brooke." Micki leaned into the angel. "I'm staying with Bradley."

Brooke's face darkened.

He floated up, keeping himself hidden. Bradley scanned the area, but wouldn't sense him, unless he used much more power.

As Jared followed them, he couldn't keep his eyes off of Micki's taunting body. Her hips swayed back and forth, hypnotizing him.

That sweet little piece of ass last night really charged your batteries—both yours and the angel's.

Jared shook his head to clear the memory.

He needed to be focused on the shadows and what threats they might hide, demons and ifrit wanting to taste Micki's bloodline power.

Her red energy swirled around her. Growing with each minute. Being so close to her clouded his thoughts with want. Micki brought sensations out of him he feared, emotions someone like him should never have.

Images of their night together, her sexy naked body warmed from the penetration he and Bradley gave her seized his consciousness. A triple embrace, savoring Micki's scrumptious shape. Kissing her soft skin...

I've got to snap out of it!

Jared watched Bradley move protectively closer to Micki. He admired the angel's skills and trusted he would be quite adept if any darkling attacked.

"Why don't you join them, Jared?" David voiced, invisible.

He thrust a picture of Gwyneth, chained and dying under his thrusts to the archangel. "That make it clear why I can't, prick?"

"I only ask because I believe it might—"

"Who do you have guarding them?"

Since Micki, Bradley, and the other woman were more than two blocks ahead, Jared decided to conserve his energy and ended the invisibility spell.

Seconds later, David materialized next to him. "You should guard them."

"Only me?"

"Of course not. She is too important for that. I have dozens of my best sentries flying above them. The rest of my troops are searching for the Dark's lair."

"You've really lost your mind over the last two hundred years, David."

The archangel shrugged. "If you need me, send word. I can be there with some additional troops in seconds."

"I heard what Jezzel said."

"She does not rule here."

"No, but she isn't about to let Micki fall into the Dark's hands, even if that includes killing her."

"She is one of the Seven of the Alliance. We don't kill humans."

"So you say," Jared interjected. "What if she has other plans for Micki?"

"I have warriors and familiars everywhere tracking all the darklings movements. If they make a move toward her, we will be there."

Jared scanned the sky. He sensed angels, but too few. "Like you did for her brother? And Gwyneth?"

David hesitated. "Why do you constantly want to challenge me?"

"We need more guardians, at least a hundred."

"Can you not handle guarding her, Jared? This morning you told me about taking out eight or nine demons by yourself."

"Eleven." Jared corrected. "And don't forget the Seven's asses I kicked."

David glared at him. "Jared, I understand you want to be noble, but the truth is none of you can get energy without the other two. If you don't get over your shit, you, Micki and Bradley will die, most likely at the hands of the Dark."

The archangel's words sliced through his denial. Jared knew first-hand the horrors the Dark dished out. He tensed when he felt another presence approaching them fast from Zone Three's direction.

He turned and looked back. Greg flew toward them.

When the angel caught up with them, his look let Jared know he hadn't warmed up to him.

"What do you have to report, warrior?" David asked.

"Most of the Dark are south of the city with more arriving every hour."

Jared's ears perked up at that statement. A battle clawed at the starting gates. He needed to get to Micki and fast. Thankfully, she and Bradley walked north, away from the Dark.

David asked Greg, "And the location of their lair?"

"Still unknown."

"Go to her, Jared. I will take care of this battle. You take care of her." David waved his hands and disappeared.

Greg snarled at him. "You better be on the right side this time, jinn." Then he vanished.

Resuming his concealment, Jared watched Bradley, Micki and the blonde walk into a parking garage.

He floated in, but stayed out of range for Bradley to detect. After some discussion, the woman sped off in her car. Her face showed confusion as she passed him driving onto the street. His former lovers remained behind and talked quietly.

Jared couldn't catch their conversation, so he took a fleck of power to enhance his hearing.

Bradley put his arm around Micki.

"I need you to stay with me until my bank opens tomorrow." She opened her purse.

Jared felt hunger press inside him. Not for food but for the triad these two promised. Powerful cravings stirred inside him.

Fuck!

Chapter 15

David keeps asking about the book. He must know I have it. How? Magic? It's the only leverage I have with him. I don't doubt he would drop our project, and me, if he ever gets his hands on it. So, I used my new bloodline magic today to put the book in a safe place where no immortal can get it.

If we succeed, he can have the damn book. I still have the scanned images of all the Bloodline's genealogical pages on this flash drive. Once healed, I will find all the living bloodliners if it takes my entire life, and I will get them the cure they need to live.

Eric's Flash Drive: day 68—entry 2

* * * *

Bradley watched Micki dive into her purse. "What are you looking for?"

"Courage," she answered him. Then she laughed.

Still, he grappled with the news David had told him when they'd gotten the drinks for her and Brooke: Micki was a bloodliner.

That explained the enormous power she'd produced for him and Jared.

"Courage? Why do you need courage?"

"To ask you exactly what you are. David told me that you're not human."

Bradley's normal firm footing slipped.

"Well, he didn't say it, but he did let me know. Apparently, I'm a mind reader." Micki fixed her gaze on him. "So, what exactly are you? I assume you are immortal."

Alliance protocol: wait for David's official blessing. *Fuck it! She deserves to know.* He swallowed hard. "Yes, I'm an angel."

Her brow furrowed. "An angel? You were no angel last night."

"Angels aren't like what most people have been taught. At least not the kind of angel I am."

"Good to know. And Jared?"

"A jinn." Bradley tried to read her thoughts, but nothing broke through. Had she already learned how to block her mind from others?

"David told me that the horned people on the street have Eric." Micki's voice cracked. "He'll help my brother, but he needs Eric's flash drive."

"Sweetheart, I'm so sorry." He hugged her tight against him.

"Well, Angel Bradley, I need your help. Tomorrow, you're going to escort me to get my brother's flash drive."

Micki's determination to help her brother didn't diminish even after all she'd learned. She amazed him.

"Where is it?"

"In my safety deposit box."

"Why wait until tomorrow?" he asked.

"Because the bank is closed."

He grinned. "I'm an angel. Locked doors don't stop me."

"Angel magic?" Micki asked Bradley.

"Something like that," he cupped her chin. Shivers of delight spread over her. "Picture the place in your mind and send it to me."

"Send it to you."

He smiled. "You're a mind reader, now be a mind sender."

She closed her eyes and visualized the parking lot just outside the bank.

"Got it, sweetheart. You ready?"

"What should I expect?" Blue light flashed, her stomach lurched, then she and Bradley stood in the place she'd brought in her mind.

The magic he preformed and his presence added to both her

excitement and her uneasiness. She kept thinking about Jared. She longed for him to be there with them.

Bradley's hand moved to the small of her back. Did he sense her anxiety?

"Close your eyes. Picture the room where your safety deposit box is."

"Why didn't we go there first?"

"I thought somewhere outdoors would be better. I didn't want to materialize inside a brick wall." He smiled. "Plus, you're new to all this magic stuff. Small steps, Ms. Mind Reader."

The gentleness of Bradley's tone spread through her, and she felt the knots in her shoulders loosen. As instructed, she closed her eyes and brought up an image of the room.

"Got it," Bradley said. "I'm going to kiss you, Micki."

"Out here?" she squeaked.

They'd traveled by magical means to the back of her bank, and all he wanted to do was kiss her. She wasn't sure why she liked that, but she did.

"Okay."

Not waiting for any more consent than that one word, Bradley took her in his arms and planted a deep, slow kiss that vibrated down her entire spine and made her toes curl.

When their mouth embrace ended, she remembered what she'd read about immortals needing humans for energy. David told her that she was a bloodliner. Maybe she tasted like some kind of life force dessert to immortals' taste buds. Had Jared and Bradley wanted only the power she could give them last night? A taste of a bloodliner?

"Inside," she ordered breathlessly.

Bradley complied and the next moment they stood inside the bank. Again, she felt dizzy, but a little less.

"What about alarms?" she gasped.

"I've taken care of that."

Micki stepped past him, noticing the arousal their kiss had given him. She'd loved touching Bradley at Zone Three, in the club and upstairs. She wanted to touch him again. Standing in the empty room with rows and rows of safety deposit boxes, he smiled back at her.

Micki felt her cheeks heat up. "Was I just a meal for you, Bradley?"

A look of confusion clouded his face, "A meal? No."

Her shoulders relaxed. Maybe not a meal, but what did she mean to him? Could immortals and humans have relationships beyond the bedroom?

She spotted her box. "There it is, number 272, but it needs the bank's master key besides mine."

"I'll take care of that." Bradley shot blue light out of his hand.

She heard one click and then another. She held out her key to him.

"You don't need that. I unlocked both locks."

"You'd make an incredible bank robber." Micki opened it, and pulled out Eric's flash drive.

"May I see it?" Bradley asked.

She felt her stomach flip-flop. Her only bargaining chip and he already wanted it.

"It's okay, sweetheart." Bradley gaze froze on her. "If you want to keep it until we get back to David, no problem."

Micki slipped it into her jeans. "I do. I know that's crazy, but having it makes me think there's still a chance that Eric…"

She couldn't hold her worry back any longer. Those hideous creatures had her brother.

Bradley pulled her into him. "We'll find him."

"Those monsters that have him, what are they capable of? I don't know, and it's killing me."

"Micki, you are more to me than any woman I've ever known, and if your brother means that much to you, I promise, I'll find him."

She felt tears streak down her face. He meant it, but was that enough? Could she break the passwords on the flash drive, and if so, would she learn anything that might help her find Eric?

She had to try. It could be her last chance to find him. Her stomach tightened. What if it didn't work and they couldn't save him?

She leaned into Bradley for strength again. *Just for a few minutes. I need his touch to escape, to feel there is really a chance to save Eric.*

She reached for the light switch, but his hand stopped her from turning it on. When Bradley's fingers curled around hers, she felt a blaze of heat pass between them. Instinctively, she closed her eyes and licked her lips.

A silhouette of blue burned in her mind—of Bradley. Then she scanned herself—hot red light.

She wanted him, wanted what had been born in her the other night.

Wings. Smoke. Rainbow.

"Lose yourself to me, sweetheart."

She needed Bradley—selfless and strong. His long fingers touched her waist. He leaned her up against the table in the middle of the vault and his lips found the side of her neck. She hungered for the warm wetness of his mouth.

Bradley pressed his lips to hers, hard, filled with desire. Micki's toes curled.

"Tonight, I'm going to make love to you, Micki."

Her breathing sped up. Trembles shot through her.

He lifted her and eased her gently to the floor. For an instant she thought she saw a halo of blue around his head.

She moved her hands to his wide shoulders. Her hands met behind his thick neck, and in a single motion, he moved down on top of her. Strong and powerful. She felt safe with him.

His sky blue eyes seduced her in closer. When he leaned into her, she felt his stiff cock behind his camos.

Bradley fixed his stare on her. "You've changed me, Micki."

She shivered. *And you've changed me.*

Again, he dove into her mouth. His tongue danced with hers,

pushing in deep. The kiss called to her entire body to submit. Moisture coated her pussy.

Bradley no longer held back his lust. A man changed with an appetite for her that would not be denied. To feed on her? *Probably.* It didn't matter. She craved him.

The rainbow, wings and smoke seemed to loom close. Micki felt them.

I will drive my cock deep inside your tight pussy.

She loved hearing his thoughts. Her body vibrated with desire.

Bradley's hard sexy body pressed against her. When he slid off of her and stood, she missed the weight of him on her.

He unsnapped her jeans. A promise that her unspoken wish would be granted.

Dreamily she said, "This is so strange and wonderful."

"Sweetheart, I will taste every part of you."

Bradley pulled her jeans down between her knees, keeping her from full movement or escape—not that she wanted to leave. He leaned down, and he kissed her navel. Her panties, still in place, kept her from feeling his full hot breath on her, but her stomach trembled at his deep gusts of heat.

His lips wandered around her belly and found her sides. She was normally too ticklish to touch there, but tonight, the sensitive nerve endings responded differently. Excitement and acceptance. The whole time his hands moved and explored more of her legs, the more desire grew in her and the less she resisted.

Bradley rasped, "I love your body."

His voice became a touch to her soul. Masculinity flew out of him from head to toe, and especially from his bulge that would pierce her very soon. She licked her lips. Desire like she'd never known before had been born inside her the other night with Bradley and Jared, and now it stood full grown and ravenous.

Micki slipped her panties down to her half-off, half-on jeans. The air felt good on her swollen folds. Bradley smiled a wolfish grin. She liked that she pleased him. She took his large hands and kissed each of them on the palms, on the back. She took one of his index fingers and swallowed it whole, sucking on it with all her might, hard and slow.

Without warning, Bradley dipped down between her legs and she felt his hard tongue dive deep inside her pussy.

A monstrous quake shot down her spine and up to her erect nipples under her top. She took Bradley's hand and guided it underneath the fabric to her breasts. His powerful hand touching her nipples made them throb, and her back arched away from the floor. His thumb and forefinger pinched her nipple erection. She took her hand and pressed on the back of his head.

Ohmigod! His touch works magic.

Electric shocks shot through her. Every part of her vibrated. She had to have more.

Bradley came up from his meal with his eyes burning a bright fiery blue. His lust shot out of him.

Leaving his kneeling position, he stood. She could see that his erection stretched the fabric of his shorts to the maximum. The animal in him unleashed.

In seconds, Bradley stripped Micki's top over her head. Another split-second and her bra landed in the corner of the room, releasing her chest to the air. Then he pointed to his pants in a single commanding gesture.

She trembled and obeyed, stripping him of his jeans and freeing his manhood. His cock pulsed with each breath he took.

Make love to me, Bradley!

"Oh, I will."

Her heartbeat quickened. With her hands, she explored Bradley's muscles, hard as steel. Her internal temperature moved up several degrees. His hands continued their work on her mound. He pulled her in close to his hard body. Micki offered him no resistance. She felt safe.

He dipped down and licked her left nipple. Then he put his lips around the pinkness and sucked hard.

"Mmm."

His tongue traced her areola.

"Do you like that, sweetheart?"

"Ohh!"

"Your other breast is getting jealous. I think I better rectify that."

Then he switched to her right side and proceeded to expertly deliver the same treatment to her right breast.

Lick. Suck. Trace.

Back and forth.

Over and over.

O-Ohmigod!

His lips moved up to her neck and delivered more kisses and sucking up the side of her face to her ears. He sucked hard on her ear lobes. She'd never experienced that, but found she loved the sensation. A newly awakened erogenous zone.

"I love your lips on my body," she panted.

She closed her eyes. Bradley touched her in the places she knew aroused her and in places she didn't know could arouse her, but definitely did. The man should put together a class for all the men on the planet on how to please a woman.

"Kick those jeans and panties off."

She obeyed him. Micki felt the pleasurable release teasing her at her boundaries. God, she couldn't get enough of him.

A second helping, please. And a third. A fourth.

She wanted to try to please him as much as he pleasured her. His body felt so good against hers. She leaned down and kissed his nipples. His chest felt hard as a concrete wall. Something harder still waited for her between his legs.

"I want your lips on my dick," he growled.

She leaned down and took his throbbing member in her hand. She pumped it, and it grew even harder in her hand.

"Oh, sweetheart."

Micki licked the tip of his dick. His slickness oozed and she tasted warm saltiness.

"Yes, Micki. That's it."

She wanted to spur his lust to a raging fire, loved having that power. Micki swallowed to the base of his dick, desire taking her completely over.

"Micki, yes!"

Sliding up and down his shaft, she moved her hand to his throbbing balls and caressed them. She moved her other hand between her own legs and rubbed her clit. A tremor erupted from deep inside her.

Bradley started bucking inside her mouth. She pulled off of his cock, but as she let it leave her mouth, she flicked its head with her tongue.

"I have got to get inside you, Micki."

Bradley rolled her over on her back. The air touched her naked front and delightful shivers moved over her skin.

He fed his dick into her waiting pussy.

"I love being inside you," he gasped.

Bang! Bang!

He pounded deeper into her.

Harder and harder.

"Y-yesss."

She matched his rhythm and moved up on her elbows. She kissed his rocking chest. He slowed and pressed her back to the floor with his weight.

Then the strokes of his cock inside her pussy began again, more urgent.

Her waiting orgasm inched to the forefront.

His dick drove deep into her. Bradley knew just how hard and fast she needed it. He would get her close to the brink of an orgasm and then he would slow his charge.

Over and over.

Pound. Pound. Pound.

Her ache thundered, inflamed by Bradley's onslaught.

Pound. Pound. Pound.

Bradley's thoughts swirled in her head, *I'm—*

"Yess!"

Going to come!

Bradley's body became stone-like with his deepest push filling her insides. Her orgasm exploded in her like a wave of bombs hitting every target inside and outside her body.

Ohh!

She tasted warm chocolate.

She stared into her champion's blue eyes, his wings spread out over her. Micki closed her eyes and saw her red energy swirling hot.

And green smoke? Jared's smoke.

Chapter 16

Only three weeks until D-day. Death-day. Birthday. Odd to think how I didn't believe any of it at first. Now, with all the symptoms—weakness, fever, visions—I don't believe I can save myself.

If I fail, maybe Micki can use my research, the book, and what I've recorded here to save herself, our cousin Eve, and the other bloodliners. She still has a year and a half left. But first, I have to tell her about the Bloodline. Next week.

Eric's Flash Drive: day 76 —entry 2

* * * *

Closing his eyes, Jared's lust thundered out of him, consuming his concentration. Every thrust Bradley drove into Micki's cunt pushed blood into his own cock. As his two former lovers enjoyed their juicy orgasms, her red energy lured him.

No more holding back, he would crash through the front door of the bank and join them once again. Hot bodies wrapped together in powerful, raw sex, devouring her red light.

A beacon for the ifrit and demons to find her.

Jared's eyes popped wide open. But the darklings were already here. He could not see the demons, but he could feel them.

Where were David's sentries? Why weren't they moving in?

Not wanting the monsters to sense him, he let his awareness move out gently. The heat grew. Black flames appeared in his mind, only thirty feet from him. They'd come out of the darkness. He opened his eyes and watched as, one by one, they transformed into crows. They all flew to the tree outside one of the bank's windows.

Twenty of them perched on the branches of the old oak.

Though the darklings seemed unaware of his presence, he held no hope for Micki or Bradley. Twenty. He'd been able to best thirteen darklings that morning, yes, but it had taken twice the power spinning inside him now. These darklings' combined power would deny him saving his former lovers's lives if they attacked. He hoped that they wouldn't.

Then three black wolves ran up to the tree from out of the shadows, demons in disguise, much older and powerful than the darklings in the trees.

Jared considered trying to send a message out to David but decided against it. It would be too risky this close to the demonic birds and wolves. He might be able to slip outside their psychic reach and get a message off to the Alliance sentries. They'd been flying above, but now, Jared couldn't sense them. It was like a total black out. Again he cursed the archangel. Some fucking leader. Micki would die because of David's ineptitude.

Jared couldn't help but think of Micki, an innocent brought into the Eternal War by her idiot brother—and David. Why the fuck had he followed David's request like some kind of new enlistee of the Alliance? Because he hadn't just guarded Micki but had given in to his desire for her, he, too, had helped bring her deeper into the war.

She would soon be dead *or worse* if the wolves and birds attacked. Perhaps they had other designs.

Terrok's words had played over and over in his head since he'd taken the last taste of Micki's ancestor's life. Now, the words screamed.

Welcome, my new dark brother, to your destiny. Count the bodies as they fall!

Jared couldn't bear to think about either Micki or Bradley suffering these monsters' devices. He knew too well these creatures' methods to satisfy their evil appetites.

The birds' hot blood lust for Micki and Bradley dried out most of the leaves of the tree on which they perched, turning them brown. Suddenly, all the birds took flight with the dead leaves falling to the ground from the disturbance.

A ring of black flames surrounded and enveloped the canines, taking them from Jared's sight. When the flame died down, the wolves had changed into their true forms, high-ranking demons.

"Where is the jinn?" the archdemon asked.

Jared recognized him to be one of Terrok's next in command, Vincorte.

"We lost track of him."

"But the angel is still with her," the other offered.

"Excellent."

The creatures opened their giant bat-like wings and flew to the window. They hovered for a moment and then passed magically through the glass, shimmering black as they did.

Without any thought or hesitation, Jared pushed hot smoke out of his body. It exploded around him. Whether he failed didn't matter anymore. He had to get to Micki and Bradley.

He changed into the shape of a lion and leapt up after the darklings.

Bradley! Darklings!

Raw rage erupted inside him.

He sent a message to David. He hoped the archangel would get it, but Jared feared David wouldn't make it in time to stop the carnage and save Micki.

* * * *

Drifting in and out of sleep, Micki reached for Bradley, but couldn't find him with her fingers.

"This can be easy or this can be hard," a voice filled with malice said.

She opened her eyes.

Bradley floated above her, his eyes filled with pain and rage, fighting against some invisible chains.

Still in the vault, Micki saw three other men. They looked wicked and evil—*with horns*. One wore mirrored sunglasses.

She reached to cover her naked body with her arms and one of the monsters grabbed her wrists. Fierce pain flowed down into her.

"I hope it hurts," the pain giver said.

Micki felt the heat moving up her arm into her chest. A wave of nausea rose in her. *Think. Calm down.* She closed her eyes and fashioned an image of her tub surrounded by candles. The pain eased a bit.

Tricky bitch.

The words from the intruder pushed into her mind along with images of Eric writhing, covered in blood.

Ohmigod! What are they doing to you, Eric?

Bradley's thoughts, *Don't let them in your head, Micki. Resist.*

She tried to quiet herself. She thought of her favorite beach. *Breathe!*

Again, the pain receded.

You're very powerful. More than your brother. Excellent.

Eric's severed head bobbed to the surface of her mind and formed a painful wail. She couldn't hear a sound from him, but she did hear a scream—her own. A sting of pain shot throughout her entire body to her very core.

Micki opened her eyes to release the image.

She'd never felt such agony. Would she ever know what happened to Eric? To Bradley and Jared?

No, my little morsel. You'll not die tonight, but you will be coming with me.

Just as she thought she would pass out, a blast of blue light filled the room.

And wings. Her champion had broken free.

The light shot out of Bradley's hands to the three horned men. They recoiled.

Her pain went down a notch.

The man with the mirrored sunglasses growled, "I thought you had him."

"I did, master. And I will again," the smallest of three answered.

Fire shot out of the creature's hands toward Bradley. Her lover dodged the flames easily and shot back a blue ball of light. The creature wailed and disappeared.

More men materialized in the vault. Bradley took on four, five, six. Screams of agony erupted from them when he sliced them to bits with his sword followed by more flashes of black.

She looked in her champion's eyes. Blind fury and steel determination remained, but there were too many.

Mr. Sunglasses stepped beside her and sent a ball of black flames at Bradley.

When the fire hit her soldier, he fell to the floor with a thud.

Total despair consumed her. *He can't be dead.*

Wanting to go to him, she tried to sit up but couldn't. Wincing at the pain inside her, she saw his white feathery wings bloodied by the fall, his face hidden under them.

He didn't move.

"No!" she screamed.

She fought the urge to pass out as the pain waved through her like a freight train, delivering aches at each stop inside her body. As quickly as the pain intensified, it weakened. Why?

Micki heard a roar of a wild animal. In the bank?

She looked up and saw a green-colored lion. Its claws ripped at one of the three strangers. Fire shot out from one of the intruders toward the giant cat.

Micki's head hurt and spun.

One of the horned men turned back to her. His eyes showed a deep black, and the evil smile morphed into a snarl.

A black flame materialized in the man's right hand. He raised it and tossed it like a baseball toward her. The light shot into her chest, burning every inch it penetrated, skin, muscle, bone—and still it went deeper.

The pain she'd experienced earlier had been infantile to this fully-grown thing. She felt like discarded slop being dropped into an incinerator. Her eyes filled with liquid as unconsciousness pushed in to help her escape the agony. Flashes of *smoke* kept her awake. Another roar.

Micki, fight it. Don't give in. Not Bradley's voice—Jared's.

Where had he been? She must've been dreaming again. Tomorrow she would wake up. Wake up to Eric's silly laugh. Wake up free of hurt.

Now, she felt pain, and it grew. Soon, that would be all that existed in her entire universe.

Jared's thought, *Stay with me, Micki.*

Micki opened her eyes and saw some of the strangers writhing on the floor. Thick green smoke surrounded them. Then she spotted Jared. How she longed to touch him again, for him to touch her, for him to make the pain go away. She remembered his words from when she'd seen him last. *What have I done?*

She wanted to tell him that he'd changed her. That the feelings she had for him could not be quieted. She longed for him, but couldn't speak.

Hell's fire rolled into her body as she lost consciousness.

* * * *

Jared flung more smoky ropes toward the dark monsters to keep them bound. They thrashed on the floor against his restraints. He didn't have much power left after the surge he used to immobilize the two demons, and he didn't think he could keep them down for much longer. He must find the remaining one, their leader who'd went invisible.

Bradley had taken out at a dozen darklings, but they'd finally bested him knocking him out.

Jared turned smoky, floating to the ceiling and disappearing from sight.

He looked down at Micki, unconscious. The dark spell burned inside her. She would die or—if she were some kind of human immortal, as David believed—she would slip into the Ether's prison. She needed to be treated and soon.

The archdemon hid in the room. Just as the smell of putrid sulfur burned Jared's nose, a power blinded his eyes, a revealing spell. Very strong. Jared defended himself against it, pushing a bit of energy around it.

Come out, come out, wherever you are, the demon taunted.

"You first, Vincorte." Jared remembered him to be the demon that had held Gwyneth's legs while he—

Another blast. This one blinded Jared.

It took more of his power to shake off the dark spell. When he could see again, Vincorte stood below him: handsome face, wearing sunglasses, sharp horns, leathery wings, and sharp claws. The monster let his lips form into a grin.

Jared formed a dagger and sent it sailing toward the creature. It hit its mark, and Vincorte let out a howl of pain.

Jared mocked, "You remember me, asshole?"

He could sense the anger in the archdemon rising.

The monster rose to his feet and sent out a pulse of black energy that stripped Jared's invisibility.

"Yes, half-dark jinn, I remember you."

"Still one of Terrok's old lap dogs, Vinnie?"

The darkling's glance darted around the room, as if he feared his master to appear any moment. Then he turned toward Jared who still floated on the ceiling.

"I see you are not half-dark at all. Fully dark, I would say. You just need a little taste to push you over."

The memories from that dark night flooded into him. The taste of human life had pulsed into him as Gwyneth died. And Terrok's evil laugh.

"Fuck you!"

"Oh, I'll be the one doing the fucking later, but first, you can make this easy on the little morsel. Easy or hard, either way, she's leaving with me."

"I don't give a damn what you want."

"But you would give a damn what our master would say."

"Your game is up. Terrok is in the Ether, with no escape."

"No escape? Really?" Vincorte asked. "Why he takes an interest in you surprises me."

Could Terrok be out of the Ether? If true, Jared knew too well what that would mean.

Lost in his thoughts, Jared made a critical mistake by not dodging the demon's two dark fireballs. Though time seemed to slow, Jared didn't have time to avoid or stop the deadly blasts. He braced for the impact, but then out of the corner of his eye, he spotted a white wing. It came between him and the fiery weapons.

Jared looked over at Bradley as he stood up patting out the flames on his wing. The angel never let his eyes leave the demon. The brave fool's act surprised Vincorte and saved Jared's life.

The demon sent a black flame toward Bradley. Jared shot a green blast, shielding the angel.

Bradley flew to the ceiling and sent a blast at Vincorte, hitting him in the chest.

Jared fired two missiles. A direct hit.

The archdemon's face twisted in pain.

Bradley produced a long sword and rushed Vincorte. The archdemon grabbed the angel's wrists before he could deliver a deathblow.

Micki stirred.

Jared positioned himself between her and the archdemon. He threw smoke daggers toward the creature.

Bradley broke free, swung again, but Vincorte dematerialized.

Was he still in the room? He couldn't sense the archdemon, but he did sense more immortals approaching.

Micki moaned as the dark power grew inside her.

He readied himself for battle. Bradley positioned his sword for attack. If they failed, Micki would die.

* * * *

Bradley lifted his sword above his head. The darklings would not take Micki. He'd do whatever necessary to keep her from them.

The door splintered into a million pieces, then David, Nash, Kronos, Rafiq, and others charged the room with weapons drawn.

Jared shouted, "Nice timing, assholes!"

David's face darkened.

The memory of the terror in Micki's eyes snapped Bradley to her side. He touched her chest. He could feel the dark energy growing inside her each second. He moved his hurting wings to cover her naked body.

The jinn rushed to the other side of her.

He'd judged Jared wrongly. The jinn had fought hard along side him to keep her safe.

Micki couldn't die. Bradley couldn't let her. He must heal her, this beautiful woman who had changed him more than anyone or anything.

"Help her," Jared growled.

Bradley scanned the power left him after the battle. Only a half-inch ball of blue remained. With the bulk of it, he formed a sphere and pushed it into Micki. She groaned.

The dark spot stopped growing and retreated, but its blackness didn't fade.

Micki needed more from him. He knew the risk. He would take all of it if it could save her. He must save her. A sliver of power. Another. And another. With each that entered her body, a small change—detectable to immortal eyes—shrank the demon wound.

He must get to the core of the ill. He let his mind search out the root.

He found a dark seed. The darkest seed.

Some being had taken hold inside her, but existed somewhere else. The creature lusted to control Micki's power and succeeded bit by bit. Cell by cell.

The monster saw him. From where? From inside Micki? Saw into his very core.

Bradley reached for all his energy left him. The tiny bit of energy inside him anchored him to the physical world. He took the sphere and guided it down his arm to his hand. The Ether would take him instantly once he released it into Micki, but she would be saved. He extended his hand to reach her and release the power. *One last touch of that beautiful ivory skin...*

Pain erupted in his jaw from a surprise punch that knocked him to the floor across the room and pushed his power back into him. The punch came from Jared.

"You'll pay for that, asshole," Bradley said, stumbling to his feet, rubbing his jaw, extending his singed wings to full.

Jared shrugged. "Okay, but you won't kill yourself. Not while I'm here."

"You and what army?" he said.

"This army." David pointed to Nash, Kronos, Rafiq, Trey and the others.

"Some army. Where the hell were you? Where was my backup?"

David hesitated. "Above the bank. Somehow, the archdemon shielded the attack from our detection."

"Some fucking leader you are."

"Enough," David's voice boomed.

"She has to live," Bradley shouted back.

"Don't be stupid," Nash said, with fists at his side. "You don't have enough power to save her."

"We won't let you kill yourself," Kronos announced.

Bradley sent, *If I don't heal her, she will die.*

David glared back at him.

Bradley looked hard at the archangel. Even though he knew that David, being a Seven, had power enough to heal Micki, Bradley's unease and doubt about him demanded he keep his commander from touching her.

Had all he believed about David been a lie? Anger exploded in him. He would get through the deception, whatever it took.

"An archdemon and dozens of his underlings attacked us," Bradley spat out.

"I know," David acknowledged.

"I trusted my backup." Bradley looked at the Alliance warriors in the room. Their shoulders dropped. "And I trusted you, David."

David sheathed his sword.

"You came after the motherfuckers left. This jinn," he pointed to Jared. "The one I didn't trust came through for me—and for Micki."

"What are you implying, Bradley?" David extended his wings to their widest, more than two feet wider than Bradley's reach, showing his anger.

"No, David!" Jared shouted.

The archangel didn't budge.

Desperation mixed with Bradley's frustration, creating a sour brew. He'd seen the monster's hold on her—in her. "I have to heal her, asshole. We are…"

"What?" David asked.

Though he'd never remember his past human life, he'd never felt alive as an immortal until Micki. "We are connected."

She had to live even if he had to die. Bradley took the last of his life force.

"So, you don't trust me anymore?" David asked.

"Not one bit." *Micki, I'm sorry I have to leave, but it's the only way to save you.*

He shaped the energy into a healing spell.

"Pity. I'm not letting you commit suicide." David raised his hand, and blue light shot out his hand wrapping itself around Bradley.

First, he felt the cold cords binding his arms and legs, then the archangel's sleep spell enveloped him.

Bradley's healing sphere lurched back into his center, away from Micki.

"D-David, you're s-so d-dea…"

Chapter 17

Brooke leaves tomorrow. She'll be back in a week.

Nothing we've tried is working. David has his theories but we are running out of time. Maybe tonight will be the charm. I just can't give up hope.

No matter what happens this evening, I'm telling Micki tomorrow. Brooke I'll tell when she gets back from her mother's.

Eric's Flash Drive: day 79—entry 1

* * * *

Micki's shoulder felt cold. She trembled and opened her eyes. She recognized the room as the place where Jared and Bradley had first ravaged her to bliss.

Another dream? No.

She pulled at the silk sheet covering her naked body up to her chin.

What about the intruders in the bank? Monsters. Did they have Eric? She trembled remembering their murderous faces, but when she spotted Jared sitting in a chair against the door to the hallway her anxiety subsided.

His gaze locked on her. Her skin electrified and warmed.

How long had he been there? The look in his eyes told her that he wanted something from her that she was willing to give. Heat rolled through her like liquid fire.

She turned and spotted Bradley. Unconscious, his head and back against the wall, legs outstretched, hands and feet bound with blue light, he looked very pale.

"Jared?" She sat up. The blanket fell away, exposing her breasts, but she didn't care. "What happened to Bradley? Why is he tied up?"

Jared didn't answer, but the lust in his stare spoke volumes.

She wasn't in a dream or a nightmare. The horned monsters at the bank, just like the ones she'd seen with Brooke on the street, were real, too. Had they seen her exposed—making love to Bradley? Had Jared?

She remembered the fight, the fear, the pain, and the man with the mirrored sunglasses.

"Untie him, Jared." She couldn't bear seeing her angel tied up and unconscious.

"It's David's spell. Only he can release him."

Tears flooded down her cheeks. She closed her eyes tight, hoping to stop the downpour.

"Micki, everything is going to be okay." She felt Jared's hands on her, around her, and she melted into him. "David knocked him out for his own good."

"He's okay then?"

"He's fine."

Micki pushed in closer to Jared. His muscular body felt good. Safe. He could make her forget.

Boom! Boom! Boom! His heartbeat or hers?

"Not human." Micki felt more of his rock hard body as she pushed in closer. "A real jinn."

Jared nipped her ear. "Yes."

"Why did you leave me our first night?" She needed relief from the madness of the last couple of days, needed relief from her own mind.

"I had my reasons, but now I know I should've stayed."

"I wish you had. I missed you."

"I missed you, too."

"And the men at the bank? What are they?"

"Demons and ifrit."

"They have Eric." She needed him to take her so that her body would be the only thing talking to her, to silence the craziness that swam freely in her mind.

Even more, Micki needed Jared.

Snuggling in closer, she said, "I understand that triplings are for exchanges of power. Is that right?"

"Yes."

"Is that why you had sex with me and Bradley the other night?"

"No."

"But you did want me?"

Jared didn't answer her with words, but his body seemed to be getting warmer the more she wiggled.

"Do you still?"

"I do, but that isn't possible. In fact, it is very dangerous." Jared's body tensed, but he didn't let her go. "We may have to work out how to have another tripling so that the angel recovers faster, but it will have to be more…"

"What?" She turned her head to look up at him. His dark hair touched her cheek igniting her cravings. Still, he didn't move.

"Controlled."

"I want you." Micki kissed his throat. "Need you."

He swallowed, and she felt his Adam's apple move against her lips.

Jared remained like a statue, but still he held on to her. "You don't know what you're asking."

"But I do. I've had you inside me and without that again, I think I'll die. "

Jared opened his mouth to say something, but then closed it tight.

She had to push forward. He'd liked when she talked dirty that night. Could that work again?

"Your cock felt so amazing inside me." Warm dampness slipped out of her slit.

Beads of sweat popped out on Jared's forehead. Tingles spread over her body.

She continued her verbal charge. "You opened me up to anal sex. I thought I couldn't go there, but you taught me. Now, I want more of that. More of your cock. Don't you want to teach me more?"

Micki hoped that her words worked on him as much as they worked on her. She squeezed her nipples, still raw.

"Mmm, don't you want to suck on my hard nipples, Jared?"

His eyes turned smoky and hedonistic.

Micki enjoyed voltage shooting through her body. *Let go, Jared. Whatever is troubling you, let it go.*

"Won't you put your thick, hard cock into my hungry pussy? I want to feel it there, too."

The glacier broke. Jared's hands came around her and landed on her chest. He pinched her berries, and liquid fire danced in her belly.

"So, there's a wicked tart inside Micki Langley. Let's just see about that." He pinched her even harder, and she couldn't hold back. Her hips instinctively ground back into Jared's body.

In a split-second, Jared had flipped her on her stomach on the bed. She turned her head to get a better look at him. He stood over her like a conquering warlord.

"You're not in charge here. Ever." Jared smacked her ass hard. "I'll let you know when I want you to talk. Nod if you understand."

A thrill shot through her. Jared would teach her more. More about sex. More about herself. She nodded.

"Good. First, I'm going to tie you up."

Micki felt unseen ropes circle her wrists and ankles.

"Next, for all that dirty talk, I'm going to spank your cute ass until it is bright pink. Understand."

Micki nodded and her ache deepened and spread out. Red flames poured out of her. She could see Jared's green smoke much more clearly than before.

"You can talk dirty, but only when I ask you to do it."

When was he going to start smacking her? The waiting drove her crazy, adding to her desire.

"You'll get your punishment when I decide." Jared shed all his clothes. His fully-erect cock promised more to come.

She wanted to squeeze her thighs together imagining him filling her pussy up with that thick monster, but the ropes tightened leaving her spread-eagle on her stomach.

"You want me to fill your pussy up?"

His hand came down hard on her ass. A sting of heat burned her cheeks. Micki swallowed hard and grabbed the sheets in her fists. She would not let the tears flow. She'd show him how strong she could be.

Another smack. And another.

She bit the pillow, resisting the urge to cry, but tears welled up. Hot waves inundated her backside, and she imagined him taking her there again.

Smack. Smack. Smack.

Her ass felt like molten magma that bubbled up desire.

"Not gonna cry. You're a very strong woman, Micki."

She felt strong, amazing.

Smack. Smack. Smack.

He never hit the same spot twice, ensuring every bit of her ass received his commanding touch. Rivers of warmth crested her boundaries.

"You promise to do what I say?"

She nodded, still face down on the bed.

Jared threw her a curveball as he began kissing her fired-up ass. Then she felt his tongue bathe her heated flesh. When he spread her backside apart, her excitement encompassed every part of her, from head to toe, pussy to tight ring.

Jared growled, "Okay, vixen, now, you can tell me what you want."

Her voice quivered, "I want you in me."

Smack.

A sting shot through her, sending a tremor of lust along the way. Red light shot out of her to the ceiling of the room.

"I want to hear vixen talk. You were so good at it earlier."

She swallowed hard. "I want your big, fat cock in me."

"Where, exactly?"

"In my ass."

Jared's breathing changed as it skated along her backside. "Keep talking."

Her lust swelled. "I want you to drive your dick hard into my ass. Deep."

She felt his tongue slip between her cheeks to the ring of desire. He pulled back and blew warm currents over it. She shuddered, and drove her hand between the bed and her clit.

"That's what I'll do then. I'm going to slide my dick into that tight hole of yours. I'm going to split you wide until you think you can't take it, but I won't stop."

Her head spun deliciously. "No, please. Don't stop."

"Then I will slow down. Let you think it is about over. But it won't be. I'll pound deeper still."

"Y-Yessss!" Micki had both hands working over her clit and pussy. His talk pushed her to an unrelenting frenzy.

"That's it, Micki. You wanted me to let go. You need to let go, too."

She felt the weight of his body cover her.

She felt his lubed-up finger drill into her.

O-Ohh!

Jared's mouth tightened over her left ear.

His cock slithered between her cheeks. Up and down. Teasing.

"Beg me to do it."

"P-Please!"

His cock pushed pass the tight ring and invaded her completely. When the shock subsided, electric spasms flared up inside her. She moved her hands frantically into her pussy. Faster and faster.

"That's it! You like me inside your ass?"

"Y-Yes!" Her body exploded with electric heat. *Jared, I'm so glad you're here. Please, don't ever leave me again.*

I won't!

An orgasm boiled to her surface.

"You come when I tell you that you can, understand?"

She was so close, she couldn't hold back.

He bit down hard on her ear and then released. "Do you understand, Micki?"

"I understand." She rocked back and forth. Her hands totally soaked from her slickness.

"That's my bad girl."

Pound, pound, pound.

Yes! God, yes!

Jared brought her close to the edge, and then as if he knew she couldn't hold back, slowed his pace. Bringing her down bit by bit. Then he increased his speed again, taking her higher and higher.

Ohh!

How many times did he bring her to the brink and then pull her back? Ten. Eleven. Twelve.

Still, he didn't let up. The enormous coming orgasm that converged inside her would not be denied much longer.

Please, I need to come…

Jared's rhythm changed inside her. His cock slammed in and out of her. The strokes lengthened with his tip slipping out of her ring and then slamming hard and deep back into her.

He yelled, "Now, you can come!"

Jared's last and final stroke inside her ass went to the deepest parts of her.

Micki plunged one hand into her channel as if trying to touch the tip of his dick through her fleshy wall, and the other she pressed against her clit.

A cyclone shot through her from clit to pussy to every fiber of her body. She came and came. Summits of vibrations, higher and higher. Liquid oozed out of her.

Jared guided her to her side. Facing her, he kissed her gently. He wrapped his arms around her tight. She felt safe.

Micki enjoyed the waves rolling through her. They continued for some time, weakening little by little.

* * * *

Bradley opened his eyes. Jared engulfed Micki's tied-up body.

He recalled the night he'd seen something similar. Gwyneth, spread-eagle, Jared on top of her. That night, Bradley had arrived too late.

"Get your fucking hands off of her, Jared!" Bradley shouted.

She turned to him, her eyes wide. "Jared said that only David could wake you."

"That's how it usually works." Jared stood up and grabbed her hand. "I guess your red energy broke David's spell, but he's still tied up by the archangel's cords."

Bradley wanted to pull her away from the murdering jinn. "Micki, you think you know him? You don't know a damn thing about him."

She sat up. "Bradley, please…"

"No. Tell her, Jared." His gut tightened. "Tell her how well you know how to fuck a woman."

Jared's eyes darkened. "Angel, I just made love to her, and she's fine."

"What about next time? Can you restrain yourself when you triple? I don't think you can."

Jared's eyes closed. Had his words hit their mark? Could he actually be reaching through to the jinn?

"I don't know if I can restrain myself," Jared glared at him. "But either way, you need to triple with me and Micki, soon."

Bradley gnashed his teeth. If he could just free one hand to punch

Jared… "Spoken like a Fallen."

Jared spat, "Look at how much energy you have left."

Bradley scanned his life force. The battle at the bank and his initial healing spell on Micki had drained almost all his energy.

Only a small speck of blue remained inside him. "Fuck that. I'll never triple with you again."

"It's me as your jinn-third, or no one."

"Are you threatening me?" Bradley clenched his jaw.

"I'm not surprised that David did tell you, so like him. Well, angel-boy, apparently you, Micki, and I formed a permanent bond the other night, what the Seven call a perfect triad."

Bradley had seen the cords, heard Micki's thoughts, felt the connection. It made sense.

Micki folded her arms. "What does that mean?"

"We're bonded together, forever." Jared's stare fixed on him. "Like it or not."

"You wouldn't know a damn thing about the truth." He turned to Micki. "You want to know the truth. Jared is a murder. He killed a woman. He fucked her to death with darklings surrounding them. He's one short fuck away from becoming a darkling himself. Do you want to be his next victim, Micki? Is that what you want?"

"Bradley, you think *you* know him, but you don't." Her eyes welled up. "I do know him. I know he carries a heavy burden, but he is good."

Bradley didn't trust the jinn, but he did trust Micki. Could the jinn be duping her somehow with his thoughts?

Jared stepped up to him and growled. "You think I didn't try to hold back. I tried. What was I supposed to do? David and Nash hadn't come."

"You broke your vow! You killed a human being!"

"You think you can control yourself? You think you're that strong?"

"I would never break my vow. No matter what happened. Ever!"

Jared's green smoke whirled around him. Was the jinn about to kill him? *So, be it.*

"Micki!" Jared shouted.

Not Micki! Don't you hurt her, you bastard!

She jerked up.

I won't ever hurt her, Bradley.

Jared turned to Micki, fresh lust spilling from his eyes. "Micki, say, yessir!"

She squeaked, "Yes, sir."

Red light shot out of her toward Bradley. His balls filled up, and his cock lengthened.

"We need to make sure that this angel can resist any temptation."

Part of Bradley wanted to pummel the jinn into the Ether, the other part, the part the jinn tested, wanted to fuck Micki into delirium—in a tripling with Jared.

What the hell is the matter with me?

Micki's cheeks flushed. "Yes, sir."

Jared walked over to him. When the jinn got next to him, he slid down the wall beside him.

"What the hell are you doing, Jared?"

"Making sure your mettle is as strong as you say."

"Fuck you!" Bradley twisted his arms and legs trying to break free. David's magic held.

Jared said, "Micki, I want you to crawl over to us."

She didn't move.

"Now!"

Bradley watched her tremble at the command. Her beautiful breasts heaved, naked and inviting. Lust washed over him. He wanted to triple like never before, wanted her between them, exchanging power and orgasms.

"Yes, sir!" She slid off the bed and down to the floor, her body totally exposed for his visual delight.

She moved toward them like a tigress, on hands and knees.

Bradley's gut tightened, this time, not from anger or fear, but from infinite want.

Jared's voice rumbled, "Go slow. That's it. Nice and easy. Don't touch either of us until you're told."

She nodded and licked her lips.

Holy hell! She's so hot!

"She is hot, Bradley. She's on fire. But I want her hotter." Jared pointed at Micki. "Now stand up."

Only inches from Bradley's feet, her scent wafted over him, and his cock hardened. He should tell her to stop, but he didn't.

Micki stood up. Tiny droplets of moisture decorated her tuft. Electric charges shot through him down to his dick.

"Step forward and put one foot on either side of his legs." Jared growled. "Remember, no touching until we say so."

"Yes, sir." Her power multiplied and spread out over him.

Bradley wanted to taste her, to fuck her, to turn her lust-filled red into an orgasmic rainbow. Every nerve vibrated in him.

Jared's green energy circled around Micki. "That's good. Move in closer. I want him to get a real good look at you."

Fuck these cords!

"Closer…"

At this distance, if Bradley's hands were freed, he could reach out and touch Micki's hot little pussy.

"Now, I want you to put on a show for us. Pinch your nipples."

Micki nodded. Her hands drifted over her chest, each one finding a hard berry nipple. She pinched them and let out a sigh.

Bradley's cock stiffened, and heat boiled inside him.

"Good. Now move one hand down your body. Go slow. That's it."

Micki followed Jared's command to the letter. How Bradley wanted to command her, to possess her.

"Press on your clit for us, Micki."

Instantly, her hand slipped to her bud of nerves and flicked it.

"Mmm…."

"Take your other hand and suck on your fingers imagining that they are a hard cock."

Bradley imagined that her fingers were his cock with her mouth inhaling it. The frenzy crashed inside him. He tried again to break free. If he did, he'd jump up and take her then and now.

He turned to the jinn, "Okay, Jared. You've made your point"

Jared shook his head. "Oh, no. Not even close. Micki, that finger you're sucking, tease your backside with it."

Bradley turned back to Micki. She had one hand working over her clit, the other rubbing her ass.

"That's a good girl," Jared's tone deepened.

Bradley's body burned. Hunger consumed him.

Jared conjured a dildo and he brought it up to her mouth. "Suck on this, Micki."

Her tongue shot out and licked the tip of the thing.

Bradley's control melted.

"Get it nice and wet," Jared instructed.

She swallowed the dildo.

"Good girl. Keep working on your clit." The jinn's breathing elongated.

Bradley couldn't imagine how hard his dick had become. He needed to be inside her. The teasing drove him wild.

"I want you to hold this toy."

She grabbed it with one hand, the other continued pressing her mound, then Bradley's head swam as Micki plunged a finger into her hot pussy. Her red power pulled on him, drawing out lust. Every muscle tense, ready to pounce. *Damn these cords!*

"Imagine your finger is Bradley inside you."

Yes, that's my cock inside you, Micki.

Bradley, put it into me. Pound me. Please!

"I've lubed up that dildo for you. Tease your backside ring with it."

Though Bradley couldn't see from his position, when she let out a moan, he knew the toy touched her entrance. Her red fire mingled with his blue light. He needed her. Needed a tripling. Fuck the consequences.

"Imagine that's my dick." Jared's green pulsed. "Push it into you. You can do it."

A second later, Micki jerked.

Bradley said, "Breathe, Micki."

"Micki, that toy is getting you ready for my dick."

Micki rocked back and forth with one hand in her cunt and the other in her backside. She jackhammered herself.

"Fuck yourself real good, Micki."

"Y-Yessir!"

Jared had proved his point, Bradley couldn't resist. Everything about her called to Bradley. He would not be denied.

"You getting close, Micki?" Jared asked.

"Mmm." *I-I'm so close.*

"You want to come?"

She breathed, "Y-Yes."

"Yes, what?" Jared snapped.

"Yessir! I-I want to come."

"Should we let her, Bradley? You give the order."

Waves of blistering heat rolled over him. He wanted to watch her come. "Yes. Come for us, Micki. Do it!"

Her fingers went in and out. "Ohmigod!"

"Do it!" he screamed.

Her head tilted back, her mouth opened. She let out a moan. Then she delighted him with an orgasm that caused her body to shake and her eyes to shed tears.

"Y-Yes!"

Bradley broke free of the cords. He wrapped Micki in his arms. He felt her climatic trembling, and his cock demanded release. "Get up, Jared! We have to triple now!"

Jared's eyes fixed on him. "Do you understand how control is an illusion? Anyone can be brought to the edge and then…"

"Yes, I understand. No one has absolute control." Supernova lust shot out of Bradley.

Jared nodded.

Bradley turned Micki back to him. "Micki, if you think the other night was amazing, just wait. We're going to fuck you so hard and so long that you're going see stars."

He pressed his mouth over hers. She moaned. His body quaked with desire.

Get in her, Jared!

The jinn fingered her backside.

Micki's red output warmed him.

Bradley reached around her and spread her cheeks for Jared. "You ready for him to plunge into your tight ass?"

"Yessir!"

Bradley pressed his dick against Micki's mound. He wanted in, but not before the jinn. "Do it, Jared!"

Without hesitation, the jinn drove deep into her.

Micki's eyes closed tight. "O-Ohh!"

Bradley felt her tense up. "Take his cock, Micki! You know you can! We were easy on you the other night, but not now!"

She opened her eyes, and he stared into those hazel-gold beauties. "God, you're extraordinary! Gorgeous! Fucking wonderful!"

"P-Please, Bradley. I need you."

Bradley couldn't hold back any longer. He needed to give her pleasure, to give her another orgasm. Needed to be inside her hot pussy. Needed the tripling with Micki and Jared. Not for the power, but for the connection. For the sense of belonging.

He drove his cock deep into her channel. He felt her rocking between him and Jared, her pussy and ring tightening around their dicks.

He brought his wings out, no need to keep them concealed. Jared's smoke swirled around them.

Micki's red power pulsed hot. "I'm—"

"Do it!!!"

She griped his cock tight with her inside muscles. He let his hot liquid spill deep into her channel.

Then he watched as part of Micki's red power flowed into him and turned blue. Another part went into Jared and turned green. But the last of Micki's power circled around her and became the colors of a rainbow.

For a split-second, a portal began to form out of rainbow light.

Bradley cupped her chin. "No, Micki. Don't!"

"I'm not doing anything." Her eyes widened with fear.

Before the opening to the Ether materialized completely, it dissipated.

He realized that he and Jared would have to teach Micki how to control her new powers, especially when tripling.

Chapter 18

The demons didn't know I could see them. My bloodline magic does come in handy from time to time.

I've locked all the doors and windows, all the good that will do. I've called David, but no answer. Where the hell is he?

Thank God Brooke left for her mother's this morning.

If anything happens to me, David better make sure Micki is safe.

God, I hope these creatures don't know about her.

Eric's Flash Drive: day 80—entry 12

* * * *

Micki woke up feeling wonderful aches. She felt guilty feeling so happy when Eric was in the hands of those…

Demons!

She sat up.

We've got to find Eric.

Jared looked up at her, head still on a pillow. "I told you, David is looking for him."

"We have to help him," she pleaded. "Find him."

Bradley stirred on the other side of her. "Sweetheart, that's too dangerous. The Alliance will find your brother."

"That's not good enough!" Somehow, she knew Eric was still alive.

She'd been having sex instead of looking for him. Micki put her face in her hands. But what could she do? Eric's captors were demons she knew nothing about fighting.

"Micki, my only concern is you." Bradley rubbed her shoulder.

"You're an angel, Jared's a jinn, and I'm a bloodliner. That's got to count for something. We're a... What did you call it Jared?"

"A perfect triad."

"Right. I've got powers now. I can feel them."

"That's true, Micki. But it's dangerous. David told the Seven about us. He also told them about how you've been changed."

Bradley glared at Jared. "Changed how?"

She turned to Jared. "I know I am some kind of bloodliner person, but what else has changed?"

"You aren't mortal anymore."

Not mortal? That couldn't be right. Try as she might to deny it, Jared's words rang true in her ears. A jangle of questions erupted. Not mortal. Would she live forever? What did that mean for her?

Micki asked, "Am I an angel or a jinn?"

"Neither."

"Then what am I, Jared?" she said, fighting back tears.

He put his arms tight around her. She pressed into his solid torso. It could've been a brick wall for a fortress to keep out the enemy. He felt good, but she couldn't stop shaking.

Jared cupped her chin. "You are an amazing woman, Micki. A human woman who is immortal."

"How can that be?" She needed Eric's flash drive. Where was it? She'd put it in her jeans at the bank.

"I am not sure, but your brother and David knew something about it."

"Eric?" Her lip quivered. "He did this to me?"

"No, but he did know something about it."

"Where are my jeans?"

"Over there, sweetheart."

Micki jumped from the bed, straight to them. She checked every pocket. Nothing.

"Where's the flash drive?" Her jaw clenched.

Jared stood up. "Damn it, I'll bet David took it."

"I think I'll ask him." Bradley leapt from the bed. "I don't want her near him."

Jared nodded. "He's downstairs. I think you and I should go see him together. If he doesn't give us the answers we want, well…"

"He'll give us answers. All of them."

Micki swung her legs off the bed. "I'm going, too."

"No, sweetheart. You're not." Then Bradley vanished.

Jared kissed her cheek. "We'll be just downstairs, and we won't be long."

Green smoke surrounded him and he dematerialized.

Micki heard the door lock. "Assholes!"

* * * *

Micki felt something oppressive, like the humidity of decomposing bodies. She stood in a dark corridor filled with creatures scurrying by her as if she wasn't there. The walls leeched globs of black liquid where the only light came from flickering lanterns. She was underground, but where? How had she gotten there?

A scream.

She ran toward it. Could it be Eric? Would she be next?

When she rushed by the crowd of horned people, she saw her brother, his body naked and shackled to a circa-Salem Witch Trials' stockade. He bled from cuts, both fresh and old. The crowd laughed. The creature closest to Eric took something metal, what looked to Micki to be some sort of poker with a sharp blade attached to the end of it, and rammed the thing into her brother. Micki expected to hear Eric scream, but she only heard her own. 'No!' she cried out in the dream.

The nightmare dissolved, and the Persian room solidified around her.

Oh dear God! Could the vision be real? All her other visions had come true.

Micki pulled her knees into her chest. Despair took her.

She'd seen Jared and Bradley in action at the bank. They could take on several demons without any help from anyone. If they could triple again, they could create a fucking magical nuclear bomb to blast Eric out of that hell she'd seen him in.

She didn't have much to go on, but she would act. *By myself?* How could she face the monsters alone? There had to be another way.

There is, a stranger's thought offered.

"Where are you? And who are you?" Micki pulled the sheet from the bed and wrapped it around her body.

She felt horror grip her. The man with the mirrored sunglasses that had attacked them at the bank appeared. How had he made it past David's guards, past Jared and Bradley?

Not at Zone Three. I am with Eric. What you see is only a projection of me.

With Eric? Panic ripped her to shreds.

Yes. His powers are helping me to reach you. Micki, I am reasonable. You have been seduced into something you have no business of being a part of. Both you and your brother.

"So, what do you want?" she whispered.

Micki closed her eyes. Now, she saw not just the man, but Eric in shackles, naked and bleeding, next to him.

That's right. You have power now. Power that will only cause pain for you and Eric.

She should scream for Jared and Bradley, this was the closest she'd been to answers about her brother and she wasn't stopping now.

This war is not your war. What do you need of this magic?

He seemed to be looking directly at her, a handsome face. She wanted to open her own eyes and end the vision of him, but she didn't. She must find a way to get Eric to safety. This might be the only way.

"How can I trust you?"

Do you trust David? He wants you for a book. Isn't he the one in charge there? Aren't you his prisoner?

It hurt her, but she couldn't deny the truth of it.

The voice continued, *I only want one favor from you. Do it, and I will release Eric, and you and your brother can be free of this insanity.*

Micki wanted to believe him. *This might be the only chance.*

"What favor?"

First, you have to get out of Zone Three.

"And how do I do that?"

With some help from me. Concentrate, Micki. You have the power. You just don't know how to use it. I do.

Micki closed her eyes tighter. Jared and Bradley's faces came into view.

Concentrate!

The faces disappeared replaced by dark eyes. She felt the pain in her left side return, difficult to tolerate, but she did. A black cord appeared in her mind.

Good. That's it. Just a little more.

Micki smelled an acidic odor. Then she heard a crackle. She opened her eyes and saw five horned men in the room with her. She pulled the sheet tight around her.

Immediately, two of them grabbed her and walked her right into the wall. It melted around them, and then she floated between her new captors on the outside of Zone Three.

You promised to let Eric and me go when I do this favor.

Come to me, Micki. It will all be over soon.

* * * *

Bradley scowled. "Where's the flash drive, David?"

"Better answer him, my friend." Jared liked Bradley's directness.

"Or would you like to face our triple juice bloodline power first hand."

David downed a shot of tequila and slammed the glass next to four other empty glasses. "I'm having it decoded."

"That drive is the only connection Micki has to her brother." Bradley's face darkened. "Did you ever think of that? You could've let us know."

David shrugged.

"Did you even think to ask her for it? In Eric's absence, it's her possession. You need to give it back to her, right now."

Jared's stomach tightened. "You set this whole thing up. Her brother's voicemail, that was you wasn't it?"

"Yes."

Bradley asked, "Why didn't you tell me at the club about this perfect triad business when we were getting drinks for Micki and Brooke?"

Jared wanted to know as well.

"You wouldn't have believed me, Bradley. Besides, at the time, you didn't trust this jinn or me."

Jared hated how well David manipulated everyone, always three steps ahead.

Bradley glared at the archangel. "I still don't trust you, asshole."

Rafiq bolted down the stairs. "There's been a breach in the stronghold!"

Micki!

Jared and Bradley flew up the stairs to the locked door of the Persian room where they'd left her.

Jared felt a crackle of power vibrate from behind the door. An odor of foul sulfur drifted out from the gap under it.

He knocked the door off its hinges and formed green smoke scimitars. Next to him, Bradley conjured his blue sword.

They didn't find Micki. Instead seven high-level demons stood, weapons ready.

Jared yelled, "If you've done anything to her—"

"You'll do what?" one spat.

Jared's rage pushed, and he attacked, deciding in a split-second to show—and not to tell—exactly what he would do. Bradley flew by his side, sword swinging.

He and Bradley hit an invisible wall before they could get to them. Superhuman energy filled the room. The potency of the magic slammed Jared to the floor. He tried to get up, but the weight of something like a mountain held him down.

I can't move, Bradley.

Neither can I. He heard angels and jinn heading up the stairs.

All too often, the Dark seemed to out-maneuver the Alliance. The impenetrable Zone Three had been *penetrated.*

Bradley, she's close. I can still feel her.

I can, too. Bradley sent out to her, *Micki, can you hear me?*

Nothing.

As Alliance warriors entered the room, they exploded into nothingness with a single flick of one of the creature's fingers.

"Enough of this," one of the monsters said.

"Bind the jinn and angel," another commanded.

They fashioned potent invisible ropes around his and Bradley's arms and legs. Jared struggled to free himself, but the energy held fast.

David materialized in the room in a flash of blue flame. "You will not take them!"

At first the creatures stumbled back as the archangel shot rays of hot light in every direction.

Then Jared saw David grimace.

The archangel stumbled back, enormous black flames wrapped around him.

Vincorte sent from outside the room, *That's right, David. So predictable.*

David fell to the ground. *Vincorte! Where are you? How are you doing this?*

Your darling Micki isn't the only human power plant.

Is that how you got through my defenses at the bank?

Vincorte laughed. *You're much smarter than the others on your council.*

Has Eric opened the portal for you?

Maybe not so smart. Why would I be here if he had, David? But I've been able to tap into some of that wonderful bloodline power. And with Ms. Langley, Jared and Bradley, I have no doubt that my master will be free from the Ether tonight.

David had played right into the archdemon's hand. If David stayed three steps ahead, Vincorte stayed three hundred.

Bradley, we have to let them take us. It's Micki's only chance.

I know.

Vincorte sent from outside the room, *We will dine together on her delicious suffering.*

"You'll fucking regret you ever met me, Vincorte. You motherfucker!" Jared spat.

The darklings slipped them through the wall to the outside.

"Struggling is futile," one of the brutes said.

"I won't kill her," Jared informed.

"I understand you've promised that before."

* * * *

At Zone Three, the demons had placed a black bag over Jared's head. He sensed its dark enchantment. He'd tried to call to Micki and to Bradley, but the thing blocked out everything.

He and Bradley had been split up immediately. At first, he'd heard some clashes, probably a few Alliance warriors trying to take on Vincorte's band, then silence. If an archangel couldn't take them on, Jared held no hope for any others.

"Move it, jinn!" one of his captors yelled removing the bag.

Jared's eyes adjusted to the dim light. A curved concrete ceiling, about ten feet above his head, closed out the world above. His captors bound him with powerful magic before forcing him across some tracks. The place reminded him of another residence of the Dark from long ago, and he felt remorse rush in like a flood. The commotion inside his head eroded his willpower drip by drip.

Gwyneth was bound with her legs spread apart. She still wore her corset—though no other clothing covered her. At least a hundred darklings surrounded her. Being the lone Alliance warrior in shackles, Jared felt helpless.

Terrok led him up to her.

"The choice to save her from the torture I can give her is yours, Jared." Terrok's eyes danced in the firelight.

Gwyneth turned to Jared, her hazel-gold eyes wet and pleading.

Her skin glowed in the firelight and her deep gashes bled. A demon, one chosen for their tripling, stood at her side waiting for him. Vincorte.

Jared did not move. He just stood there. Gwyneth was Nash's woman. Nash, his friend, his fellow warrior, his student.

Jared wouldn't harm her.

"Very well," Terrok said. Black lightning shot out of his talons and sliced Gwyneth's stomach. Blood splashed everywhere, like a fountain.

She screamed so loudly Jared's ears felt like they would bleed. If it weren't for his restraints, he'd blast Terrok with every ounce of his remaining power.

The demon prince lifted a finger and the wound closed.

"You can not stop her suffering by fighting me," Terrok informed him and grinned.

Jared's hope evaporated. He dove into her. At least he could take her quickly—end this.

Jared had tried to keep the evil lust at bay, but as he and Vincorte fucked Gwyneth, it consumed him bit by bit.

"Please, no," Gwyneth begged. "Do not, Jared."

Her pleas went unheeded, and dark tendrils wrapped around his heart.

He bit into her flesh, nearly drawing blood. He felt a smile grow on his face as she screamed. God, forgive me, he loved hearing her scream.

Finally, Jared did stop Gwyneth's suffering just before the warriors of the Alliance, with David and Nash in the lead, entered Terrok's lair discharging immense energies.

The Ether opened and Terrok's eyes went wide as he was sucked into the immortal prison.

Jared shook off the barrage of images and emotions that bore into him. He knew his own guilt. It had been his one and only constant companion for so many years. He cleared his mind of the past, and images of Micki chained and writhing in pain floated to the surface of his consciousness.

He knew, too well, what mind games these fuckers could play.

Jared, welcome! Terrok's voice exploded inside his head.

Pain. Pulsing pain.

It couldn't be. He'd escaped the Ether?

Not yes, but soon, the evil creature answered.

"But how can you reach through from the Ether, Terrok?" he asked fighting back the acute hurt between his ears.

Terrok's sent, *All in good time. I hate unfinished business. And you, Jared, are at the top of that list.*

Jared felt the intruder leave his mind. The pain eased with Terrok's exit, leaving a hot stinging in his head as a reminder of the visit.

As the monsters took him deeper into the mine, he saw more demons and ifrit, many with their victims. Some of the victims screamed. Others stared blankly at nothing.

The chaos felt too familiar.

They passed through one tunnel where he saw a man chained to a table, spread-eagle. Two females, one demon and one ifrit, bit chunks of flesh from his body while stroking the man's cock.

The sight brought on a longing for the energy that he'd received tripling with Micki and Bradley. With it, he could blow the doors off of this place of horror, but that was the very essence of the dark lust: the desire for power.

Jared shuffled along but studied all he passed as his captors walked him deeper into the evil lair. The flickering lantern on the left, the discarded shovel by the last entryway, the board with the single nail, each turn, later he must recall to ensure Micki's escape. He needed to find a way out for her. He must.

The darklings pushed him into a large expanse. A natural limestone cavern filled with dripping stalactites on the ceiling and receiving stalagmites on the floor. It looked like the inside of a shark's jaw. Hundreds of the creatures of the Dark bustled in every direction.

Then Jared spotted a figure he recognized. Unblinking eyes stared back at him.

"Over here," Vincorte ordered.

The two holding him walked him toward the man.

Now, no mirrored sunglasses hid the archdemon's steel-blue eyes. He let his leathery wings stretch out and then folded them in with a yawn.

Arrogant bastard!

"Welcome, Jared," he greeted.

"Vinnie, you need these guys to keep a little weak jinn of my level from harming you? And I thought you were a badass."

The demon smiled. "I am."

Vincorte waved the guards away. Jared still had his arms behind his back, the power rope tight.

"I see the Dark hasn't changed their love of the underground," Jared said, tilting his head to the cavern.

"It is necessary to keep our secrets."

"Sure. Subterranean. I get it."

"But everything will change soon."

"Really?"

Jared wanted to keep Vincorte talking. From his peripheral vision, he spotted a glimmer of light on the far side of the cave. *A way out?*

"You will help with that. You and the woman."

Jared clenched his teeth. The game had begun, but this time he would not be a pawn. Not again.

"Where is she?"

"Close. But you should not concern yourself about that."

This fucker was about to release Terrok on the world, and he expected Jared to help. Anger flooded into him, and guilt.

"I won't kill Micki."

The perpetual sea of bodies that the Dark had murdered over the ages stretched across the horizon of his mind. Terrok seared Jared's mind with the vision from all those years ago.

Visions of millions dying at the Dark's hands. Killed in plagues, famine, war—and even up close and personal. They specialized in painful deaths.

Jared would not add Micki to their numbers. He desired her, every part of her, more than any woman he'd ever wanted in his long life. He would never touch her now.

"You know the choice," Vincorte taunted.

He would make sure that he didn't have to make that choice. He would find Micki and get her out, hopefully to Bradley. Then he would come back to Vincorte and his gang of assholes and would blast to hell as many as he could with all the power inside him. Until every bit of energy vanished. Then he would join Terrok—in the Ether, right where both he and the evil monster belonged.

Chapter 19

Micki paced inside her cell. She clung to the sheet around her body, willing it to transport her back to Zone Three—to Jared and Bradley. Nothing happened, of course. *So much for my new power.*

Decaying smells filled her nostrils, and nausea took up residence in her stomach. She pinched her nose. Even breathing through her mouth, the stench of the place made its way to her olfactory receptors and the acid in the air landed on her taste buds.

When the freaks had flung her inside the filthy place, she hadn't uttered one syllable.

Eric's life hung in the balance and now her life, as well.

Her captors had the upper hand. No, she didn't say anything, wishing not to provoke them. Best to just follow along, but wasn't that exactly what had got her into this nightmare in the first place? Following along?

Micki grimaced at her own foolishness.

She needed Jared and Bradley, but they were far from here—and her. Could they find her in this hell hole? She didn't know, but she prayed they would.

Micki looked beyond the steel bars. The beast outside her cell stayed immobile. Though more dreadful than any she'd seen this night, he didn't move to harm her. He was at least eight feet tall with four arms as massive as tree trunks, and in place of legs—tentacles. The only thing that resembled a human on the thing happened to be its face, though fangs jutted out from its thin blue lips.

As Micki paced, the monster's head turned, following her back-and-forth pattern inside the cell. She felt utterly helpless, and she expected she would die—and soon.

Footsteps pulled her from her thoughts. They came from the end of the hall where she'd entered the row of cells earlier. Time's up? She felt a sudden rush of cold—like ice water—pulse through her, overpowering and pushing out what little hope she held onto.

The tentacled creature shuffled away into a dark corner. It feared whatever the hell headed her way.

She didn't have any place to hide from the horror that approached.

When the footsteps ended, a man stood on the other side of the bars. He looked human on the outside, but she suspected something much different on the inside. She'd seen the horns back at her bank, though now they didn't appear. About six and half feet tall, his body muscular.

He'd been the intruder at the bank wearing the mirrored sunglasses, now his steel blue eyes fixed on her.

He held a bottle and a brown sack. *Is he having a picnic and I'm the main course? The food?*

"Hello, Micki."

She recognized the voice immediately, the same one she'd heard that promised to free Eric. But would he?

"I apologize for the crudeness of my children. I hope you will forgive them their bad manners. We don't entertain the likes of you very often."

His voice pretended comfort, but hidden just under its surface lived an oppressive confidence and an ever-present threat.

"I hope you are hungry."

Swallowing hard, Micki pushed her courage to the back of her throat and spoke. "Where is my brother?"

"Everyone seems to be in a hurry tonight. Lost on this modern world are the occasions that require deliberate contemplation."

"What have you done with Eric, you bastard?" Micki kept the sheet snug around her body as if it were a suit of armor.

The man mocked her with a smile. He waved his hand, and the

bars changed to black flames. He walked through them into her cell, and the bars turned back to steel.

Micki's heart sank. She'd been a fool to come. She should've screamed for Jared when she'd first heard this man's voice at Zone Three. Instead, like a tiny mouse to a pack of rabid cats, she'd walked into an evil trap.

"I am Vincorte, and I am happy to be your host this evening."

He held up the bottle that looked to be white wine.

A picnic it is.

"Humans like you and your brother were thought to be…"

"To be what?"

"How do I say this delicately? Extinct."

Vincorte pulled out two glasses from the sack and motioned for her to sit.

Micki wondered if he served her liquid poison.

"You mean bloodliners?"

"So, the do-gooders did tell you some things. You are of a very special breed of human."

Micki sat. Her nerves didn't relax, but she would comply, hoping she might still have a chance to save Eric and herself.

Vincorte sat down on the ground with her and crossed his legs. He pulled a bottle opener from the same brown sack. Micki watched as he poured a generous amount of libation in each glass. He held one out to her. She took it but didn't drink from it.

Looking inside the sack, Vincorte said, "I have cheese and crackers, if you'd like. You must be starving."

"What doesn't that sack have?" Micki answered nervously.

He laughed. His manner eased some of her terror, though she didn't know why. So strange.

"I'll give you whatever you want, but I want you to free my brother."

"I promised you as much." He took a long swig on the wine in his glass. He sat it back down, half empty.

Micki gazed into her glass. The yellow liquid sloshed inside it, disturbed by her shaking hand.

"What is this favor you want? How did I get this new power inside me? How do I get rid of it?"

"Shh." he commanded, whispering, holding his index finger to his lips.

He picked up his glass and drained the rest of its contents. Then his steel-blue eyes found hers.

"Too many questions. You are definitely a product of this age, my dear."

"Yes, and I'm only going to keep getting more impatient until you give me a straight answer about my brother."

The man had poured the wine from the same bottle into their glasses. He'd taken a long drink. Not poisoned. She needed courage, and liquid courage would have to suffice. Micki put her lips to the glass and sipped the wine. Its sweetness danced on her tongue.

"Delicious, isn't it?" he asked, his voice musical.

"Yes." Micki's head spun.

"You fell into power that is very dangerous for someone like you. I will free you from it and from the memories of all you have seen these past few nights."

How could he erase everything? Even her memories of Jared and Bradley? That just wasn't possible. She knew Vincorte lied.

Unless he meant to kill her.

She took in another drink. She missed her champions. They weren't riding in on white horses and scooping her up and away. Why? Because this wasn't just her fantasy. This was real. A real nightmare.

Micki felt her body slump. Her head spun.

"Lie quiet, Micki."

He'd poisoned her wine.

"You d-damn liar." She heard her voice slur.

* * * *

Micki awoke to low moans. She opened her eyes to find she'd been moved to another cell, much larger than the first. The sounds of disquiet came from a figure chained to a table.

Eric!

She ran to him. His wounds went deep and dark. His eyes were swollen shut, but he stirred when she put her hand over his.

Thank God, he's still alive. He meant so much to her. Though seeing him in this condition pained her, she didn't care. She needed to be with him, no matter what. Her heart softened. They were together. She'd finally found him.

"Eric, it's Micki. Everything is going to be fine," she lied and felt the tears stream down her cheeks.

She gingerly touched his face.

He choked out, "Sis, is that really y-you?"

"It's me."

"Thank God, you're okay."

"Eric. Don't talk." If they had to die tonight, at least they'd be together.

"Micki?"

"I'm here, Eric." *I can't face this!*

"We are blood…" he wheezed.

"Bloodliners, I know. It's okay."

Dark liquid shot out of his mouth.

"Please, Eric. You don't have to tell me anything."

"Brooke?"

"She's okay. She's safe." Eric's girlfriend would never know what happened to them.

"I-I'm so glad."

"Rest, Eric." Micki hummed a lullaby, and shed more tears for her brother.

"There's a book. I put it in a place that I thought was safe."

The book of Timu? The thing all these assholes wanted. "Eric, where did you put it?"

A fit of coughing took him.

Her gut wrenched. "It's okay. Don't speak."

Sis, I never opened the Ether for them. No matter what they did. I never opened it.

He must've put the book in there to protect her.

She swallowed back her tears. *I know.*

Eric's body convulsed.

A crushing black hole weighed down on Micki's heart. She hated seeing him this way and knowing what lay ahead. She put her head in her hands and sobbed uncontrollably.

"David, Brooke is not to be a part of this."

She'd brought Brooke to Zone Three. If something happened to her, it would be Micki's fault.

"Make sure our cousin is safe."

Cousin? Eric continued rambling, drifting in and out of reality for several more minutes.

Finally, he seemed to rest, breathing slowly.

Micki sensed they weren't alone. She looked left, and saw Vincorte magically appear.

"See, your brother is alive just like I told you."

Micki screamed, "Vincorte, you fucking asshole!!!"

She pounded her fists on his chest. He grabbed her wrists, stopping her.

"Guilty!" Vincorte patted Eric's leg.

"Don't you touch him!"

"Micki, all you have to do is open the Ether for my master, and Eric lives."

"You're lying."

"Maybe."

Her gut tightened. "I don't know how I did it before."

"No worries, my dear. Best to recreate the scene of the crime, if you know what I mean."

* * * *

Jared's head pounded from his attempts to contact Bradley. Every thought had just bounced back into him after they hit the demonic magic in the walls of the cell. Then he'd tried to contact David at least a dozen times. Same result, no matter, he would keep trying to find an opportunity to rescue Micki.

"She is amazing," Vincorte said, stepping out from the shadows.

Jared yelled, "You are a dead immortal!"

A toothy smile appeared on the archdemon's face. His looks matched any leading man's in Hollywood. Twenty dark warriors accompanied him.

Vincorte raised his left hand up, and bile grew inside Jared until he thought he might spew. If he did, he planned on projecting the entire contents toward the bastard.

"I would not if I were you," Vincorte quipped.

"But Vinnie, you aren't me."

"I love how you never miss the obvious, Jared."

"I love how darklings never realize when they've lost."

Vincorte lowered his hand. Jared felt the grip of nausea ease.

"Arrogant. You will so fit in."

"Fuck you!"

"Excellent, Jared. But for now, we do have business to conduct."

"I told you, I won't have anything to do with it."

"That is your choice."

"Let her go, motherfucker!"

The archdemon glared at him. "Not likely."

"What do you want then?"

"In exchange for Ms. Langley's release? Well…"

"Do you want me?"

As the words left Jared's mouth, he realized what he offered.

Himself. His soul.

If Vincorte would release Micki, he would join their dark brood. He couldn't kill her, but he couldn't see her tortured, either. The only way he could escape both possibilities was to accept rebirth into the Dark. He knew what that meant.

"That is interesting."

"Vincorte, if I join you, will you let her go?"

"You're already one of us. You just haven't accepted it yet, but you will."

"You are wrong."

"This above all, to thine own self be true," Vincorte quoted from the centuries old play. "Would you like to see her?"

"You already know the answer to that."

The door opened, and he walked out of the cell. The darklings escorted him and their master down the corridor—a corridor like the one he walked with Terrok all those years ago—to his victim.

He silently repeated his vow to never let that happen, ever again. Jared's former plan stayed at the forefront of his mind: get to Micki, use every bit of power left him, and get her to safety. No matter the cost.

Then he heard Micki. "Like what you see, assholes!"

Why?

As they approached the cavern, he heard her thoughts.

I wish I'd told Jared and Bradley how much I love them.

Love? He'd never felt it before. Now he knew he loved her, and for the first time, understood what that really meant.

When Vincorte turned him to their final destination, Jared realized how fruitless attempting any rescue would be.

Dimly lit, he saw an assembly of at least two thousand dark immortals. Not one whisper, one sigh or one word passed any of the crowd's hideous lips. Their collective attention centered on two naked figures chained to a stone altar—an angry *Micki and an unconscious angel.*

Bradley!

"When the angel comes to, I believe he will be hesitant. You can help," repeated Vincorte.

"Want to resurrect Terrok?"

"Yes."

"Vinnie, don't you know what Terrok will do if this does work?"

"Oh, yes."

"I don't think you do."

"Jared, the choice is yours."

Vincorte raised his hands and the evil crowd inched toward the pair that held Jared's every thought captive.

"Stop them, Vincorte!" Jared shouted, defeated.

The archdemon lowered his hand, and the crowd stepped back.

A path cleared for him to Micki and Bradley.

Jared would not kill again, but he could guide the angel to ensure the evil deed occurred without pain.

Chapter 20

Micki struggled against the shackles on her wrists and ankles that chained her naked body to the stone table. She shivered from the cold touch of the slab against her backside and the gazes from the throng of lecherous demons around her.

She missed the sheet she'd stolen from Zone Three.

After Vincorte had secured her to the stone, he'd brought in a comatose Bradley, wings hanging limp. At first, she'd thought him dead, but realized, watching his chest rise and fall, he did breathe.

Like her, Bradley had been stripped and shackled to chains that went through holes on the table. On his back, his semi-hard cock jutted against his stomach. She wanted to touch him, to feel his strength, but her chains were too taut. They were attached to some kind of crank under the table that Vincorte had tightened before leaving.

Bastard!

She screamed at the crowd. "What do you assholes want from us?"

Some smiled wickedly, but none made a sound. What were they waiting for?

Micki turned her head to the side, and looked again at the other table. The contents terrified her: chains, whips, clamps, paddles—and knives.

She turned the other direction and spotted Vincorte returning. Next to him...

Jared! You're here!

His face sunk. Micki felt her heart jump. She wanted him close.

She needed him.

He walked up to her, but stopped just out of reach—for touching.

She wanted to shelter herself in his strong arms, wanted him to lie to her that everything would be okay.

Why wouldn't Jared hold her?

Her mind reeled. She held no hope of survival, but at least she had Jared and Bradley with her.

"Jared," she called out.

He looked up but didn't move. What held him back? She didn't know. He wanted to protect her, but his eyes showed defeat. She wanted to ease the struggle inside him.

"How this ends depends on what you do, Jared." Vincorte walked over and pinched her nipples hard.

Micki shrieked.

Jared grabbed his hands and pulled him away. "Get your fucking claws off of her!"

"Then get on with it, jinn. Or, I will."

"Loosen her chains," Jared commanded.

Vincorte nodded. "If you try anything, jinn, it will only make things worse for her, do you understand?"

He nodded.

Micki felt her bindings relax,

Jared stepped closer. "Wake the angel."

Vincorte raised his hand, and a black flame flew from it to Bradley's body. "Done."

Micki watched as Bradley attained consciousness in seconds. He fought against his shackles with such strength she thought he might actually break free, but he didn't.

When he turned his head toward her, recognition filled his eyes. His face went blood red, and he pulled his massive arms up. One chain broke. For a moment, she actually allowed herself to hope.

"You darkling assholes will pay for this!" Bradley screamed.

Micki heard the thought Jared sent to Bradley. *Angel, we've lost.*

Bradley turned to him. "You! You're actually going to give in to these fuckers!"

"Bradley, look around."

Shivers of terror ran up her spine.

He continued, "There's over two thousand of them, and that's just the ones in this room."

Her angel scanned the room. After a few seconds, he, too, realized they were fucked.

Vincorte laughed. "Excellent."

Her biker glared. "Loosen his chains."

Micki heard the clank of the metal unwinding from the crank.

Bradley rolled over to her. Skin to skin. Red hot fire shot through her.

He covered her body with his. Her angel, her hero.

"That won't do, angel." Vincorte spat. "We're here to see all her pleasure and pain."

"Fuck you!" Bradley shot back.

"No, fuck you. And if you and this jinn don't do what I want, then I'll let my children at Ms. Langley. They've been hungering to chew on her hot cunt for sometime."

Micki whispered into Bradley's ear, "You don't have to do it. They're going to do whatever they want anyway, and I don't want them to hurt you."

Bradley placed his hand between her legs and nibbled her ear. He kissed her. *I'll be gentle. It will be okay.*

His wings hung limp around her.

Jared commanded, "Bradley, they want to see."

I don't give a damn what they want.

Jared sent, *You better or they'll torture Micki beyond anything you can imagine.*

She looked into Bradley's blue eyes seeming to darken and glaze over.

Her angel crawled between her legs and kissed along the inside of her thighs. She needed his strength, his caring to help her make it through this nightmare.

A jolt shot through her when Bradley flicked his tongue over her clit. She looked up and saw Jared. He stood at her shoulders, closer, but still he didn't touch her.

Bradley slid another finger into her and kept licking her clit. She felt the pull of unconsciousness again. She cried out.

Their audience sighed with every moan she took. She hated them for it. She wanted to stop but couldn't. Her body burned, and without someone's touch, agony.

The wine Vincorte had given her? An aphrodisiac?

She wanted Jared, needed him. Why didn't he touch her? She could tell he wanted to, wanted to be with them, wanted to join in what they had enjoyed that first night together. She knew it. Still, something continued to hold him back.

Was it because Vincorte wanted the three of them to join together in sex?

She didn't really care why. Her mind spun wildly, illogically. She wanted to comply. Every cell in her body tingled red hot, anticipating both her men inside her. Micki loved Jared and Bradley.

Please, Jared. I need you.

He didn't answer either in thought or word. He closed his mind off to her.

Oh God! He's losing himself to darkness to save me. Despair locked down on her heart.

Micki longed for him to touch her. She looked up at him, his features upside down from her view. His dark eyes nearly closed as if he couldn't bear to look at her.

When a tear fell from Jared's eyes and touched her cheek, Micki felt a sudden rush through her entire body—exploding as it went—from her cheeks, down to her chest, to her stomach and between her legs where Bradley continued to work with fingers and tongue on her clit. An earthquake of movement rocked inside her body.

She closed her eyes.

"Get to it!" Vincorte hissed. "I've given her a potion that will have her begging my children to take her if you don't."

The rainbow shimmered. The wings stretched out. The smoke warmed.

"Enough of the sweet stuff," Vincorte spat. "Use something from the other table. I want to see her feel some pain."

O-Oh no!

"I do, too!" Jared laughed wickedly.

She grappled with her fear, shooting through her like a million needles.

Vincorte smiled. "Excellent, my brother."

Bradley's head shot up. *I'll kill you, jinn!*

Jared sent, *Bradley, it's the only way. Hold your thoughts to only Micki and me. Can you hear my thoughts, Micki?*

Yes.

Good. You know we'd save you if we could. Jared's hand brushed her hair back from her face.

Yes, I know.

If we play along, we can keep them off of you. We can make this as painless as possible.

Bradley shot back, *And if we don't?*

Micki stroked the top of Bradley's head. *Oh, my loves, don't. It's too high a price.*

She reached up and touched his hand. Bradley moved up and kissed her abdomen. Micki shuddered. She looked down at him.

"I love you, Bradley."

"I love you," he whispered.

She looked up. Jared's apprehension entered her entire mind. She must reach him.

Jared commanded. "Roll her over, angel."

Bradley rolled her on her belly. The stone pressed against her moistening mound and hardening nipples.

"Give me a paddle," Jared pointed to the table.

The crowd's gleeful cheers echoed in the cavern.

A shout from one of the darklings echoed. "She will open the Ether as she dies, and our Prince Terrok will be free!"

I'll never open it. Never!

"Quiet, children!" Vincorte yelled.

A hush followed.

Jared sent, *Micki, I have to make this look real. You understand?*

Yes.

Smack.

"O-Ouch!" Her flesh stung. Sweat poured out of her.

"Did I say you could talk, slut?" Jared yelled.

He landed more strikes with the paddle on her backside. One. Two. Three. The stinging felt blistering hot.

Tears poured out of her like rushing water.

Stop it, asshole. Bradley's thoughts to Jared blasted into her.

No, Bradley. He's right. I'm okay. Really.

"You want a crack at her, angel?" Jared asked. *You've got to do this, or Vincorte will unleash these motherfuckers on her.*

Micki looked over her shoulder and saw Bradley clench his teeth.

"Yes, give it to me," her angel extended his hand for the paddle.

"I will, and then you give it to her."

She felt the paddle land a bit softer on her than before.

"Pussy-boy," Jared taunted. "You can do better than that."

Bradley's next strikes drew out tears from the hits to her ass.

Micki saw stars. The pain shot through her and mixed with her growing desire. She wanted Jared and Bradley inside her. Needed them.

"Blister her ass!" her jinn continued.

Smack. Smack. Smack.

O-Ohh! She bit her lip trying to hold back the outburst trying to slip from her lips.

An ache of lust bore through her. She ground her mound into the stone, rubbing it raw.

Jared commanded, "Roll over, slut!"

She obeyed. When she looked up, she saw Bradley's eye color had darkened to a grayish blue, and his wings took on a gray cast.

What's wrong with you, Bradley?

I'm still here, sweetheart. I'm holding on.

Something more than his eye color changed inside him.

Then she looked over at Jared, his face darkened. Had he changed, too?

"Give me two clamps for her nipples." A wicked grin spread across his face.

Her stomach flipped over.

Jared got right up to her face, his breath felt hot. *Hang on to your chains. It will help with the pain.*

Micki reached past her shackles and grasped the metal cables in both hands.

"Angel, kiss her hot cunt!"

Bradley dove his tongue deep into her pussy. Micki vibrated from the work over of his mouth.

Jared fastened both clamps onto her nipples. Red light and massive pain exploded behind her eyes.

He sent, *Breathe, Micki.*

Bradley agreed, *Yes, just breathe through it.*

The pain subsided. She felt like she floated above the scene.

Then her champion's thoughts left her. She couldn't reach him, no matter how hard she tried.

"You making her cunt hot and wet for your cock, angel?" Jared asked.

He answered, "This slut is drowning in desire."

Now, madness seemed to overtake Bradley.

Jared?

Yes? He took off the clamps on her nipples. An ache replaced the pain they'd been causing her.

I want you to know that I love you.

He didn't answer, but his mind opened fully to her. No more walls. No more boundaries.

Jared's memories rushed into Micki's mind. First, a woman who trusted him came into view, then a demonic crowd surrounding the woman—and Jared. The monsters wanted to harm the woman—harm her in horrific ways.

He struggled in the image. He could stop it, but only through one way, take the last of her energy and her life.

The evil spidery-like man laughed, because right before the woman died, he'd used her power and opened a portal. But an instant later, David and other warriors arrived on the scene, and the monster fell into the Ether just as the portal snapped shut, imprisoning him. Many of the monstrous crowd had been sliced to ribbons but a few escaped including Vincorte.

The good guys won the day, but came too late for the woman. Jared had saved her from torture, but his guilt stayed deep inside him to his very core.

Micki pushed deeper, into his blackest pain and deep suffering that Jared had carried all those years.

Tears streamed down Micki's cheeks.

Jared couldn't touch her no matter how much she wanted him to, and she would never ask given what she knew now about his torment.

Bradley positioned himself on top of her. His eyes gaped apart, showing only the animal left inside him. A pang of sadness filled her as she realized he would share the same kind of pain and guilt as Jared. Changed forever. She hated the thought of it. She knew what it would mean for him to invade her body. The coupling would pull whatever life she had left out of her. No knights saddled up to ride in to save her. She wanted it to be over. All of it.

Her maddened angel lover plunged deep into her pussy, lost to whatever darkness the monsters fed him.

Micki clenched her teeth tight as pain shot through her body.

Soon, the pain subsided giving way to pleasure. The electricity felt more like lightning shocks, but she breathed through them.

Bradley's wings spread out above her as he forced his cock in and out of her pussy. His wings evolved into a lifeless gray with the more and more feathers dropping to the floor as he fucked the life out of her.

He pulled out of her and then slammed deep into her channel like a sledgehammer. With each stroke, she felt her heartbeat skipping. Her body shuddered as the first waves of orgasm took her.

The image of the spider-like man in her mind smiled. His voice entered her seductively like a lover's embrace.

Open yourself and my prison's gate.

No!

Micki wanted the nightmare to end. She willed her eyes open and the image of the man disappeared. She looked at Bradley and then at Jared.

A small cry escaped her lips as her angel lover found deeper parts of her insides with each thrust of his massive dick. She shivered as she felt the sweat fall from Bradley's body. When she looked up, a single tear dropped out of Jared's eyes onto her face. Every nerve in her body exploded.

Jared?

Yes, Micki?

Take care of Bradley once this is over. Take care of each other.

Chapter 21

Just as demonic hosts are ordered by rank, so are the hosts of Light. The first sphere that walk in the Heights are the Seryphims, Cherybims, and Ophaynims. The second sphere that walk in the Ether are the Dominions, Virtues, and Thronos. The third sphere rulers that walk among the world are the Archangels and Archjinn. The last sphere that walks among men are the angels and the jinn.

The Book of Timu: Verse 3—Chapter 27

* * * *

Bradley floated on the outside of his own body looking down on the horrific scene. He plowed into Micki, consumed in his own lust. He didn't even try to stop. He couldn't stop. Something pushed him forward, faster and faster, as he lost himself and his soul to the dark. The lust for power.

Now, he understood Jared's past. It would become Bradley's future.

The tendrils of a void spread around his mind, leading him to insanity as more of Micki's life force poured into him.

Bradley wanted to die but instead Micki was dying under him. And he was her killer.

* * * *

Jared's cock hardened as he watched Bradley drill into Micki's cunt. He hated himself for it. The dark lust called to him.

Bradley seemed oblivious of his presence. The angel's attention remained on Micki, not truly aware of her but of what she provided to him. *Power—dark seductive power.*

The angel tasted more of the immortal drug with each stroke, and each stroke into her pussy took more of Micki's life—bit by bit. Angels and jinn sent energy back into their human partners during a tripling, demons and ifrit never did.

As she slipped closer to death, the angel became more corrupted and controlled by the Dark.

Jared had shared memories of that terrible night with Micki. Though she knew that he could make her dying easier, she didn't ask him to take her. Instead, she asked him to help Bradley at the end of this terrible night.

She astounded him. No woman he'd ever known matched her will and goodness.

He looked around and knew that no angelic cavalry would arrive. Even if they did come, they would not be able to save Micki. Thousands of faces looked on in fanatical concentration, and he doubted that David had more than six hundred warriors in the city.

During Jared's long life, he'd kept humans and immortals at arm's length. Now, everything changed.

Micki held his desire like no woman before. Her loyalty and honesty surpassed any he'd ever known.

And Bradley, the idealist, threw everything near and dear to him away to save her from the likes of Vincorte and his horde. The angel flew head and shoulders above the rest of the Alliance.

Their tripling had changed Jared, accepted and forgiven. He wouldn't let Bradley face the guilt alone.

The demonic crowd seemed satisfied with what they'd seen. He blocked them out of his mind. He needed to focus on what he was about to do with Bradley. He must keep his mind on Micki.

"Jared, are you there?" she voiced weakly.

A coward no more, Jared put his hands on her shoulders. "Yes."

Heat shot through him. Her red output expanded beyond what It'd been at Zone Three. Every moment he'd spent with Micki and Bradley swirled in his head. Sealed by their love, together.

He watched Micki's chest rise and fall as if each breath might be her last.

Bradley continued pumping into her, his eyes blank and clouded with dark lust.

Micki's thought floated toward him, *My love, please forgive yourself. You saved that woman, even though you lost yourself.*

Jared felt like he couldn't breathe. Micki understood. No one had broken through his walls of guilt. Not him. Not any mortal or immortal. Until Micki. He'd been an island, alone, living on the edge of the Light. An island filled with skeletons.

Micki saw all of it. She forgave him.

The memory of their tripling rushed into his mind. He remembered the passion and joy he felt in their connection. Once he tasted her, he would lose himself to the Dark but he didn't care.

Micki and Bradley needed him. He would make sure that Micki's last experience in life would match their night in the Persian room.

He grabbed Bradley's head. The angel didn't respond. He might be able to keep the dark lust at bay from Bradley, at least temporarily. He needed to try. He shook him hard. The angel looked up with growing hate in his eyes.

Bradley, look at her. It's Micki.

A snarl on Bradley's lips emerged, but he continued to pump into Micki as the blank stare returned.

Jared punched Bradley in the face, knocking him off of her and off the stone altar.

The crowd laughed wickedly.

Bradley jumped to his feet in a split second, filled with a passion for murder. Jared wasn't sure he could reach him since the angel neared the change to a full-blown demon. He hoped he could reach him. He must.

"Look at her," Jared pointed down at Micki. Bradley moved closer, not responding. The next step, Jared would have to stop him with deadly force.

Bradley, remember the rainbow. Remember Micki's rainbow. Remember Micki.

Bradley blinked. The fog lifted. He looked down at Micki. His wings dropped to his side. Guilty.

The angel stood silent for a while. Then he backed up. The crowd pushed him back into the table.

Bradley, we can't save her. We can only make her passing something different then what these motherfuckers would like it to be.

Bradley looked at him. *I felt it. I felt the dark power.*

I know.

I wanted it. Wanted to kill innocence.

Jared wanted to help him, but their time evaporated. Like sharks with the scent of blood in their snouts, the crowd patience and sanity ebbed away.

Remember Zone Three.

Bradley nodded.

Let's give her that.

Bradley looked up from his feet. His eyes no longer the brilliant blue Jared remembered them to be, but still blue—grayish blue.

"We owe her that," Bradley said aloud.

"Yes."

I don't know if I can control myself, Jared.

Remember that night. You said you would keep an eye on me.

Yes.

Jared sent, *Well, tonight, let's keep an eye on each other.*

Bradley nodded.

He motioned the angel to the other side of the table, putting Micki between them. They would give her all that they could. Let her experience their connection, their love, until her last breath.

He looked down at her body. He couldn't remember ever seeing such beauty. Her perfectly proportioned breasts, her thick full lips, her swollen pussy, all of her—exposed for the demonic throng.

He hated them.

The angel sent to him, *Forget about the Dark.*

She slipped fast.

He and Bradley didn't have much time. He closed his eyes and called to her.

Micki?

She stirred, but her eyes stayed closed.

Even in her dream state, sexiness poured from Micki. Jared felt his cock harden.

Micki?

Her hazel-gold beauties fluttered open and hypnotized him.

Yes?

He forgot about the crowd. He forgot what the results of their actions would be.

I love you, Micki.

And I love you. She turned and looked over at Bradley. She touched his chest. *And I love you.*

I love you, sweetheart.

Micki spread her legs apart, revealing her tiny tuft. Jared knew she wanted them.

"Micki, I don't know if I can," Bradley announced.

"You can. We both can—and must." Then he leaned down and kissed her delicious mouth.

Her eyes glazed. *That feels so good, Jared.*

He continued kissing her as Bradley dove between her legs. She vibrated under him and hooked her hands around his neck. Jared drifted down her neck to her chest and devoured her left nipple, then her right nipple. His erection pulsed.

She kissed him on the top of his head. Her moans of delight drove him wild.

Yes. You both feel so good.

Jared sent, *You're amazing, Micki.*

"So are you," she whispered weakly.

Jared continued down her abdomen, stopping at her navel, giving it extra attention. He watched Bradley's tongue rush in and out of Micki's cunt.

"My turn," he commanded Bradley.

Bradley's work with his tongue had left her swollen and wet.

The angel pulled his mouth off of her and his lips traveled down one of her inner thighs to the soft underside of her knee.

Jared's tongue stabbed inside her moist pussy. She rocked feverishly back and forth against his mouth, her motions creating huge waves inside him. He surrounded her in his green smoke. His cock pulsed. She slid her hands down her breasts, massaging them to the beat of his plunging tongue.

I want you both inside me.

He spread her apart with his fingers and teased her clit, rubbing it with his other hand. He heard her suck in a mouthful of air. She seemed to be gaining strength.

She'd been moments from death, but now she could roll onto her side giving him easy access to her mound.

Bradley stared down at her ass, enveloping all her in his blue light.

Lick me. Make me squirm.

Bradley disappeared from his sight, but Jared felt Micki react to the angel's licks on her backside. Jared continued his work on her front side, sinking a finger into her hot folds.

Yes, that's perfect. Micki's red power wrapped around Jared's green and Bradley's blue, binding them together.

Jared put another finger inside her channel. Micki's hand grabbed his wrist. She worked it like a jackhammer pushing his fingers in and out... and deeper. Jared flayed his digits out with each stroke inside the walls of her pussy. Her other hand caressed his fully loaded balls. He growled as her caresses moved up the base of his cock.

"I want to taste you, Jared."

Jared swung his legs onto the table, positioning his cock so it touched her hungry lips, and his lips touched her swollen folds between her legs in a perfect sixty-nine. She licked the tip of his dick. He sampled her juices, which flooded out of her even faster. Jared's heart skipped a beat as the colors of her rainbow body filled his mind. Adrenaline shot through him.

Micki moaned with a mouthful of his cock. She slicked him up.

Bradley's hands spread her legs wide so that Jared could dive in deeper. Desire exploded inside him. Time slipped away. If he didn't take her soon, it might be too late.

He twisted around and kissed her on the mouth with her own juices still on his tongue. Bradley's hands reached around and cupped her breasts. Her head turned back to Bradley, and they kissed deep and long.

Jared smiled. He loved them.

Even more than their first tripling, they all let themselves go free. Micki wiggled back against Bradley and pulled Jared closer to her. She pushed him on his back. Her face burned with desire. She rolled on top of him sitting up. His cock felt the slipperiness between her legs. Micki stood up above him like a conquering queen. Energy exploded out of every part of her.

She looked down at him, her eyes brilliant and alive. She slid down on his erect dick to its base. Her head tilted back as she did. His dick grew inside her.

Jared felt her cunt tighten around his cock. She leaned into him, her hair blinding him.

Her red power exploded around him, and an idea came to him. If they short-circuited their tripling, it might end her suffering instantly, and her life.

Bradley?

Yes. Vincorte won't leash the crowd much longer.

I know.

We can end this quickly.

The angel sent, *How?*

Her power needs to drain off. If we both are in her pussy at the same time, it might work.

Micki's thought pushed into him like a megaphone. *Do it! Please!*

He sent back, *It will be painful, at first.*

I know.

The three of them worked together to get into position, Jared on the table, Micki against him with his cock inside her cunt, and Bradley coming up from behind almost crouching.

Jared felt Bradley's cock against the base of his dick. Micki tensed. Slowly, the angel moved the head of his cock at the bottom of her slit.

Then he felt the angel shove his dick into Micki's pussy. Jared could feel Bradley's hard cock side by side his own. She gasped.

Too much! Oh G-God! Burning! So much! Stretching!

He and the angel stopped moving. Jared felt the tears well in his eyes. How could he live one second without this woman?

Micki's thought slipped into his mind. *I'm okay, now. Just go slow.*

He and Bradley began again, easing into her body. She shivered against him.

Her hips rocked up and down. Her pussy clamped down on their combined monster dicks pounding deep, deeper.

Her insides warmed—being in Micki with Bradley felt incredible. The vibrations grew like lightning and thunder in the sky. The room whirled around them.

Bradley drove in and out of Micki, and he matched each of the angel's thrusts.

Micki mewled sounds of delight.

So tight, so incredible.

In and out. Faster and faster.

Jared saw Bradley's mouth widen as he exploded inside Micki.

On cue, he unloaded his balls' contents deep inside her, too. Her orgasm seemed to consume her totally. She pulsated like a live wire between them.

Then light exploded in Jared's eyes, blinding him.

"No! I didn't mean to open the Ether!" Micki screamed.

* * * *

Wings. Smoke. Rainbow.

Micki looked around. Black void surrounded her. Her lovers floated with her in the emptiness. The man she'd seen in her mind hung near them. His black wings stretched out. Long, sharp horns jutted out from his forehead, more menacing than any she'd seen on the other creatures.

Power surged through and around her.

A ripple from the demon pushed into her mind. *Power that you don't know how to use, my dear.*

Jared exploded. *Fuck you, Terrok!*

Micki turned and saw the image of the nightmarish cavern appearing in what seemed to be some sort of passageway. The beastly crowd stood cheering like loyal fans at sporting event. She couldn't let this evil into the world.

Terrok smiled.

What can you do about it, human? I will join my children, and you will be trapped here, just as I have been for two hundred years thanks to your fucking ancestor.

Jared's green smoky body heated to a firestorm. Bradley's blue power grew blistering hot. She sensed they prepared to launch an attack.

Don't try it, angel. You broke your vow. Do you think you can harm me here or anywhere?

Bradley's wings shrank back.

And Jared, my son, you and my new demon will return with me to enjoy my delicious destruction on mankind.

Woman, you will remain here in the Ether, not quite alive and not quite dead—forever. And let me tell you, there are creatures here that make my children seem like toddlers. They will give you a welcome to the neighborhood in a fashion you will find unbearable.

The monster's voice reminded her of murder and disease. Terrok folded his wings and dove for the opening, an opening that she'd helped fashion though she didn't know how. The world would suffer if he made it through. Eric's bravery would be for naught. She didn't know much about her power but she could feel it. How to use it?

Goodbye, human. And thank you! Come boys!

Without stopping to consider, Micki pulled at the strands of power in her rainbow body and pointed them to the magic doorway. The multi-colored lights rushed past Terrok and encircled the passage. The portal exploded in bright white light and vanished.

She could no longer see the cavern and its crowd. Only Terrok remained in her view.

He screamed inside her head and lunged toward the three of them.

Jared and Bradley moved in front of her.

Fire erupted around them. Micki could feel the heat of it.

Terrok flew past them, again and again, each time shooting giant balls of black fire. Jared and Bradley sent out power that shielded the three of them from the flames. With each pass, their green and blue energy shrank back.

As Terrok prepared to dive bomb once again, Micki wasn't sure that Jared and Bradley could hold him back. She pulled at the colors in her rainbow and guided them into her lovers. She felt their powers multiply. Jared's green smoke heated and Bradley's blue light brightened—they burned like the surfaces of two exploding stars.

She looked at Terrok's face and saw fear.

Her jinn and angel hurled thousands of magical missiles at Terrok.

All of them hit their marks, piercing the monster's wings. His face twisted into a hideous scowl of pain.

Today the battle is yours, but the war is still mine.

Terrok waved his hands, creating a flash of black fire, and he vanished from their view.

Micki felt Jared's warmth engulf her and Bradley's light illuminate her. She loved them. The three of them had kept Terrok from the world of mortals.

Hey? Bradley's thought entered.

Yes, she and Jared responded in unison.

Look down.

Micki did and saw what appeared to be a black cloud growing. It wasn't a cloud. Hundreds of the creatures that Terrok told them about—Ether creatures-- headed their way.

How do we get out of here? Jared asked.

I don't know, Bradley answered.

You mean neither of you can get us back? Micki questioned. They could be trapped there with...

Jared sent, *I think I might know how to open a way.*

But how? Bradley asked. *Immortals can't open a portal out of the Ether.*

But Micki can.

Bradley sent, *Of course, she can. It's your power, Micki.*

My power?

Jared sent, *Yes, your bloodline power.*

Their belief and enthusiasm warmed her, but looking down again at the creatures that seemed only a football length away doused her in a chill.

How do I do it?

How did you close the portal? Jared asked.

I don't know.

Waves of fear rolled over her. They would be lost to the tortures of these creatures that even Terrok feared.

Jared floated in front of her. *You can do it. Try. Immortals make portals in the world by seeing where they want to go in their mind.*

Then they feel the place.

Micki moved closer to him. *If you two can't do it, how can I?*

But you can. You did it when we first made love together, without even trying.

Bradley agreed. *You can do it, sweetheart.*

Micki felt the cold growing. The monsters approached, only seconds away from them. She imagined their first tripling, at Zone Three, on the pillows. Jared, Bradley and her. She loved them. She wanted to be there again. She closed her eyes and brought the picture of the place into her mind.

Then she thought of Eric.

Eric! We have to save him.

Jared sent, *You know where he is?*

Yes. I know. In a large cell Vincorte put him in.

Jared started his objection, *But...*

She didn't hesitate. Her brother needed her. She pictured his cell, and a shimmering portal appeared.

You did it! Bradley exclaimed.

In a flash, Jared pulled them through the portal and they landed in Eric's cell.

"Close the passage before the creatures or Terrok breach it!" Jared shouted.

Monstrous eyes, as big as serving plates, stared at her from the portal. A claw pushed past the magic opening.

"Close, damn it!" she screamed.

The portal disappeared. She looked at the floor. A claw the size of a tractor tire oozed green thick liquid on the floor. It'd been severed from the creature when the magic passage closed.

Micki felt dizziness overwhelm her and she passed out.

Chapter 22

Jared watched Micki place another cold cloth on Eric's forehead. He doubted that her brother would last more than a couple hours.

When she'd passed out after closing the passage to the Ether, Bradley had swept her up into his arms. Jared had scooped up her brother, and had opened a portal back to Zone Three.

"Isn't there something else we can try?" Micki's eyes remained red from her night of crying. "David doesn't know everything, does he? The three of us could try again."

The Persian room radiated with their magical attempts to heal Eric. They'd tried for hours, but nothing worked.

Jared put his arms around her. "He's a bloodliner. With all he's been through, and without forming his own perfect triad, there's no helping him. I'm so sorry, sweetheart."

She put her head into his shoulder, and a fresh round of sobs came out.

A knock on the door.

He and Bradley took defensive positions.

Relax, both of you, David sent. *I've brought Brooke Caldwell as Micki requested.*

The door opened and the blonde woman bolted to the bed.

"Oh, Brooke!" Micki folded her arms around her.

David walked in behind Eric's girlfriend.

"This can't be happening." Brooke's tears fell on Micki's shoulder. "He can't leave us."

A cough sounded from the bed.

Both women leaned over Eric. Jared saw his eyes open. With all the man had been through, he had a toughness that would put fear in any demon's black heart. So like his sister.

Eric choked out, "Brooke, is that you?"

"Yes, Eric. It's me."

"S-Sorry. I wish…"

She kissed his cheek. "Don't worry. It's okay. David told me everything. I understand."

Jared found that hard to believe given the archangel's standard behavior. When he looked over at David, gaze fixed on Brooke, he wondered.

Eric coughed violently. Then, he whispered, "I love you, Brooke."

Jared watched the woman's face change. "Then stay. Fight this. You can do it, damn it!"

Eric tried to speak, but instead, convulsed, and passed out. David leaned down and shot blue energy into him. The man settled back.

David looked at Brooke and Micki. "I've kept him alive for as long as I can. It's time."

"No!" Brooke screamed. "He can't leave me alone to raise our baby."

Micki's head shot around. "You're pregnant?"

Brooke nodded.

"When did you find out?"

"You know my mother's a doctor, and very overprotective. She ran a pregnancy test on me when I complained about being sick every morning during my visit. It came up positive."

"How far along are you?"

"About a month. I wanted to tell Eric when I got back." She eased her head into her hands.

Micki said, "It's okay, Brooke. I'm here for you."

Jared watched David start pacing. The possibility of a bloodliner baby changed everything in the Eternal war.

Eric's coughing quieted. "Micki?"

"Yes."

"Sis, I love you." Then he fell back, unconscious.

Micki's hands shot up to her mouth. Tears rolled down her cheeks.

Eric's body turned ashen.

David stated, "I've done all I can. If I keep him alive any longer, the pain will come back ten-fold."

Micki and Brooke looked at each other, and both nodded.

"Let him go." Micki held Eric's hand.

David waved his hand over her brother. Then Eric died.

What happened next surprised Jared and everyone else in the room. A green smoky cloud shot out of Eric's body, then it coalesced into ball.

"Do you see that?" Micki asked, excitement in her tone.

"I see it, too." Brooke looked confused. "What is it?"

The ball whirled, and then a smoky image of a smiling Eric materialized for a few seconds.

"Oh my God!" Brooke screamed.

The apparition faded into nothingness, and Eric was gone.

"Does the green smoke mean he will come back?" Micki asked. "It looked like yours, Jared."

David stared at Brooke. "He might."

Jared thought he should tell Micki that even if Eric did return as a jinn, her brother wouldn't remember either her or Brooke, but Jared couldn't add another blow to her right now. She suffered enough.

Micki ran to Jared. She wrapped her arms tight around him. He felt Bradley's wings and arms envelope Micki and him.

She pulled away and went back to Brooke still kneeling next to Eric's body.

Micki asked, "Can you guys leave Brooke and me alone for a bit?"

"Of course." Jared walked to the door and motioned for Bradley and David to follow.

Before closing the door behind him, Jared looked one more time at the woman that had stolen his heart. She put her arms around Brooke to comfort her. Even in grief, Micki amazed him.

* * * *

In their room at the stronghold, Jared stood with Bradley on either side of the bed that Micki slept in. She'd finally fallen asleep after hours of crying.

David, Parkor and Jezzel walked into the room unannounced.

"Keep quiet." Jared commanded. "She just got to sleep."

"What the bloody hell?" Parkor said. "This is power on a level I have never seen before."

"I told you," David answered.

Jezzel looked at Jared, her disdain for him evident to all in the room.

"I don't care if he is part of this triad; the jinn shouldn't be here given his past."

Jared watched Bradley take a step toward the two nobles, his wings extending in defiance.

"I know his past, and I'll be damned if he isn't allowed to hear whatever you assholes have to say." The invisible cord to Bradley vibrated and tightened. That pleased Jared.

"Very well," Jezzel conceded.

Jared asked, "Where are the other council members?"

"They've been briefed already." David looked tired. "When our troops arrived at the Dark's lair, they found it empty. No surprise."

Parkor paced around the room. "So? Terrok is still in the Ether. Is Vincorte's army disbanded?"

"Terrok is still in the Ether because of Micki," Jared stated proudly.

David leaned against the wall. "Not disbanded but in disarray—for now."

Jezzel said, "Vincorte still has grand plans."

David nodded. "Plans to bring Terrok back"

"Damn fanatics!" Jezzel spat.

Jared tensed. "All I care about is Micki and Bradley."

"Will they come back for Micki?" Bradley asked.

"We don't know. If Vincorte knows a perfect triad is possible, he may try to form his own," Parkor mused.

"We don't even know how we became a perfect triad. How can they know how to make one?" Bradley spread his wings out wide.

"Even if they do not create one, they might have the book of Timu. Then they would have the advantage," Jezzel answered.

"Where could the book be?" Parkor folded his arms.

"I think it's in the Ether." Micki yawned, notifying everyone of her state of wakefulness.

"Darling." Bradley leaned down and kissed her on the cheek. Jared kissed the other one.

Jezzel scowled. "How did the book get in the Ether?"

"My brother put it there to keep it away from the Dark."

"And what if Terrok finds it?"

The thought chilled Jared.

"We'll find it first. We are a perfect triad," Micki pointed out.

"On the Alliance's side?" Jezzel asked them.

I'm in, Micki sent him.

Bradley agreed: *Me, too.*

Jared shrugged. "Apparently, I am outnumbered."

Jezzel asked, "Where's the human that is carrying the bloodliner's baby?"

"Her name is Brooke." Micki snapped. "She needs time to adjust to all this immortal business. And she just lost the man of her dreams, my brother."

"Brooke is here," David answered. "Under my protection."

Jezzel's dark eyes smoldered. "If the Dark got wind of a bloodliner baby…"

"They won't," David informed.

Micki turned to the archangel. "Eric put most of his findings on the flash drive."

"We cracked the code. The genealogical records are there. I have warriors searching for all the names of the bloodliners."

Kronos bolted into the room and exclaimed. "Eve is missing."

"How long has she been gone?" David asked.

"I saw her last night," Kronos huffed. "We have to find her."

David looked at Micki. "Eve is your cousin."

* * * *

Micki stood looking around the Persian room, no longer a play chamber of Zone Three. David gave it to her to share with Bradley and Jared, there private place.

Though her grief over losing Eric stayed with her, she took comfort knowing he'd been happy to learn her future had been secured because of him.

She vowed to get the book back from Terrok. She'd also make sure Brooke was safe. She owed Eric, Brooke and their new baby that.

Micki also worried about Eve, her cousin that Eric had located and brought to Zone Three for protection. Micki remembered meeting her that first night at the club.

Several warriors searched for her with Kronos in the lead.

"So?" she asked as Jared shut the door to the hall.

"So?" he mimicked.

"Don't think just because I quit my job at the bank and moved out of my apartment that you can order me around," she teased. "I have options. I am a bloodliner."

"Is that right?" Bradley laughed and dove onto the bed. "Then we better power up."

"It is our duty." Jared joined him.

Micki stood looking down at the two of them, her old life fading into memory and without any hold on her. Her two fantasy men, a jinn and an angel, would protect her and she them. They were her perfection.

"I love you, my immortals."

"We love you," they said in unison.

She dove in between them, anticipating the extreme power and pleasure they would create together—forever.

THE END

www.kriscook.net

ABOUT THE AUTHOR

A military brat to the core, Kris Cook never put down deep roots in any particular geographic location. Until Texas. Why? Kris loves the sun.

A voracious reader, Kris loves many genres of fiction but this writer's favorite books are romances that are edgy, sexy, with rich characters and unique challenges. Kris' influences include JR Ward, Lora Leigh, and Shayla Black.

Kris has won and placed in several writing contests in the past couple of years.

Kris' motto: I like cooking up really hot books for my readers. The hotter, the better.

For news, info and upcoming releases, be sure to stop by www.KrisCook.net

Siren Publishing, Inc.
www.SirenPublishing.com